This is a cracking good read... A story that brings a...
heat and the underbelly of life in a Mafia controlled Sicilian village.

Ann Gough

The charm of reading this book is that: always, and I mean always, the reader is satisfied with the result... a confrontation between raw, unpolished power (men) and the sophistication of women's minds.

Manuela Iordache

Vaffanculo.................I love the word as much as I love this book. Talk about attitude! Sicilian women are a surprising bunch according to Linda Lo Scuro's book "The Sicilian Woman's Daughter." Abused, scheming, vindictive, connected, murderous, victims and victors.

I loved discovering the story of Maria aka Mary who came from a poor Sicilian background to recreate herself in England as a successful and wealthy teacher and wife to a high flier bank executive.

I was fascinated by this story and can completely understand the fascination Linda Lo Scuro has also. The excitement of danger is enthralling.

Andrea Brown, New Zealand

I felt I w ... es can
be turne ... try to

remove ourselves from (in this case the Mafia). Insightful, well written and I found the pace just right. The storyline took an interesting twist at the end which didn't disappoint.

Dawn D'Auvin

Wow – this is a great story! The writing is superb throughout and I see Linda Lo Scuro progressing to great success.

Phil Rowan

Linda Lo Scuro weaves the story about the daughter of Sicilian immigrants with layer upon layer of substance. It's a must-read for mystery lovers.

Carolyn Bowen

An interesting and thought provoking read this one... this separation of identities and anonymity is crushing to read about.

Maria tells her story of her Sicily and the image the world has of that place – its mafia connections and how she and everyone from there is tarred with the same brush. As the story takes us on that (very fascinating) train journey across to the island, secrets start to float to the surface, as do the bodies...

A fascinating look at the mafia stain on a family of women and what they have to do to survive, bring justice and not be a victim. There are four generations of women's stories to immerse yourself in and this is a real treat, never too much nor too long. Sicilian words pepper the text as they would the pasta.

An enthralling read on many levels.

Book Trail

Certainly exciting and riveting reading. An enthralling glimpse into another world where grandmothers keep a gun close to hand... it was a fast moving book, included plenty of surprises, and gave an insight into a different way of life and family ties.

The book has left me wondering how much of it is based on the reality of life in some of the regions of this island. Thought provoking!

Emma B Books

I have always considered women to be the "power behind the throne" ... and this book proves it to be true. It was fascinating to read about how different her lives were depending on where she was or WHO she was that day.

This is an addictive read from page one to last and thoroughly enjoyable! Great book!

Janet Cousineau

The story tells of all the things that the mafia has done in Sicily and brought over to London... very interesting and very easy to follow.

Mary Weimer

I enjoyed reading this book immensely. Even though it's fiction it gave you an insight into what might happen in this sort of family. Plus, you learn great words in Sicilian!

Doris Vandruff

An exciting plot, great characterisation and an unexpected ending all add up to a thoroughly enjoyable read.

Millie Thom

OUTSTANDING. This book makes very interesting reading and a lot of research has gone into it. I also like Linda's writing style, and the plot flowed. I have awarded this book 5 deserving stars.

Haley Norton

No matter how many rosaries you say, how faithful you are, there are always excuses to take revenge if that suits you well. Female sophistication and guns, poison, and network connections do the trick. The plot's convincing and rich in local flavours.

Henk-Jan van der Klis

The Sicilian Woman's Daughter

Linda Lo Scuro

Sparkling Books

This story is a work of fiction. Names, characters, businesses, organisations, associations, enterprises, places, events and incidents are either the products of the author's imagination, or are used fictitiously. Any resemblance to actual persons, living or dead, businesses, organisations, associations, enterprises, events or places is entirely coincidental.

British Library Cataloguing in Publication Data. A catalogue record for this book is available from the British Library.

ISBN: 978-1-907230-69-1
E-book: 978-1-907230-70-7

1.2

Printed in the United Kingdom by Short Run Press, Exeter

@SparklingBooks

"All those women saw their men down and under."

James Joyce, *Ulysses*

With thanks to my editor Lynn Curtis,
and the Sparkling Books team

Linda Lo Scuro

Characters

Unless stated otherwise the characters are in relation to the protagonist Maria (Mary). Some minor characters and spoilers have been left out of this list.

Nuclear family:

Humps (Humphrey), husband

Clara, daughter

Emma, daughter

Mark, Emma's husband

Little Benjamin, grandson. Emma and Mark's son.

Extended family:

Zia, aunt (mother's sister)

Tony, uncle (Zia's husband)

Silvio, cousin (Zia's son)

Stefano, cousin (Zia's son)

Susi, cousin (Zia's daughter)

Peppina, aunt (mother's sister)

Gloria, aunt (father's sister)

Giuseppe, uncle (father's brother)

Ziuzza, great aunt, (grandmother's sister, on her mother's side)

Old Cushi, cousin once removed, (Ziuzza's son)

Young Cushi, second cousin (Old Cushi's son)

Adele, Young Cushi's daughter

Elena, step-mother

Teodoro, Zia's brother-in-law. Tony's brother.

Bella and Rosa, Teodoro's daughters

Adriano, Teodoro's son

Carmela, Teodoro's wife

Elderly neighbours when Maria was a child:
"Auntie" Marge
"Uncle" Peter, husband of Marge
Dorothy, Marge's sister
Belinda, Dorothy's daughter
Charlie, a visitor to Marge and Peter's house

Visitors to Zia's house (and their connections):
Giusy, a hair stylist
Alberto, Giusy's lover, owner of an amusement arcade
Olga, Alberto's wife
Nancy, manageress of arcade
Angelina, Zia's Sicilian friend
Provvi (Provvidenza), Angelina's daughter
Giulio, Provvi's husband
Beatrice, Angelina's twin sister in Sicily

Maria's friends in Sicily when she was eighteen:
Franca
Patrizia

Riverside View inhabitants:
Ruth and Ian – 1st floor
Richard and Barbara – pensioners – 2nd floor
Charlie and Sarah and their children: Nigella and Tristram – 3rd floor
Maria and Humphrey – 4th floor
Pablo and Consuelo – 5th floor

Dorset:
Yvonne and Henry, neighbours
Nigel, gardener

Sicilian / Italian Words and Expressions

* standard Italian
(otherwise Sicilian dialect)

asetta – sit down

biviti – drink up

buco du culu – arsehole

buon appetito* – enjoy your meal

bagascia – slut

bagasci – sluts

du big bagasci – two big sluts

campagna* – countryside

cannolo – Sicilian cakes with a ricotta filling

cannoli – as above, but plural

capisti? – have you understood?

cassuni – a big drawer (bodies stacked one on top of the other in a cemetery)

cugliuna – balls, testicles

disgraziatu – unfortunate

donna d'onore* – woman of honour, a woman high up in the mafia hierarchy

fittente – stinking, rotten

futtiri – fuck

maliducato – rude person

maliducati – rude people

mangia* – eat

mangiare* – to eat

minghia – prick (word also used to express surprise or to call someone an idiot) minghiuni – big prick (big idiot)

picciotto – thug

picciotti – thugs

piglati chissu – take that

pignata – cauldron

puttane* – whores

salute e figlie femmini – cheers, (drink to) to female daughters

stra-minghiuni – extra big prick (enormous idiot)

trasi – come in

troia* – slut

troie* – sluts

uomo d'onore* – man of honour, a man high up in the mafia hierarchy

vaffanculo* – fuck it / fuck off

vileno – venom

zoccula – slut (literally, sandal)

zoccule – sluts

PROLOGUE

Rumour had it that Ziuzza, my grandmother's sister, on my mother's side, carried a gun in her apron pocket – both at home and when she went out. She wore her apron back-to-front, resulting in the pocket being propped up against her belly. She kept her right hand poised there, between her dress and apron as if she had bellyache. I had noticed this suspicious behaviour when on holiday in Sicily with my family when I was twelve. At that stage, never could I have imagined that she was concealing a gun, while she stood there in my grandmother's kitchen watching me have breakfast. I never saw her sitting down. She brought us thick fresh milk, containing a cow's hair or two, in the early mornings and often stayed to chat.

She had a dog, Rocco, white and brown, which she tied to a wooden stake in my grandmother's stable downstairs. It was a lively animal, snapping at whoever passed it, jumping and yapping. The mules, the rightful inhabitants of the stable, were out in the campagna with my grandfather from the break of dawn each day.

A tight silver bun stood proudly on Ziuzza's head. Her frowning face always deadly serious. Fierce, even. An overly tanned and wrinkled face. Skin as thick as cows' hide. Contrastingly, her eyes were of the sharpest blue – squinting as she stared, as if viewing me through thick fog. I was scared of her. Truly scared. And all the other women were frightened, too. You could tell by the way they spoke to her, gently and smiling. Careful not to upset her, always agreeing with her opinions. They toadied up to her well and proper. An inch away from grovelling.

And, I found out the rumours about the gun were true. Ziuzza would come and bake bread and cakes at my grandmother's house because of the enormous stone oven in the garden. I helped carry wood to keep the flames alive. Did my bit. One day the sisters made some Sicilian cakes called cuddureddi, *meaning*: 'little ropes.' They rolled the dough with their bare hands, into thick round lengths in the semblance of snakes. Using a sharp knife, they then sliced the snake-shape in half, longways, spread the lower half of the butchered snake with home-made fig jam. They put the snake together again, slashed it into chunks. Then the chunks were dealt with one-by-one and manipulated into little ropes by pinching them forcefully into shape with their nimble fingers.

As Ziuzza bent over to wipe her mouth on the corner of her pinafore, I caught a glimpse of her gun. I was sitting at the table sprinkling the first trayful of cuddureddi with sugar. No doubt about it. It was there in Ziuzza's big inside pocket of her pinafore. While I was looking at the bulge, she caught me out. We exchanged glances, then our eyes locked. She narrowed her hooded eyelids into slits and crunched up her face. I blinked a few times, then looked around for some more wood to replenish the oven, grabbed a few logs and vanished into the garden.

After she received a sickening threat, Rocco's bloodied paws were posted to her in a box, she, like her dog, came to a violent end. Ziuzza was shot in her back, in broad daylight, by someone riding by on a Vespa. People with line of sight, from their windows to the body, hurried to close their shutters. Nobody saw who it was. Nobody heard the gunshots, though the road was a main artery from one end of The Village to the other. And nobody called a doctor. It would be taking sides. Which you certainly didn't want to do. Added to that was the fact that Ziuzza at that moment was on the losing side. She was left to bleed to death in the road like an animal. It wasn't until the dustcart came round that they removed her body because it couldn't get by. But nobody commented, it was as if they were removing a big piece of rubbish. It was nothing to them. But instead of throwing it away, they took the body to her home. Nobody was in. So they brought it to my grandmother's house instead.

This was the lowest point in our family's history. With time, though, Ziuzza managed to triumph through her son, Old Cushi, who began the escalation. And, later, her grandson, Young Cushi, completed it by becoming the undisputed boss of our village, of the region, and beyond. But the transition was not easy. A bloody feud ensued. Lives were lost on both sides. Some might know who Ziuzza's enemies were. I didn't get an inkling. Most of the information I came across was from listening to what the grown-ups in our family were saying. And they never mentioned her rivals by name. Some faceless entity fighting for control of the area.

This is just one of the episodes I remember from our holidays in Sicily. There are many more. Every three years, I went to Sicily with my parents. Those I remember were when I was nine, twelve, fifteen and eighteen. The last time we went my mother was ill and we travelled by plane. All the other times we travelled by train because poverty accompanied us wherever we went. I think we had some kind of subsidy from the Italian Consulate in the UK for the train fare. It was a three-day-two-night expedition. I remember setting out from Victoria Station carrying three days' supply of food and wine with us. Especially stuck in my mind was the food: lasagne, roast chicken, cheese, loaves of bread. We'd have plates, cutlery, glasses, and an assortment of towels with us. At every transfer all this baggage had to be carried on to the next stage. No wheels on cases in those days. Then we'd get the ferry from Dover to Calais, and so began the first long stretch through France, Switzerland, until we finally pulled into Milan Station. Where our connection to Sicily was after a seven-hour wait.

We used to sleep on the waiting-room benches, though it was daytime, until someone complained about the space we were taking up. The Italian northerners had a great disdain for southern Italians. They saw us as muck, rolled their eyes at us, insulted us openly calling us "terroni", *meaning:* "those who haven't evolved from the soil." Even though I was young, I noticed it, and felt like a second category being – a child of a minor god. There was the civilised world and then there was us. My parents didn't answer back. And it was probably the time when I came closest to feeling sorry for them. For us.

The journey all the way down to the tip of Italy – the toe of the boot – was excruciating. The heat in the train unbearable. When there was water in the stinking toilets, we gave ourselves a cursory wipe with flannels. Sometimes we used water in bottles. Every time we stopped at a station, my father would ask people on the platforms to fill our bottles. Then came the crossing of the Strait of Messina. At Villa San Giovanni, the train was broken into fragments of three coaches and loaded into the dark belly of the ferry. My mother wouldn't leave the train for fear of thieves taking our miserable belongings, until the ferry left mainland Italy. While my father and I went up on the deck to take in the view. But we had orders to go back down to the train as soon as the ferry left. Then I'd go up again with my mother. She became emotional when Sicily was well in sight. She would become ecstatic. Talk to any passengers who'd listen to her.

Some totally ignored her. She'd wave to people on passing ferries. Laughing and, surprisingly, being nice to me.

Reassembled together again, the train would crawl at a tortoise's pace along the Sicilian one-track countryside railway, under the sweltering heat. Even peasants who were travelling within Sicily moved compartment when they got a whiff of us. Another event that excited my mother was when the train stopped at a level crossing. A man got out of his van, brought a crate of lemons to our train and started selling them to the passengers hanging out of the windows. My mother bought a big bag full and gave me one to suck saying it would quench my thirst. Another man came along selling white straw handbags with fringes, and she bought me one.

By the time we reached The Village our bags of food stank to high heaven and so did we.

PART I

London, 2017

ONE

Sunday 20th August

It all begins quite innocently enough.

"I just got an email from our landlord asking us to remove our bikes from the garage," Humps says, as we are having dinner. He's in his stay-at-home clothes today – a Tattersall shirt worn loose over his jeans and rolled up at the sleeves, frayed at the collar from countless washes. I still find him attractive, even in his rumpled look and with his receding salt-and-pepper hair.

"Why?" I ask.

"Apparently, someone pointed out, at the Annual General Meeting, that our bikes are taking up precious space, have cobwebs on them, and that we hardly use them."

"Look, darling, you know they're snobs here. They just don't want our old bikes next to their latest generation, shiny contraptions."

We have lived in the Riverside View Residence in West London for four years. I've never felt comfortable here with the attitudes against foreigners of some of our neighbours. That irked me. But the proximity to the Thames with a spacious balcony within a stone's throw of the river, where I can sit sipping tea and reading, helps me overlook their behaviour towards me, especially when Humps is not around.

"What are we going to do?" I say to my husband, "You do realise that there'll be friction, if we don't comply, don't you? Shall we remove them?"

"Never!", he says firmly, over his salmon en croûte. "Mary, as you know, mine is a memento of my Oxford University days. I've had that bike for over forty years, and there's no way I'm getting rid of it – it stays where it is! What's more our sky-high rent gives us the right to keep as many bikes as we want in that bike-store. One resident has six!"

So Humphrey said 'no.' Emphatically.

"Well, I'm getting rid of mine because it's so old," I say. "There's a charity, I've heard, that does up old bikes and sends them out to Africa. They can have mine, and I don't think Clara will want hers now she's moved to central London. She should have taken her bike with her, anyway."

"Even if we get rid of your two bikes, it won't free up any space because all three are leaning next to each other against the wall," Humps says.

"Well, I'm giving mine to the charity. Make a child happy. I'll phone Clara and ask what she wants to do with hers."

I had my left kidney taken out when I was young due to a violent kicking. My doctor suggested that I give up cycling in traffic so as not to endanger my other kidney. No motorbikes or skiing either. "Look after it," he said, "if I damage one of my kidneys it wouldn't be as serious, but for you it's a different kettle of fish..." I only cycled in parks and on towpaths after that.

I phone our daughter in the evening, ask if I can give hers away. "Yes," she says, "no way do I want to cycle in London traffic, I'd rather take the tube. Less hassle. Anyway, it'd only get pinched." There have been some nasty accidents involving buses and lorries lately, cyclists have been killed in their prime. It is a relief to me that she wants to do away with hers, too. She tells me a little about her job. How her boss at the interior design studio exploits her, charging excruciating prices to clients and giving her a miserly salary. She reckons she's the flair behind the studio's success.

Right, I have to grab the bull by its horns, or the bicycles by their handlebars, and sort this out. Humps is busy with his high-powered job as a senior banker managing the bank's own account investments. He still also manages a few important clients' portfolios. I have more time. I've worked part-time since we got married, then I gave up work altogether when we moved to Riverside – we don't need the money. I taught English. Whether to kids in comprehensives, smart public schools, or adult education. It feels as if, over the years, I have taught the whole of London and her husband. I have given enough, and it is time to think about myself.

The next day, I phone the charity. "Yes," says the bright young voice on the other end of the line. "We've got a man and van. We can send him round to collect the bikes, if you want."

"That would be great."

Down I go to the bike-store. Our bikes are a sorry sight – huddled together in the corner against the white wall. I need to clean up the two bikes before handing them over. Separate the three, brush away the cobwebs, and give them good soapy water and sponge treatment. I remove the black saddlebag from mine. A keepsake. Cycling back home after shopping with my saddlebag full and, at times, a carrier bag on each handlebar, down the Thames towpath has been one of the pleasures in my life. Riding under the green canopy with sunlight filtering through it. Or the gentle drizzle falling on me rewarded by a hot cup of tea and cake when I got home. Proud not to be polluting the air and getting exercise at the same time. I can always buy a new bike.

Anyway, one bike is staying, two are going. End of story.

Not so.

TWO

Monday 21st August

My cousin Susi phones me out of the blue. Susi is the only relative I've kept in touch with, and that is only every now and then. When some major incident takes place in her life – whether good or bad – she contacts me. Her mother is my mother's sister. When Susi's parents emigrated to London from Sicily, they lived with us until they could afford a deposit on a house. This meant that she slept in the single bedroom with me, in a single bed. So, essentially, we are like sisters in that we spent a lot of time together as children. Then her family bought a house across the road from ours. So we could still play together. But, they moved again. This time quite a long way out, to another part of London. I missed Susi so much after that. I also missed Susi's mum, she was kind to me. Eventually, Susi and I developed different characters and, as a consequence, we now don't have much in common except for the strong affection that binds us.

"Hi, Mary!"

"Susi, how are you?"

"Pete and me have just broken up."

"How many times has that happened now?"

"This is the third and final time."

"You know you'll take him back."

"No, I won't, not this time. I've had enough."

Pete has been spicing up his boring married life by having an on-and-off affair with Susi. She doesn't see that. I've told her as much, many times before.

"How's work?" I ask.

"Shit environment," she says. "Things are not good, some people have been laid off and there's this threat of redundancy hanging over us."

"I'm sorry to hear that. I do hope you'll be alright. Anyway, Susi, you're so enterprising, I'm sure you'll soon find something else even if it came to the worst."

"Mary, my mum's been asking about you. She says she really wants to see you. You know how close she was to your mum. My mum's fond of you as well. Try to make an old woman happy, why don't you?"

"Well... I'll think about it, Susi." She was emotionally blackmailing me. The call was probably instigated by Zia, Susi's mother.

"How's your retirement going, then? Enjoying being a lady of leisure, are you?"

"I am, actually. It's nice to have all that time on my hands," I say, "there're so many things I want to do and books to read."

"Yeah, but if you want a tip from me, don't get bogged down with all that reading. Try getting out of the house. Why don't you try volunteer work?" Susi says.

"Could do. Yes, I've always felt passionate about defending battered women and mistreated kids. It's got to have something to do with our childhood, you know?"

"Yeah, tell me about it," she says.

"We weren't dealt the best cards in life, were we?"

"You can say that again. I've got an even better idea. Why don't you get yourself a lover? That'll pep your life up."

"Really, Susi. I'm still in love with my Humps."

"Yeah, but it must be all pretty routine in the sex department by now. You need variety. The spice of life," she says. She wasn't altogether wrong in that respect.

"Maybe," I joke. We laugh. She knows it'll never happen. "Susi. I need to go out now. I'll phone you some time soon, promise."

"Right, but you promise you'll go and see my mum. Please, Mary."

"OK, Susi, I promise. Bye for now."

And I keep promises.

Wandering round a cycle shop, I am looking for ideas about how to vamp up Humps's bike. But, every bit of it needs changing, and then it wouldn't be his bike any more. So I end up buying a snazzy silver and black cover. You'd think there is a Harley-Davidson standing under that. To my surprise, when I go back to the bike-store I notice, on the wall, someone has drawn a big hand giving Humps's bike the finger. And, under it, they have written: "ARSEHOLE." It must have been the person who asked our landlord to tell us to remove the bikes. Who is that? No idea.

If we'd been owners of the flat we live in, we would have known exactly what is going on. We decided not to buy the flat. Instead, we bought a lovely chocolate-box cottage near the sea in Dorset, and a chalet in Cortina d'Ampezzo. When Humps finally decides to retire, we can go and spend our days by the seaside or in the Italian Dolomites. Both of which we love.

While cooking I keep churning the incident round in my mind. How dare someone call Humps an arsehole? No respect. I always taught my students the importance of respect. Respect for their parents, teachers, classmates and for the elderly. At the end of one school day, I once left school with some girls, and asked them to show respect to two old ladies by letting them get on the bus before us, even though they had arrived after us. I am so respectful that I even show respect to those I don't respect at all.

I need to find out who it is. And when I find out, what will I do? Will it be an eye-for-an-eye? Forgiveness? 'For they know not what they do'? Can revenge appease anger? Or, does it make matters worse? I have always found forgiving difficult. No doubt, revenge is time-consuming, requires effort, planning, and guts. And I chafe against the Catholic Church for forgiving sinners so easily. Just kneel down, tell the priest your sins, get a gentle rebuke, a few Hail Mary's, and off you go.

Now, I have a feeling deep in the pit of my stomach, a ball of anger which won't go away. Is this what my Sicilian ancestors felt when they couldn't get justice? Shamefully exploited by land barons. Powerless, helpless victims. Whole families, including children, working all day for a pittance, bending down low to the land under the blazing sun. Not even being able to feed themselves properly. Families living in one room, without electricity or running water. Revolting against their masters who were colluding with the State. And there is no sense of State when you have an empty stomach. In those conditions the only resort for justice was to take it into your own hands. Let's not leave it for heaven to sort out. Let's get it seen to down here. That was the attitude most Sicilian land workers developed.

The Romans captured Sicily and made it their own. Created a system called latifondo, a feudal system, whereby peasants rented land from the owners, or from a sub-lessor. That system survived well into the 1950s. The mafia emerged from the latifondo. The landowner's men paid thugs to keep the peasants from revolting; to punish those workers who dared to complain. But workers also sought to rise above their station and either co-operated with their very exploiters, or organised groups among themselves to threaten their own. Thus they could acquire a better piece of land or demand a percentage from their fellow-peasants. A savage survival of the fittest ensued post World War II. Rome couldn't cope, or didn't want to cope, with Sicily any more. The island went its own way.

When they grew up, hoards of those peasant children, amongst them my mother and father, emigrated, taking with them the pitiful image of their long-suffering parents. And they also took with them their sense of the violent climate they had grown up in.

My father arrived in England with a broken pair of shoes and a big cardboard box tied up with rope. Without a word of English. When he had saved enough money for the wedding, and train tickets for them to come back, he went to Sicily and married my mother. I still have a couple of black and white photos of their wedding. She is wearing her best Sunday dress. They couldn't afford a wedding dress. And their wedding reception was in the courtyard of my grandparents' house.

THREE

Tuesday 22nd August

Susi's mother, Zia, had been another one of those peasant children. Zia means 'aunt' in Italian. But in Sicily it is used as a term of respect for older women, as is zio for older men. Also, Susi's mother is a 'donna d'onore.' That is 'a woman of honour,' which implies that she is to be handled with utmost care because she has mafia links. So 'Zia' is the least you can call her. But, as coincidence has it, she is also my real aunt. And, although she is less than transparent, I am fond of her. I've kept her at arms' length to protect Humps, but he is now nearing the end of his career, so I need not fear an entanglement as much as I did before.

Seems like a lifetime since I saw her. Years. She is eighty-seven and lives on the other side of London from us, the East End. To get there, I walk about a mile down the Thames towpath, along the edge of a football field, and up a main road to the nearest underground station. I could take the bus but I'd rather get the exercise. Then, forty minutes by train with a change. It isn't exactly next-door. But the distance isn't the reason for not going to see Zia, it is an excuse.

My mother died young, when I was still at university. For five years, during my mother's illness, Zia had helped look after her and was often round at our house. The two sisters were very close, always had been. They have another sister in Sicily called Peppina. I did what I could to help during those years, but, emotionally, I was all at sea. Trying to deal with my teenage issues as well. Because I am an only child, I couldn't share the burden. My father stayed away from home for as much as possible. I never saw them exchange gestures of affection. No conniving glances. Even worse, at times they fought each other, never mind that I was present. My mother would growl at him like she did at me, and I remember objects and even furniture flying in our living room. When her illness became serious, he moved into the spare single bedroom, and started thinking about a new wife. A dark brooding atmosphere had always hung inside our house.

As if it hadn't been black enough, it became blacker when her incurable disease was found. Zia kept my mother company and livened the place up a little. I didn't know the full force of the illness, the gravity of it. Until I accompanied my mother to the doctor one day. I had to translate what the doctor was saying to her. He wanted her to have a complicated operation. She was scared and refused point blank. Sitting opposite the doctor, and with my mother at my side, he dropped a bombshell that I wasn't, even remotely, expecting: "If she has the operation she could live for another four to five years, if she doesn't it'll be six months." I was gobsmacked. It was as if a ton of bricks had come down on me. I felt deeply sorry for her.

On the tenth ring, Zia answers the phone with a forceful "Hallo!" Zia doesn't talk, she shouts, as my mother used to do.

"Zia, it's Maria, your niece."

"Maria, I no believe you call me. Long time no hear. Why you no call?"

"Sorry, Zia, I've had a busy life, what with the house,

work, family..."

"You make excuse. You no make time for you Zia."

"But I'm calling you now," I say. "I've got a grandson, you know? His name's Benjamin."

"I know. Susi she tell me. Ah, you daughter give baby nice name?"

"Zia, he's the most gorgeous baby you could ever hope to see. Anyway, Zia, I wanted to check you were at home this afternoon."

"Cousin here, but you come. You remember Angelina and Provvidenza, yeah?"

Zia doesn't do plurals. Like many native Italian speakers of English, she finds an 's' at the end of a word difficult to pronounce.

"Yes, I remember, I think."

Actually, they aren't our cousins at all, not even ten times removed. But Zia likes to collect cousins. So any Sicilian she's been on particularly good terms with is awarded the status of an honorary cousin.

"Angelina?" she shouts even louder, irritated that it took me a moment to retrieve the women from my memory. "She has daughter, Provvi. You know, she have bad leg, she limp."

"Oh, yes!" I say. "I know."

I sincerely hope that Angelina and Provvi are in another room and the doors are closed, so that they haven't heard what she just said.

"See you later, Zia."

That's what Zia is like. If she has to describe anyone, she distinguishes them by their physical faults: the one with the crooked teeth, hawk nose, squint, big mole, shrill voice...

Though, of course, Zia herself has never been an oil painting, nor is she ugly. One might describe her as nondescript, quite short and thin. She wears flat sensible shoes, pleated skirts and blouses. I've never seen her in trousers. Her movements fast, darting around all over the place. And she throws her arms about a lot. Walking with Zia was exhausting, as a child I had to run to keep up. She has acquired a hunched back. It makes her head stick out at the front. It isn't parallel with the rest of her body. Her hair is always clipped back by a large tortoiseshell slide. Overall, she has an odd schoolgirl style. Her appearance is deceptive, though, because there's nothing, absolutely nothing, naïve about Zia.

I swing our Residence's heavy gate shut behind me and step onto the towpath. Strolling along the Thames always makes me feel good, that fresh light breeze in my face and in the trees, the clouds floating by... But today, I am more absorbed in my thoughts. Going to see Zia after all these years has brought back memories of my family as a child. I'd heard that Zia had been involved in things not quite above board in her past. I don't know what exactly. I couldn't ask and, even if I did, she wouldn't tell me.

My earliest memory of my extended family in Sicily was when I was there as a nine-year-old when we stayed with my grandparents and Aunt Peppina. Zia and her family were in Sicily, too. Though Zia's family stayed with her in-laws in the same village, within walking distance, as there wasn't space enough for all of us at my grandparents' house. Zia and Susi spent most of their day with us, though. Susi and I were very close and we loved playing together. Our grandfather didn't like us. I vaguely remember him. A severe man. He never spoke to me, or to Susi, come to that – only to Silvio and Stefano, Susi's brothers, out of his grandchildren. He had a deep revulsion for females. Susi and I were playing in the courtyard with other girls in the neighbourhood. My memories are those of hearing the sound of the hooves against the cobble stones, then looking up to see him arriving sitting proudly on his mule. You could even describe him as arrogant. Getting off, he landed lightly on the ground causing some dust to lift. Then he spat not far from his boots, led the mule to the stable, and yanked the reins hard, on the sharp corner, to turn the mule round, and force it in. At that moment, my grandmother came down to the courtyard all in a tizz, like she did every time he arrived home. He didn't acknowledge her, so much was his disdain of the sight of her.

The mistreatment was due to the fact that she hadn't been capable of giving him a son. I remember he insulted her in front of visitors and threatened to hit her by raising his hand into a slap position. Once I overheard some women saying that when my grandmother and grandfather were out in the village together, they bumped into the mayor and stopped to talk to him. My grandfather slapped my grandmother in the face, while she was standing there silently, just to prove he was boss in his house. A real man.

Our grandmother signalled to Susi and me to go back inside the house. So we followed them upstairs. He sat on a chair in the kitchen, lifted one of his feet for my grandmother to pull off his boot. She tugged so hard that she jolted backwards as the boot came off. Then the other boot. After which she took the boots out to the garden where she gave them a wash and brush up.

It was also during this holiday that Ziuzza's husband died in the unforgiving campagna. It was summer. Not understanding what was going on, all I could do was to listen to the shrills and shouts in my grandmother's house. She sat down and slid her hands into her hair, rocking backwards and forwards in the chair, in a kind of distressing trance, yelling and repeating in Sicilian dialect "Ammazzru me cugnatu, disgraziati. Ammazzru u marito di me sorru!" *meaning:* "They've killed my brother-in-law, the villains. They've killed my sister's husband." I was frightened and couldn't understand what was going on. She knew that

Ziuzza would be left vulnerable, without a husband, and on the wrong side of victory. And Ziuzza had always been defiant. Her enemies knew she wouldn't back down, that she had been the driving force behind her husband. And that she was more than capable of taking the helm.

Ziuzza's husband's body was brought to my grandmother's house because it was bigger. Ziuzza's house had a narrow spiral staircase up to the first floor and there was no way they could bring a coffin down, if not vertically. Like my grandmother's house, Ziuzza's house had a stable on the ground-floor. It would have been disrespectful to hold the wake there.

I can still remember the day when they brought his body back to The Village – it's impressed on my memory. I've forgotten a lot about my childhood, but I will never forget this episode. Ziuzza needed support when the body arrived in The Village, so my grandmother and other women were there to comfort her. Ziuzza had two sons. They had both emigrated to England and could not console her. So she was accompanied by a couple of men, while others went before them and cleared the roads by telling people to go inside. With a sheet over her head, she walked to my grandmother's house through, what was at that point, a ghost village. Even the two little grocery shops and the chemist pulled down their shutters. Only stray cats and dogs roamed the streets.

My grandfather and two other men, all on mules, went to fetch the body. They knew exactly where his land was. A man whose land was next to his had noticed that his sheep had strayed. That meant they weren't being herded. He went to inquire and found Ziuzza's husband lying perfectly immobile face down where his blood had coagulated with the dust. Flies hummed around him and feasted on his injuries. The peasant rushed to The Village to raise the alarm.

The grown-ups stood at the entrance door and in the

courtyard to wait for his body to come into sight. Susi and I weren't allowed to be there with them. Silvio and Stefano, had been sent to their other grandparents. Susi and I were told to go out and play in the garden at the back of the house. But we knew something extraordinary was happening and didn't want to miss it. So we went to sit quietly on the balcony, on the first floor, and kept our heads down. We had a wide open view of the whole courtyard and, to the left, we could see the women spilling out of the entrance door while they waited for the body to arrive.

My grandfather on his mule appeared first around the corner. Following him, close behind, was another mule tied to the first one by a thick rope. Both animals dribbling foam from their mouths. Slumped over the second mule, face down, hands and feet dangling, was Ziuzza's husband's body wrapped in a blanket with blood seeping through it. A man walked by the side of the mule to keep an eye on the body. All you could hear was the clip-clop of the hooves in the stillness under the outrageously hot sun, until the women caught sight of him and began howling to the sky, hitting themselves, pulling their own hair, and out of rage Ziuzza tore the black skirt she was wearing. It was a sorry sight.

As the body was being brought up the stairs, Susi and I scarpered to the garden. But when the body was laid in the middle of the room, we crept into the kitchen and watched through a slither of the open door. They washed the body, put a suit, shirt and tie on him, combed his hair, pulled his legs straight and folded his arms across his chest. Everyone sat in a circle around the body. Peppina led the rosary. The room filled up with visitors who'd come to pay their respects. Standing room only. The people who had killed him were there, too, offering their condolences to his widow. Ziuzza spat at one man in the face. He slowly wiped the spittle off, grinned, turned around, and left.

When my family went back to Sicily, when I was aged fifteen, my grandfather had already died. My grandmother in Sicily had a similar lifestyle to Zia's in London: family, friends, drinks, and cake. Hospitality is a Sicilian custom. Guests are always welcome. But there was a big difference between the entrance to my grandmother's house and Zia's house. Grandmother's front door was always wide open during the day. My aunt Peppina used to go and pin the door back at 6.30 every morning. From then on women, mostly dressed in black, would parade in and out of the house until sunset.

My grandfather died years before my grandmother. She died at a ripe age. Just like Zia, grandmother was a widow for years. Left on their own, aunt Peppina and grandmother used to squabble no end. Aunt Peppina had never married. And if you didn't marry in those days in Sicily, your only way out of your parents' house was in a wooden box – a white one. Grandmother used to get me breakfast: yesterday's leftover bread soaked in milky coffee and sprinkled with sugar. I'd usually have a different assortment of 'godmothers' or women relatives, clad in black, watching me having breakfast. And, as mentioned before, Ziuzza, was among them until she was killed.

Custom was that when your husband died, you wore black for the rest of your life. That included black shoes, stockings, and handbag. If you didn't wear black, it meant you were on the lookout for another husband. Widowers, bachelors, any man, both far and wide, could come knocking at your door asking your hand in marriage. For the first year after a husband's death, women also wore a black headscarf when going out. If you didn't, your sadness for your husband's loss was fake. Who made up all these rules called customs? Why were women always expected to suffer the slings and arrows of outrageous fortune?

The default for women was that they were loose, 'troie.' They were born hussies. A kind of original sin. So only by her 'good' behaviour could a woman climb out of the troia category and become a decent woman. Women were obsessed with not putting a foot wrong. And the most rigorous enforcers of women's morality were women themselves.

You could be a troia for no-end of reasons. Because you smiled at a man in the street, because you wore make-up, because you wore high heels, because you wore revealing or tight clothes... Once when I was in Sicily, Peppina decided that all the clothes I'd brought over from England were troia clothes. She ran up a couple of dresses, or should I say sacks, on her Singer sewing machine. I still remember how she saw lust in everyone and sought to cover my body in long-sleeved, baggy kimono-like things.

Zia called Ziuzza's son Cushi. The name means 'cousin' in Sicilian. He died about ten years back in about 2007. He emigrated to England when he knew he'd be killed if he stayed. After his mother, it would have been his turn as the eldest son. However, he kept going backwards and forwards between Sicily and London. Doing God knows what. With God knows whom. Cushi had worked a few years for British Rail – cleaning trains – but he was caught sleeping on seats more than once, when he should have been working, and finally got fired. Since then, he refused to look for any more work. If he was unlucky, as he used to say, work would find him.

He bought a few huge run-down old houses in a run-down part of London, and rented out rooms to anyone: prostitutes, drug pushers, all low-life seemed to be there. Weekly payment on Fridays in cash. No contracts. "If you no pay, I keep your nice things and chuck rest out of window, you no come back." He actually threw a woman out of a window once, or so it was rumoured. And he got into trouble with the police over it. He diddled electricity meters, he found a way. His hobby was poaching on country estates. If anyone questioned him about the latter, he'd say he was the gardener. The lord of the manor had given him permission.

The most horrendous episode he was involved in was the abduction and rape of a young Sicilian woman. An honour rape. His brother had fallen in love with her, she wouldn't have anything to do with him. Her family had no mafia connections. She was easy prey. To be refused by a woman from an 'inferior' family is an insult to one's honour. One morning when she was going to work, Cushi, his brother, and another man, frogmarched her into a white van. They parked the vehicle in a quiet spot. Cushi and the man kept guard while the brother attempted to rape the woman. They had the radio on loud to disguise the screaming. But, she was resistant. Cushi and the other man had to go into the van to hold her down and silence her. Word was then put around that she had been raped. She was dishonoured and had to marry him. It's called a matrimonio riparatore, *meaning:* 'a marriage that repairs.' By marrying her, he was repairing the damage he had done. Making an honest woman out of her.

This kind of mindset was exactly what I chafed against. The reason why I have been a feminist ever since I can remember. Going on marches when I was at university and standing up for women whenever I could. Though I would never tell my daughters about these heinous acts taking place in our family. I sometimes wonder how they would react given that they do not seem particularly interested in feminism. The fighting was done by my generation, and the generations of women before mine.

Back in The Village, Cushi had become bosom friends with the Mayor. Zia helped him recruit relatives and friends to go to Sicily and vote for Cushi's Mayor. Cushi would already be there in The Village piazza doing the meeting and greeting, simultaneously giving everyone voting instructions, along with subtle threats. Voting in accordance with your political outlook wasn't an option. Votes were for Cushi's candidate. The opposition would only get his family's votes. That was allowed. There had never been a woman candidate.

And Cushi's side knew exactly who you'd voted for. Although the ballot-papers were all alike, you'd think that your vote would be anonymous. Nothing of the sort. You gave your ballot-paper to the man standing behind the box. He put a sign on it. He would crease it slightly, on a corner, or tear it a little bit around one of the edges. Then he'd add your name to his list, 'to remember that you'd voted.' Next to your name he'd write how your ballot-paper could be singled out. They didn't even try to hide their dishonesty. I saw him. Right in front of me creasing a corner, the first time I voted in Sicily. Everyone knew. Nobody said anything. The result was that the mayor would be Cushi's puppet. Cushi was the mayor maker.

I arrive at Zia's house. She has two front doors, an outer one, and an inner one. The outer one being a wired-glass cage. She obviously thinks one door isn't enough to keep undesirables out. I remember her reason for this was that "People rob. Get in house." She opened the inner front door and, if she didn't like the look of you, she'd shout "No today," and shut it directly. She'd also had metal blinds fitted on the inside of her ground-floor windows, "Break glass. People come in." The blinds fastened at the bottom with a good chunky lock. But the smell of freshly baked cakes manages to escape through all the security measures. She is always on the bake. Trayfuls. Free to anyone who visits the house: "Mangia, mangia. Cuppa tea?" Eat here or take away. Incessant coming and going, to and from her house, every weekday afternoon was the norm.

"Zia. It's me, Maria," I call out after she has opened the inner door.

"Maria, Maria, trasi, trasi. Long time no see you." Zia is visibly moved. She hugs me tight then looks me in the eye and says: "You look like my poor sister."

"It's nice to see you again," I say to her, feeling guilty that I can't quite conjure up the same Sicilian effusions about seeing her, although I actually love her as much as I do Susi and Silvio. They were my childhood.

"I make eclair this morning. Cuppa tea?" Zia says to me, then she shouts "Maria here," to her guests in the living room, as I wipe my shoes on the doormat.

"Yes, please, Zia. That would be great," I say as I follow her down the yellow-painted corridor, like Sicilian sun, with prints of saints on the walls on one side, and Popes on the other, chronologically ordered so that Pope Pius XII is the first in line, and the present Pope Francis is nearer the living room door. Though there is space for more before she gets to the door frame.

The eclair is already there waiting for me. I greet Angelina and her daughter Provvi, and another woman who I don't know. This lady is just leaving. Zia goes to show her out saying "I see you next week."

The living room floor is still covered with chequered light-blue and black lino tiles. I remember Zia and my mother laying them down after brushing glue onto each tile, then stamping them down into place with their feet. Susi and I did a bit of jumping up and down on the tiles, too. The wallpaper is new: orange roses with big green leaves on a white background. Clara, as an art historian, would be horrified if she saw this décor. Zia still has her wedding photo standing on the sideboard in an aluminium frame. And next to that, she has Silvio and Stefano's wedding photos, and a few of her grandchildren. Zia has decided to forget about Susi's disastrous marriage. In the middle of the room is a big wooden table, and on this table a tray of eclairs, a teapot and pink flowered cups and saucers. All very English. Chairs scattered wherever there's a space. The room is a thoroughfare. It has four doors. Three in a row along one side: from left to right, the pantry door, the corridor, and the sitting-room door. On the opposite side is a door leading to the kitchen. I notice the pantry door is padlocked.

As Zia is still chatting with her departing visitor, I sit with Angelina and Provvi. Angelina has an identical twin living in The Village called Beatrice. Both Angelina and Beatrice's husbands died together in the same car accident in Sicily years back. There had been a lot of talk about identical twins losing their husbands at the identical time. It was too much of a coincidence, people murmured.

Angelina looks straight at me, squints and asks "Do you live near the Thames?" It comes across as an accusation. As if it were a crime to be well-off. Lucky she doesn't know about the cottage and the chalet. We keep those secret.

"Ma, you know she lives near the river," Provvi butts in.

"Yes, I live in a flat near the Thames towpath," I nod, smiling at Provvi as if to say 'It's OK, I know their ways.' Angelina, like the others in the community, can't stomach that I have moved away from them, and have thrived by that decision.

"Good place. You've got money. You don't work. Your husband works for you," Angelina goes on.

I detect a tinge of envy, and give her a half smile.

"Ma, stop it!" Provvi huffs, red with embarrassment.

A noticeable bruise peeps over Provvi's neckline as she bends down to pick up her handbag. "We need to go now. We've got to get some shopping before we go home."

They bid me goodbye, kiss me on both cheeks, pick up

their cake box and go to the front door where Zia is still yabbering to the other woman. Zia is full of flowery apologies saying that they mustn't go, that she is all theirs now. But the mother and daughter insist that they must leave otherwise they won't get their shopping done before Provvi's boys finish school.

Zia's expression has changed, softer; she is motherly towards me. "Long time no see," Zia says looking at me, smiling, and picking up her knitting. She's still making bed socks. Her bed socks accompanied me through my childhood as my feet grew. Mostly pink, sometimes yellow the colour of lemons and the Sicilian sun, Zia used to say. These were mint green. I knew the style. Ribbed above the ankles, leaving little eyelets for a crocheted cord to run through, then adding a pompom onto each end, nicely anchored so the cord wouldn't come out when you untied the bow in the morning. She used to make baby-blue ones for Silvio and we'd laugh about them.

Feeling a bit guilty, I say: "Zia, I'm only just getting on top of things. You know, I had the flat to look after, the family and work..."

"You can no make minute for you Zia."

I feel fleeting pity for her. She has aged so much. Such a thin face. I might not have recognised her, if I'd passed her in the street. I am her only niece. She has some on her husband's side of the family, but they mean nothing to her.

"Of course, I will make more of an effort in future, Zia, I promise."

"And you keep promise for Zia."

I nod. We go on talking for a while about our families. She's very interested and wants to know everything about my new grandson. Then we talk about neighbours. She tells me an Italian family from Naples lives on one side and an English family on the other. Zia doesn't have much to do with the English family, while she's great friends with the Italian lady, when they are not squabbling. "Napoli is not Sicilia," Zia says. Nobody is superior to Sicilians in Zia's view of the world. A blessed island.

I shouldn't have told her, but given it's been niggling me, I spurt out the bike incident.

"Zia, I've had a little problem with one of the residents..."

"You live posh house. You no have problem."

"Unfortunately, some people behave like children."

She doesn't look up, concentrates on her knitting until I tell her about the insulting graffiti. She stops knitting.

"Minghia! They call you arsehole?" she asks raising her voice. "Nobody call daughter of my poor sister bucu du culu!"

"Exactly. It's bad, isn't it?"

"And you no break big bastardo face? You know we have cousin, picciotti..."

"Zia, I don't even know who it is."

"We no kill. But we make revenge."

I look at her, "What?!"

"You give him my cake, give him big diarrhoea. He shit for one army."

"Zia, are you putting laxative into cakes? I don't believe it..."

"You no believe because you Englishwoman. You marry Englishman. You read book. I tell you, you find this man. I make special cake for him."

The door bell rings. Zia goes to see who it is from behind the net curtain, "Ah, Bella and Rosa," she says, looking directly at me, "they du big bagasci, my husband Tony two niece."

When they come in through the door, Zia embraces them as if they are two long-lost sisters, "Bella! Rosa! Trasi, trasi. I wait for you. I make special eclair for you."

Amongst all the greeting and shouting coming from all directions, I take advantage of the confusion, say I need to go and cook dinner, bid the ladies 'hello' and 'goodbye.' Zia grabs me by the arm and says: "Yes, you come back tomorrow. You keep promise for Zia. I have friend. She have problem, she need you help." Then she shoves a couple of eclairs in my hand, wrapped in aluminium foil, for Humps.

FOUR

Tuesday 22nd August – late afternoon

On my way back home, I start musing about being caught between two cultures. Frustration overcomes me. How many times do they have to voice their disdain at my being English? Why can't they simply accept it? Like I accept that most of the other second generation Sicilians are closer to their roots. They go to mass on Sundays and are devious the rest of the week. I am atheist like my father. My relatives go back to The Village nearly every summer. I haven't been for over four decades. This distancing of mine irks them. Obviously, there is resentment there. Some put it down to the fact that my mother died when I was young. I went astray from there. That is total rubbish. Long before that, I had taken the decision to be English, when I was about twelve, or even before. I don't remember exactly. But I do know that I can't think of a time when I wanted to be like them.

And Auntie Marge's influence contributed to that. She wasn't my auntie at all, nor was her husband my Uncle Peter. They were our English next door neighbours. She looked after me. She and Zia were the nearest I had to a mother. I could identify with Auntie Marge and her husband. And I wanted to be part of their way of life. I wanted to marry an Englishman. An educated man. Like Uncle Peter. Not one of the rough boys in our community, though they weren't all like that. I wanted to get away from their arguing, backstabbing, aggression and dodgy doings. I wanted to be part of something else.

Maybe it wasn't necessary to go as far as I did. But once I'd started, I got more and more determined. See how far I could get. It's astounding what you can do when you set your mind to it. I marched straight on resolutely towards my new life, looking neither left nor right. During university, and particularly after I graduated in English, I got myself a posh accent. Did it all by myself. Imitated the BBC newsreaders. Spoke more slowly. Got my vowels right. Pronounced my consonants properly. Was I going to teach English in my broad cockney? I don't think so.

I stepped it up: read *The Times, The Economist* and, every now and then, even the *Financial Times*. I knew who all the politicians were, who was trying to backstab whom, who had safe seats and which seats could be toppled at the next election. I knew the names of prominent foreign leaders, kept abreast of how they interacted, who was doing what and why. I was like Alice in Wonderland. And, to top it all, shame on me, I even joined the Conservative party. Went to their dinners and acted all la-di-da like them. Any awkward questions about my past were sidelined by vague answers, and quickly followed by a question which I knew would flatter their egos. That transferred the focus onto them and, from then on, it was plain sailing. They loved talking about themselves. And my interest in their lives seemed to be second to none.

Though I looked and sounded the part, there were some gaps in my behaviour I needed to tweak: not interrupting people while they were talking, not flaring up when I disagreed with someone (which happened frequently), feigning interest when they bored me (which also happened frequently), and not appearing too forward. My manners were soon honed to perfection. I quickly learnt which cutlery was used for what, which glasses were for wine, water, port... What to do with my napkin. All looked confusing at the start, but it turned out you didn't have to be awfully clever to understand it. In fact, you could be quite thick, like some of them, and understand it. At these events, I met the narrow-minded and conceited Mr. Collinses, and the tiresome garrulous Mrs. Bennets of this world. But, contrastingly, it was also where I met my Mr. Darcy.

I had already noticed him at other events. On this particular occasion he came bowling over to me while I was speaking to an elderly lady about her cello. She didn't budge, so Humps had to listen to her as well. Then he had to leave because he had an appointment. Anyway, we got each other's names. At the next event, he was there dressed in black looking drop-dead gorgeous. He had a polo-neck tucked into his trousers. And good quality brown leather belt, and cow-boyish boots. Jesus. The black set off his green eyes, his dark blonde hair was longish and swept back. He had that confidence expensive public schools gave you. My heart was in my mouth when I saw him making a beeline for me. This time I was alone. He towered over me. I'm five-foot-six, he about six-foot-two, I guessed. We went to sit at a table. After we'd spoken about the weather, he started telling me about his job in banking, and about his family; their country pile in Surrey and their barge on the Thames. While he was talking, I was thinking that, given a chance, I'd have him there-and-then under the table. "How lovely," I said, nodding and smiling.

Meeting Humps was the best thing that had happened in my life. I was enthused by his attentions. Tried to make myself as attractive as possible using money my mother had left me. I put a lot of time in making myself look tip-top. And

I thoroughly enjoyed the whole process. But I also made a point of forgetting about my appearance once I'd taken a last look in the mirror upon leaving home. Before dates with Humps, I'd go to a chic salon and have my long black hair styled differently each time. I bought plenty of designer clothes in stark and dark colours, and had great fun combining them. Shoes. Only leather. With heels. I wore the best make-up and French perfume.

When things got serious he took me to meet his parents. By then, I had nobody to introduce him to. I was the whole of my family. I admit that must have seemed quite suspicious to his parents. As I always did to start off with, I told them that my parents were Italian. "Sicilian," Humps added. "And do you speak Sicilian?" his mother, Penelope, asked me.

"Yes, I do. It's the only language, dialect actually, that I spoke up to the age of five before I went to school." She was visibly shocked. Probably thinks that all Sicilians are mafiosi. Which is rubbish. Not all Sicilians have the ability. To thrive in the mafia, you have to be laser-sharp, especially if you want to make it all the way up to a boss. Even the picciotti need to make on-the-spot decisions.

Humps's father, Jacob, took to me like fish to water. Penelope hated me from the moment she set sight on my curvaceous figure and shapely legs. I was wearing a smart electric-blue Armani suit, the pencil skirt came to about two inches above my knee. High-heeled beige Italian designer shoes. Dark red lipstick, and nail varnish, which set off my long dark hair and brown eyes. Men loved my Italian looks. I wasn't going to try looking like an Englishwoman. I couldn't even if I'd tried. Penelope looked me up and down with a slight hint of disdain.

But she was no threat to me, I'd already given Humps the whole tantalising, Sophia-Loren corset and black stockings jingbang, like in the film. And one Sunday, we spent the whole day in bed. To save time we had cheese panini in bed for lunch, then made love on the crumbs. There's a lot to be said for long wet British Sundays. Humps knew there was plenty more where all that came from. Then, to top it all, we were intellectual equals. We could talk and laugh for hours. Penelope didn't stand a chance. She could stick her nose up at me as much as she wanted. I took little notice of her. Concentrated on Humps, Jacob, and Humps's sister, Fiona, instead. Stupid Penelope. I could have had her barge burnt to ashes before she could say croissant. Even if it was surrounded by water. Poor Jacob probably only got a quick fumble around in the dark while his no-tits wife lay back and thought of England.

Fiona was nice. But she was frumpy. Hair the same colour as Humps's but straight, and lanky. As far as good looks and intellect were concerned, Humps, as first born, had got there first and taken all the good features in those departments that his parents could afford. Fiona was self-conscious, a constant nail-biter. I decided that flat-sandals-and-socks, Fiona, would be my matron of honour. She was delighted. And so was I. Not that I needed a young woman like that to set off my good looks. I made sure we decided the wedding day would be in September. When Zia and Susi would be on holiday in Sicily. Can you imagine Susi there, running after every suit, and Zia shouting minghia at anything she thought nice? Amongst all those toffs? And, what with my mother dead and my father out of my life, there was nobody at our wedding on my side of the family. I didn't even want any university friends there, in case they let out some stupid comment.

That stopped Humps's family from knowing about my relatives. Not even Humps knew about our links to the mafia. He might not have married me, if he'd had an inkling. But he was well and truly cooked. Say what you like about

Italians but they know a thing or two about culinary skills. Anyway, what did Penelope have to complain about? It was partly her own fault for making her son such a sexy and clever devil. Notwithstanding the stupid Christian name they'd given him. I ask you. He was anything but a Humphrey.

FIVE

Tuesday 22nd August – evening

Humps arrives home from work. I go and give him a passionate kiss.

"Did you have a good day, darling?" he asks.

"Oh, yes. Though quite uneventful. Had a lovely walk down the towpath. Did some shopping on the way back. And, what do you know? I went across London, and popped in to see Zia, too."

"What a surprise! Well, I'd never have guessed that. Going to visit your family now, are you? After all you went through?" He seems a little uneasy.

"Oh, darling, don't worry it was my mother and Peppina who abused me. Zia's always been kind to me."

"I'm sorry, but you're very worryable about. So what brought that on?"

"Well, it was Susi who insisted I go to see her mother."

"I've never felt the need to embrace your family connections. And you've never insisted, but that's fine by me. How is she?" Humps asks.

"Ah, very well. She's got lots of life in her yet. She has more energy than me," I laugh.

"Must be getting on now. How old is she?"

"She's eighty-seven."

"So what does she do to pass the time these days?"

"You know, she has lots of visitors. The whole female population of the Sicilian community seems to waltz in and out of her house. Always has the kettle on."

"You said she used to make some bloody top-notch cakes, if my memory serves me well."

"Yes, your memory serves you very well, Humps. She made chocolate eclairs this morning. Can you believe that? Here, she gave me a couple for you."

Bless him, he was about to take one.

"Not until after dinner. It'll spoil your appetite," I say.

"It's you who spoils my appetite by not letting me eat what I want."

We laugh and hug.

"And how was your day, darling?" I ask.

"Busy as usual. One of our big clients is playing up. He reckons he can get much better returns on his investments than he does with us managing his portfolio. He's been told that by some quack."

"Do you think he'll go?"

"No knowing what he'll do, Mary. He's done well over the years. Hope he comes to his senses. If he goes, he'll probably invest it in some dodgy scheme and lose it all."

"Oh, dear," I say. "That would be a great shame."

"I'll do what I can to stop him. But, ultimately, it's up to him."

SIX

Wednesday 23rd August – morning

Determined to find out who'd written that insult, I figure out that I'd have to circulate where I can bump into the other residents. While sitting quietly, on a bench in the communal garden reading a new novel, I am keeping an eye on the bike-store. The heavy wrought-iron gates to the complex open and Charlie drives his 4x4 monster in. He parks in the only space left. Next to our Mercedes. The garages were designed so badly, you can't get a big car in them. So I keep my VW Golf in ours. We wave to each other. Charlie lives on the third floor, just below us, with his wife Sarah and two children. He is a property developer and was involved in building this very complex we live in. They've been here since it was built in the late 1990s.

"Hi, Charlie, how's everything?" I ask.

"Trundling along," he says, "Busy as usual. And how are you and Humphrey?"

"We're fine, thanks. Listen, Charlie, I wanted to show you something. It'll only take a moment."

I walk towards the bike-store and he follows, like an obedient poodle.

"You see, someone's drawn this pretty picture here and accompanied it with a sophisticated caption. It's directed at Humps. We've decided not to move his bike."

He shakes his head. "Surprising what fully-fledged adults can do. Look, don't worry, leave your bike here. I'll see to this unacceptable behaviour."

"You must know who it is," I say, "it was the person at the AGM who insisted we move our bikes. You were there." He doesn't answer.

Because we are not invited to the AGM, when changes are made, I usually get information second-hand from Sarah. Charlie takes a picture with his phone, says he is sorry, and that he'll have a circular sent round to all the residents. He leaves. I go back to the garden bench with my book. About twenty minutes later, Sarah appears. She comes and sits next to me. We discuss the weather and the book I am reading. A man comes out of the bike-store, waves at her from a distance. "Hello, Richard," she says as she waves.

"Good morning, Sarah. Off for a ride while the sun's shining – strike while the sun's hot and all that. What-O." Mounts his bike and cycles off.

"He never speaks to me," I say. "He's always been stand-offish."

"Good old Dicky doesn't hide his feelings. He can't abide foreigners, never has done. He's a staunch Leaver."

It soon dawns on me that I am the foreigner!

"What!" I say. "I'm not a foreigner. I've got a British passport. I was born here! Was I supposed to get a taxi to Heathrow and a flight to Italy at one day old?"

She laughs at that.

"He's a great fan of Farage's. He did a lot of campaigning for Brexit in the run-up to the referendum last year. He even came canvassing us, though he was preaching to the converted."

"Well, he didn't knock on our door."

"He wouldn't what with you being Ital... You know what I mean, having Italian parents..."

So, that's how they see me. An outsider – not one of them. She tries to make amends. "Hey, you beguiled Humphrey with your Mediterranean looks. Everyone says you're a looker, even now you're in your early sixties." It gets worse. "Must be all that olive oil... Um, I came down to say I'm sorry about the bike incident. Charlie just got home and told me about it. Richard shouldn't have done that."

"Richard!"

"Yes, didn't you know? Sorry, I've opened my big mouth again and put my foot in it. I thought you knew."

"I do now. Look, sorry, Sarah, but I need to get lunch ready, otherwise it won't be ready by the time Humphrey arrives. Must run along. Bye for now."

"Bye. I'll pop round. I want to talk to you about the barbecue," she shouts after me.

SEVEN

Wednesday 23rd August – lunchtime

Humps is coming home for lunch today because he is going to work from home in the afternoon. Concentration is not easy in a chaotic office. And he needs to do some preparation for his talk at the British Bankers' Association about the effects of Brexit on banking.

"What did you do this morning, darling?" Humps asks, as he is about to plough into his spaghetti bolognese. "You don't look very happy, Mary. Are you OK?"

"I'm fine, don't worry. Sarah, downstairs, was all in awe of Brexit. She got on my nerves, if truth be told."

"Oh, just forget about her. She doesn't understand Brexit. She spouts off what she reads in the right-wing press. Danger is that even a small recession can trigger a serious depression..."

"It's not only Sarah, you know? Most people here in Riverside View are Leavers."

"Not surprised."

"No, I suppose not, darling. Sarah also said that it was Richard, you know, second floor, who scribbled the obscenity in the bike-store."

"Richard! What? A middle-aged Banksy. Started graffiti a bit late in life, didn't he? Thinks he's a teenager..." Humps laughs.

He finds it amusing and couldn't care less about the insult. Typical of Humps, he lets things wash over him. I'm livid. As I've grown older, I don't feel as tolerant as before. I wonder if, rather than ignoring the issue, doing something about it would make me feel less cross.

"Humps, do you see me as more English or Italian?"

"Mary, you're a lovely mixture. I see you as English with a dash of Italian that makes you so attractive. You wouldn't be you without the combination of the two cultures."

"Thanks, darling. You're totally biased in my favour, of course."

"Of course."

"Oh, nearly forgot to tell you. The annual Riverside View BBQ is on Sunday. Always last Sunday of August. Good job Sarah reminded me, I would have forgotten otherwise."

"Didn't we get the usual card in our letter box?" he asks.

It is Barbara, Richard's wife, who usually stuffs the invitations in our letter boxes. They've left us out!

"Well, I haven't seen it," I reply. "I'll suggest to Sarah that we'll take the dessert. I was thinking of getting Zia to make something."

"Excellent choice," he says, "nothing like Zia's home-made cakes. You'll make an impact with those."

"Yes, I certainly will. A big impact."

Richard won't forget it for a while, I thought.

Humps loads the dishwasher. That is his territory. Only he can pack it properly, so he says. I leave him to it, ring Sarah's bell on the way down and ask if I may bring the dessert for Sunday. "Yes, that's excellent," she says, "Barbara's bringing the spare ribs, I'm doing sausages and jacket potatoes. I'll get the others to bring drinks and salads. We're catering for about fifteen."

And off I go to Zia's. Zia doesn't welcome visits in the morning, she has to do her housework, she says. So I want to make sure that I'll be the first to get there and hope any other visitors arrive later, after I've spoken to her.

Another sunny day. The Thames is busy. A boat named 'The Kid's Inheritance' passes me. Amusing. A few implications there, methinks. I did inherit a good deal of money when my mother died – money she'd hidden in an old, brown, faux-leather bag at the bottom of her wardrobe. All cash. She told me where to find it. But I already knew it was there.

Not that she wanted me to have it, more that she didn't want my father to get his hands on it. She knew he'd spend it on some other woman. He'd already raided their building society account. The building society wanted my mother's presence and signature to withdraw all the money and close the account. My father took my mother's passport, and he and his sister, Gloria, took every last penny out. Aunt Gloria pretended she was my mother and must have practised her signature. The two women did look vaguely alike, they had black hair and wore it in a similar shortish-permed hairstyle, typical of the 1970s. My mother herself found out about this fraud and told me. They emptied the account. Though it wasn't much money, she was upset.

She still had a lot of money. She had worked all her life and had been frugal. When my mother went out she took the bag with her. I knew she was hiding something in there because she kept the bag locked up in her wardrobe at all times when she was at home. And she kept the key on herself at all times. But I discovered that the key to my wardrobe also opened hers. One day when she was gardening, I ransacked the wardrobe, opened the bag and, to my disbelief, it was full of banknotes. Jam packed. Tenners, twenties, and fifties. Tied in wads with elastic bands. Couldn't imagine how much was in there. As if it burned my fingers, I quickly put it back, locked the wardrobe door again. Dazed and confused I hurried to my room. Sat on my bed in a trance trying to figure it all out. Where had the money come from? How much was it? This wasn't the kind of money you could put by as a factory worker. No matter how much you penny pinched.

Shortly before she died, she said to me in Sicilian dialect: "Un ci fare arrivare dru bastardo di tu padri. Manco un penny," *meaning*: don't let that bastard of your father lay his hands on even a penny of it. The day after she died, I did a quick round trip and took the bag to my bedsit. I was living on my own by then. I had no qualms about taking that money.

In fact, not long after her death, my father was married again. He kept the marriage a secret from me. That was in November, I was at university. They got married in Sicily. I didn't find out until it was all done and dusted. I was gob-smacked. How could he do this? He'd had no consideration for me or my recently dead mother. His new wife, Elena, was Aunt Gloria's sister-in-law. Sicilian, of course. Blonde.

The consequence of the marriage was devastating. Elena forbade my father to have anything to do with me. At first, they lived in Sicily for a spell, where she had been all her life, then they decided to live in England. When I went home, my key wouldn't open the front door. The lock had been changed. She opened the door to me. I didn't know who she was. Put on the spot, I thought my father had sold the house and new people had moved in. He had taken her to live in our family home. Shocked. In disbelief. The house my mother had died in! I rushed into the house past this Elena shouting "Dad, Dad."

"Un ce tu padri. Si ni yi a circari travagliu. Vattini. Vattini" she said in Sicilian, *meaning:* your father's not in. He's gone to look for work. Go away. Go away.

I left. Tears down my face as I walked along the road towards the underground. My instinct told me to go back, confront her. But I was in a state. My heart was beating fast. I was confused. Instead, I made my way to my bedsit then cried all night. Feelings of loneliness overwhelmed me. I didn't want to lose my father. Not to her. Not to anyone. But he was gone.

To think that he had suffered as a child when his mother died at only thirty-five with stillborn twins. He must have gone through similar heartache. The difference was that my father had a big brother he looked up to, and they were both close, too. They could share their burden with each other. Grief is compounded if you carry it alone. The three siblings only separated in their twenties when they emigrated. My father came to England, his brother, Giuseppe, went to another city in Italy. Giuseppe was already married by then and his new wife refused to go and live abroad. While my father's sister Gloria, ultimately moved to London, too.

The two brothers had to leave The Village for good, whether they liked it or not. It became too dangerous for them there. Uncle Giuseppe was five years older than my father and because of this age gap between them, my father was easily influenced by him and copied everything his older brother did. As teenagers they became atheist socialists and, as such, arch-enemies of the local right-wing, fascist clans, which sided with the mafia. Post Second World War, the mafia quickly reorganised itself after Mussolini's repression. It infiltrated the right-wing Christian Democrat party. Uncle Giuseppe was the most fervid communist, both anti-mafia and anti-Christian Democrats, speaking up, not only in his own village, but in far-flung neighbouring villages, too. A big protest was organised in The Village with the brothers at the helm waving their red flags. They received warnings, threats. It got so dangerous for them that, eventually, they had to leave. It was either that, or be strung up on a tree in the barren countryside.

I needed to go back to my family house again the next day, to get some of my belongings. Those things I hadn't managed to get last time, when I rushed out in despair. This time my father was in, and she wasn't. I was happy to see him, he wasn't happy to see me. It was as if I was nothing to him. Maybe he had never loved me. "Get your things and go. She'll be back soon." He had a sponge in his hand. He went to the kitchen and started cleaning the draining board.

Following him, I said, "You didn't tell me you were getting married. I didn't even know you had found another woman. How can you just push me out of your life like this?" He was impassive. The mask had fallen. For the first time, I saw him for what he was. A man without an ounce of empathy. Selfish. Cold. Unmoveable. It was no use trying to reason with him. I went upstairs to get my stuff. As I came back down, a big bag over my shoulder, with tears blurring my vision, he turned to look at me. The sponge in his hand dripping water onto the floor, he said: "Go and don't come back."

Although Susi is on my mother's side of the family, she knew the right people in our Sicilian circle to get all the gossip available. At that time, my father's behaviour was the talk of the community. My mother's family cut off ties with him, but that was water off a duck's back to him. What did he care?

Susi kept me up to date. My father and his wife argued all the time. Elena wanted to return to Sicily. She hated England, missed the sun, her family and friends. She was expecting a baby and wanted it to be born in Sicily. After I heard that, I phoned my father at work. I told the secretary it was urgent. I had to speak to him. He'd gone back to the same factory he'd worked for previously. It took ages to get him from the shop floor to the office. He said "Hello." Right after I answered "Hello," he said, "Why are you calling? Do you know how long it took me to get here from the other side of the factory?" He didn't give me a chance to answer. He put the phone down. I sobbed.

Susi later told me that my father had sold our house, they'd gone back to Sicily to live, where she had a house, and their baby was born – a boy called Carmine. The money they'd received from our house in London, they'd spent on doing up her house in The Village. At the age of fifty-two, my father went back to the work he'd done before he ever emigrated to England at the age of twenty-five. Farming.

He never gave me any money to help with my studies. He didn't know about the bag my mother had left me. Didn't he ask himself if I needed help? I never heard from him again.

When I returned to my bedsit, after accompanying my mother's body to Sicily, I finally had time to count exactly how much money was in the bag. Emptying it on my bed it built up a good pile. I checked if I'd locked my entrance door, drew the curtains. In all honesty, I was frightened of that money. Was it jinxed? I sat on my bed and counted it, putting it into little piles of a hundred, and then, when I had ten of those piles, I'd make a wad of one thousand. So absorbed was I, that I didn't have dinner that evening neither did I sleep that night. It came to nearly £27,000. That was a tidy sum in 1976 when the average house price was £12,700.

All night I thought about what to do with the money. Move into a better flat? How would I justify that? The authorities would want to know where the money came from if I had a big rent. I worked part-time in Sainsbury's – three hours late-opening night on Fridays, and a full day on Saturdays. I couldn't give up the job because it's what appeared to be keeping me – and had actually kept me, in dire conditions, up to that point. Conclusion was I'd change as little as possible in my everyday life. So as to not draw attention. I would spend the money on 'luxuries.' Items bought in cash in big shops, no loyalty schemes, no invoices in my name, no Green Shield stamps. Nothing that could be traced back to me.

Worry stopped me from going to university the next day. I took a day off. Went shopping instead. The first item I bought was a black patent leather Gucci handbag and an entwined G leather belt to match. Then followed a nice pair of Clark's boots. New rucksack. Max Mara coat. Gone were the charity shop jeans and jumpers. With hindsight, I must have seemed an unlikely customer, when I first entered those top-of-the-range shops. And I felt self-conscious especially when the shop assistants looked me up and down. Others might have walked out at that stage; however, all the blows to my dignity throughout my life, made me impervious to their disdain.

And food shopping became a delight. Up till then, I'd mostly survived on pasta and sandwiches. I bought food I had never bought before: prawns, salmon, T-bone steak, mangoes, kiwi, strawberries out of season, good wine. Even caviar, I had to try it. To me it tasted foul. I must have been the champion of posh-nosh at our university – that included the badly paid lecturers. Gone, too, were the second-hand books – best hardbacks only. I even went to the bookshops in Charing Cross Road to look for first editions. I still have some on my bookshelves.

Of course, the money came from some dodgy source. I did eventually find out what that source was. Maybe if I'd known then, I wouldn't have enjoyed it so much. What should I have done with it? Thrown it in the Thames? Would it have sunk?

My father had fought the mafia as a youngster waving the red communist flag. He'd had his life disrupted by having to leave his native village, separated from his brother, only to end up married to my mother, a woman steeped up to her neck in organised crime. And he never knew. The women on my mother's side of the family were close-knit, inseparable, tight-lipped. No, he never found out. I'm sure of that.

EIGHT

Wednesday 23rd August – afternoon

Next day I go back to see Zia. The curtain twitches and Zia's face appears. After all the unlocking, I go through to her living room. A most delicious smell wafts through the house. "Lasagne," she says. She leads me to the kitchen and shows me two huge baking trays full of the most mouth-watering tomato and cheese topping. Closing the oven door, she says she'll give me some to take home. "You have lasagne for dinner," she tells me.

I am relieved to see she has no other guests yet. Someone would come and ring the bell soon, no doubt.

"Zia, I found out who called Humps an arsehole."

"Ah, you find the man. You good girl."

"Yes, a man called Richard. He hates foreigners. And his wife, Barbara didn't put an invitation to the barbecue in our letter box this year."

"What big bastardo and big bagascia. They need slap in the face."

"I'm so angry, I could strangle them."

"You no strangle any person. This not so serious for strangle."

"No, I didn't mean it, Zia. Let's go down the diarrhoea route."

"I make you cake. No problem. What day?

"I need them for Sunday."

"That's alright. What cake you want?"

"I don't know, Zia, I thought you might advise me on that."

"How many people?"

"Erm, there'll be about fifteen at the barbecue... What about eclairs?"

"Eclairs no good – you Englishwoman. I think ice-cream

better for outside in summer."

"Ice-cream? Do you make ice-cream?"

"No, Silvio make for you. Best Italian."

Zia sits and thinks for a moment. Then she says:

"Cassata Siciliana gelato!" That is Zia's eureka moment.

"Beautiful," I say, "Zia, you're a genius. Yes, yes! Almond ice-cream, with marsala soaked nuts and candied oranges and lemons, all covered in pistachio ice-cream!"

"Yes," Zia says, "I tell Silvio make for Sunday. Saturday you come get. Silvio put in nice wrapping for you."

The door bell rings.

"OK, Zia, I'll come back Saturday afternoon to get the ice-creams."

"You come Saturday. But now you stay," she says. "I want you meet young woman."

I follow Zia to the living room window to see who is at the door. She turns, looks me straight in the eyes and says: "She big tart. She futtiri with married man."

If only Zia knew what her daughter, Susi, got up to. That was big-time serial tarting with lots of married men. I don't think Zia has the foggiest idea about that.

"Hello, Giusy!" Zia says, as if Giusy were her long-lost best friend she hasn't seen for years.

"Hello, Zia!"

And they proceed to kiss each other on the cheeks.

"This my poor sister daughter. She marry Englishman. Good man. Best house near river," Zia introduces me.

"This Giusy. She cousin of friend. She come to me. She have man problem. She have no-good man," Zia says.

Giusy tries to argue that Alberto is a good man.

"He good when he sleep," Zia says. "He make lot of problem for you."

Giusy looks at me as if to say: 'Can I speak in front of her?'

"You speak, Maria good woman. She tell nobody. She

Sicilian blood."

Zia's eyes dart from one to the other of us and says: "Cuppa tea?" Without waiting for a reply she goes to the kitchen, puts the kettle on and comes out with some jam tarts – strawberry. "I go back, get tea, you tell all," she says looking at Giusy. When Zia comes back again tea is poured and Giusy starts.

"Alberto ain't left his wife, Zia. You know, he said he was gonna leave her but he ain't. Me mate told me he was still with his wife. Alberto's making a packet with the amusement arcade. He pays the rent of the flat I live in. He's with me three or four nights a week, and when he ain't there he says he's on business. But he ain't on business. Me mate follows him. He goes back home. I'm expecting his baby, I'm three months gone. I told him about it. He says he's happy. He wants a son. Me mate found out his wife's pregnant and all. They've already got a little girl. He was sleeping with his wife, when he was sleeping with me. I want him to come and live with me."

She finally stops, slurps her tea, then takes a tart. I can't get my head round how Zia can help, if not just to offer consolation.

"Well, he's obviously telling his wife he's on business when he's with you," I say.

Giusy looks at me, without blinking, as if I were an alien. With suspicion. It must be my accent. Zia can hardly tell cockney from toff-speak. But this young woman is intimidated by the way I speak. I try to give my words a slangy edge: "You see, he's got the best of both worlds. His wife must know he's cheating on her but she puts up with it like you do."

She looks at Zia, who says: "He big bastardo."

It is exactly what I meant. No one can sum up things like Zia.

"What you want from me?" Zia asks bluntly.

"I want him to leave his wife, and I want a baby boy."

"Alberto rich man. He alright. He have two women, he want lot baby. Wife no leave Alberto if he no pay. Goodbye wife is goodbye money." Zia tells her straight. At times, people couldn't make out what Zia is on about. But I understand her alright.

"He said he can't live without me. He'll never ever leave me," Giusy says.

"Ah, he get that from love song."

"No, Zia, I mean it, I can tell. He loves me."

"I try help you. I give you two potion. One love potion, one baby potion."

"Thanks, Zia."

Jesus, how can grown-up women believe in that mumbo jumbo?

"Love potion mean he no leave you. Baby potion mean you make baby boy."

"Does that mean he'll leave his wife?"

"If he pay lot money she leave. If he pay little money she stay," Zia says, "I make sure you make boy. No worry. I get potion."

Zia takes the key she has tied around her wrist and unlocks the pantry door. A crucifix has been nailed above the lintel depicting Jesus dying. Giusy and I watch. The door is in the same room we are in. Zia lives in one of these big Edwardian houses with all sorts of nooks and crannies and, of course, a walk-in pantry: it is big, dark, and spooky. No windows. As black as hell. And smells like it, too. Does she have garlic in there? Or what? She pulls a string attached to the ceiling to switch on the bare light bulb dangling at the end of a wire. Zia walks down three steps. From where I am sitting, I can see diagonally into the pantry. I can't figure out where it ends. But I get a glimpse of jars of all sizes with handwritten labels on them, mixed up with bottles of home-made wine and bottles of olive oil, pickled aubergines, peppers, and olives; home-made tomato sauce, and little boxes going down as far as I can see. Noticing, over her shoulder, that I am looking, she pulls the door to, behind her, as she goes in.

I smile at Giusy and say, "It'll be alright." The same sentence I often repeated to my pupils when they came crying to me. You need to give people hope, at times. Is that what Zia is doing?

Giusy is well turned out. Her make up is heavy and immaculate, her dark hair is long and styled. She has all sorts of gold jewellery hanging from her. A necklace with a big cross dangling down into her cleavage, which is well in view. Her bangles jingle as she reaches for her cup.

"Life's difficult, isn't it?" I say.

"Yeah, yeah," she answers.

"What's your job?" I ask.

"Hairstylist. I got a salon. It's called Giusy's. Alberto gave me some money to do it up. Looks nice now. Business is picking up."

Zia appears with two little bottles in her hand. She heads over to a drawer in her sideboard, takes out some labels and a pen. She writes 'Alberto' on one, and 'boy' on the other. "You put little in drink before go to bed. When finish potion you come back, I give you more."

Giusy seems quite happy, relieved even, stretches out a blue finger-nailed hand and pops the bottles into her handbag. She offers to pay Zia.

Zia says: "You no pay, potion free."

Giusy says her goodbyes and leaves saying "See you next week, Zia."

I tell Zia that Alberto has paid to do up her salon. Zia knows that already. She tells me that his wife, Olga, also of

Sicilian extraction, knows about Giusy. She's decided to stay with Alberto, unless he pays up. She is a lady of leisure and isn't going to give up her lifestyle. Though she does a bit of part-time work, selling cosmetics or something, to keep herself from getting bored.

"But she can't be happy," I say.

"Nobody happy all time," Zia says, "but she happy when she spend his money."

I ask Zia how she knows all this.

"I give Olga potion. She visit me. She no ask potion for boy. She want money potion. She wife, she no need keep husband happy. Good if he happy. Good if he not happy."

We laugh.

"Well, at least you give the potions away for free," I say.

"If work, they bring present, if no work, they no ask for more."

"What do you put in those bottles?"

"Part cod-liver oil, part olive oil, part vinegar. If it taste bad, they think it work."

"Yes, but you gave her two bottles."

"In other one, I add salt."

"Tomorrow you go speak to big bastardo Alberto. We help Giusy. Women help women. My Tony he have woman when he live. You go speak to Alberto, you young. He listen to you," Zia says.

"I can't just go and tell him what to do. It's none of my business."

"It you business. He need help, Giusy need help, Olga need help. You go. You ask what he want do with life. You know, like you naughty children at school. You sort out."

We let the subject drop. Zia holds up the mint-green bed sock and says, "This second bed sock. The first one too long. I give to you husband. He have big feet."

That's all we need to give our love life a coup de grâce.

"You want white or green pompom?"

"Erm, white, please?" If they are going to look ridicul-ous, we might as well go the whole hog.

"You good taste. When I finish, I make bed sock for you. I have pink wool."

Zia's stream of consciousness leads her from big feet to my wedding.

"I no come to you wedding."

"Yes, I know, Zia. You were invited, but it was unfortunate you were in Sicily."

"But you no tell me in time. You tell me day before I leave with Susi."

"It was all sudden."

"But you no pregnant?"

"No, I wasn't pregnant, but I thought I was," I lie. "Then after we were married I had my period."

"Minghia! So you futtiri before you marry? Pope not happy." She is shocked and stops knitting.

And she didn't know about my university days. With neither religion nor family as shackles, I was free to do whatever I wanted. It was great.

"Well, yes. But just once. We got carried away. It was a mistake."

"If only one time, God forgive you mistake," she generously concludes, and starts knitting once more.

We are still sipping tea, when the door bell rings again. It is Angelina and Provvi again. I knew Angelina as a child. My mother was a friend of her mother's. I don't know what kind of friendship they had because they always seemed to be squabbling. We met at weddings, christenings, or at house gatherings. It was at a christening party that my mother and Angelina's mother grabbed each other by the hair in the ladies' toilets.

Angelina and I weren't especially friendly. She and her

two girl cousins, little barrels, short and fat like her. All three were constantly singing Elvis songs, and sometimes took their transistor out into the street and danced to his music there. I remember passers-by joining in. Angelina had definitely lost that happy-go-lucky stance now. I had never had it. I was a wreck. Frightened. Always carefully treading on eggshells. I couldn't be happy like them. They saw me as a misery guts, for sure. Don't think I was much fun at the time. Too busy getting whipped; it made me morose. I felt Angelina didn't like me, and that stayed with me. She consciously avoids me when she walks into Zia's living room. Or maybe she is simply absorbed in her thoughts. We've never fallen out, or anything like that.

Provvi is in a state. She wears sunglasses. One side of her face is swollen, her cheek is somewhere between reddish and purplish. Her lip has, what looks like, a cut in it. Of course, I realise, there and then, that her husband must be the cause of this. Zia says: "What happen? He big bastardo." Provvi takes her sunglasses off. It looks awfully painful. She pulls her sleeves up to show us the aubergine-like bruises on her arms. "What's worse is that he insults me and shouts in front of the kids. Says I make him do it because I don't do what he says. Says he'll break my spirit, ruin my face, break my nose, break my teeth... That I'll need plastic surgery by the time he finishes with me..."

On hearing that, I think that she has just put into words what my mother tried to do to me: break my spirit. Knock the fun-loving girl out of me. And she succeeded. She made me melancholic. Downcast. It was only when I went to university that my real personality surfaced. Vivacious and always up for a laugh. Though resentment and anger have never left me. Even as an adult I can't get my mother's violence towards me out of my system. It makes me particularly sensitive to the plight of mistreated women and children. I had always sided with them and wanted to help. That's the way I channel my anger. If my mother were alive today, I would revenge what she did to me. The other abuser was Peppina, and I haven't given up on the idea of getting my own back for all the suffering she caused me.

Zia is fuming and shouts "Big, big bastardo. We show him. We make Giulio pay."

Giulio, Provvi's husband, lashes out at Provvi for no valid reason. Provvi says he picks on things like dinner isn't ready, or because he trips over the children's toys, which he says Provvi hasn't put away because she's untidy. "Anything is reason enough to beat me."

Angelina listens, looking down at her shoes, and mutters insults, curses, and threats directed at Giulio. Angelina says she's spoken to Giulio's mother to see if she'd intervene in Provvi's favour. Giulio's mother sent Angelina packing. She defended her son saying that Provvi was useless in the home and made her son angry. He wasn't a bad man, he needed to be treated in the right way, and Provvi couldn't do it.

"She needs to be strong and take some brave decisions like I did with my husband. It's the only way," Angelina says, as she keeps nodding, "the only way," she repeats in a soaring sour tone. Then Angelina turns around and addresses her daughter: "When he threw you down the stairs and broke your leg, you could have landed on your head instead and been dead by now. Think of your children."

I gasp. Jesus. This man is a beast. It has to stop. Provvi can't go on living like this. But, what were they thinking of doing? Of course, he had to be made to see sense. That's the reason why Angelina and Provvi have come to see Zia. To get help. To sort it out. Zia gets up, goes over to the sideboard, takes a Bible out of the drawer. "You swear on Bible you no speak about what we say today. This secret. Only me and you three know. You put hand on Bible, you swear you no say a thing."

"Zia, look, it's no use me swearing on the Bible, you know I'm not religious." Angelina and Provvi look at me as if I'm the devil incarnate.

"She no believe," Zia says to them. "She strange, she not normal woman like me and you." Zia looks me up and down and says: "Eternal God have mercy for you. I pray for you. You mother no like what she see from heaven. You promise."

"Yes, I promise I won't say anything about this," I say.

Angelina and Provvi swear on the Bible according to Zia's wishes. "You forget you ever come to my house," Zia says to the two women. Now looking at Provvi, Zia says: "You take Giulio to Sicilia. You find reason. When arrive in The Village, Peppina, my sister, she give him education he deserve. She look after him. I come to Sicilia, I help if I no ill. I stay with Peppina."

Aunt Peppina lives alone now. My grandmother died in 1975. I remember because it was a year before my own mother's death. My grandmother had never left the village in her life. Not even to have her children; her three daughters: Zia, my mother, and Peppina were born at home, in that order.

Angelina and Provvi discuss how they can persuade Giulio to go to The Village to get some education. Zia suggests inventing a seriously ill relative, a family celebration... anything that gets him there.

Zia asks: "Provvi you agree we take Giulio to Sicilia?"

"What will you do?" asks Provvi.

"Depend on him. We talk to him. If he no stop, we teach lesson. We take care. You no worry."

Tears come to Provvi's eyes. She knows Zia will stop at nothing. And she also knows that Giulio is obstinate. Angelina sighs. She is getting irritated at Provvi's lack of resolve. "Look, do you want to carry on like this, or what?"

"You silly girl," Zia says to Provvi. "If social service people know he hit you in front of children, they put you and children in state refuge. You want that? If you husband no go to jail, he come to kill you. Think about. Come back Monday, quiet day. We talk again."

We all go down the corridor towards Zia's front door. Angelina and Provvi leave. I am about to follow them. Zia shouts out to me: "Maria, I forget, I forget the lasagne!" She hurries to the kitchen, and comes back out with a big rectangular baking tin wrapped in aluminium foil.

"For you, dinner."

In the meantime, another woman has arrived at Zia's door. Still in turmoil, I take the lasagne, say thank you, and leave.

NINE

Wednesday 23rd August – evening

On my way back home, my brain is spinning with what has been said this afternoon, especially Giulio's violence towards Provvi and about Giulio being tricked into going to Sicily. I suppose he deserves everything coming to him. In all honesty, if that had been me in Provvi's place, Giulio would have been counting worms for quite a while. I would have to go back on Monday afternoon, to find out how things have progressed. Zia, who is so endearing and funny when she speaks English, Zia who gives women hope, has a dangerous sinister side. You do not want to have her as your enemy.

And what about her sister, Peppina, in Sicily? Zia said Peppina would 'look after Giulio.' She would make him see sense. No hesitation there. Peppina had had a few vicious outbursts towards me when my family stayed at grandmother's house, during holidays in Sicily. The garden behind the house was beautiful. Right at the bottom of the garden, before the drop down a slope, was a row of tall cactus-like Indian rubber fig plants. Just outside the kitchen door stood a large cement sink, where we washed clothes by hand. A little further along there was a hen house with lots of chickens clucking around in the sun. And a lamb. So sweet. I spent time with it everyday. Fed it grass. On the other end of the scale from the innocent lamb was Aunt Peppina, the demon.

Once, when I was looking at myself in the mirror, about to go out with some young relatives of ours, she crept up from behind startling me when, from the corner of my eye, I glimpsed her reflection in the mirror. In Sicilian, she snarled: "Cu pensi di essiri?" *meaning:* "Who do you think you are?" Adding that I wasn't as beautiful as my mother had been when she was young. Compared to her, I was dirt. I became terribly afraid of Peppina and tried not to be alone with her.

One late afternoon I was quietly playing solitaire in the living-room-cum-Peppina's bedroom next to the kitchen. A shrill shrieking sound pierced through the kitchen door. I'd never heard such a desperate cry for help. It was clear something barbarous was happening in there. "Tenilo strittu," Peppina was shouting to my mother, *meaning:* "hold it tight." As I put my head round the door, I saw the most stomach-churning sight that has stayed with me to this day. There was a big sheet of polythene covering the middle of the floor, on it was this poor helpless creature writhing in pain, blood all over the place, some had spurted onto the women themselves. Peppina was trying to cut the lamb's throat and making a hash of it, while my mother held it down. I screamed "Stop it," over and over, then ran out to the bottom of the garden, where I howled my disgust to the barren parched land below. And vomited over the edge of the fence.

During that holiday, my mother tried to bully me into staying in Sicily with Peppina and my grandmother, rather than going back to England with her and my father. My mother had no scruples in trying to get rid of me. I was twelve. I was horrified. I wanted to go back home to Auntie Marge, my friends, my school, and to Miss Davies, my teacher. I didn't want to stay amongst those weird women dressed in black, a few were slightly bearded and some had discoloured and missing teeth. My mother was just as vicious as Peppina. She got me up against a wall and slapped me in the face again and again. "I don't care if you kill me," I yelled to my mother, "I'm not staying here." I was desperate, howled and screamed till I was hoarse and couldn't yell any more, pulled hair out of my head, slapped my own face until it was bright red. All worth it. In the end, she caved in. I came back to England with, what were supposed to be, my mother, and my father.

Back home in London, though, my mother made my life hell, even more than she had done before. The novelty was that she tied a length, about a yard long, of clothes line to her pinafore. That way, she'd have it at hand when she was overcome with the urge to whip me. I was very careful not to provoke her. Being terrified of her, I tried to keep out of her way. Whichever room she was in, I'd try to be in another one. When I bumped into her my heart pounded with fear.

She was in the kitchen one day. I thought I ought to make an effort, ask her if she'd like any help, and smiled at her. She grabbed hold of the clothes line (the sort that had wire running through the middle) swished it high above her head. I turned round to run away, but it came down on my back. She ran after me whipping me, and growling "I'll kill you," until I managed to get to the bathroom and lock myself in. I tried to look at my wounds in the mirror, red stripes criss-crossing my back. I applied cold water to my wounds, thankful that at least they wouldn't be visible to others. Her reason for whipping me was that I was taking the piss when I smiled at her, she said. My opinion was different, of course, I think she simply wanted to whip me. She had no pity. None at all. I bellowed: "I hate you," from behind the door.

Hitting her back wasn't an option. It would only make things worse in future. She was my mother and, above all, when she became incensed like that, it was as if she were possessed by some powerful force, she gritted her teeth, squinted her eyes into narrow slits, but worst of all she'd hiss terrible insults at me. She was like a beast. Terrifying. Strong.

Of course, I'd also thought of suicide or running away. But I didn't. I loved school and my life outside the house, when I was allowed out. She wouldn't let me go out with my friends. Once my schoolmate, Pauline, came round and knocked on our door. When my mother noticed it was for me, she said: "Don't let her in. Get rid of her," in Sicilian dialect. My mother always spoke Sicilian. She never learnt to speak English. Although it was raining, poor Pauline had to stand in the porch. We chatted there for a while. I didn't apologise to her about not letting her in. I wouldn't have known what to say. My mother came to the porch: "That's enough. Send her away now." I told Pauline, I had to go shopping with my mother, and that I'd see her the next day at school. Bless her, Pauline was very good about it. She didn't hold it against me. I'd tried to hide my mother's vicious nature.

Yes, I was quite good at concealing it. I didn't want people to know what was happening to me. I wanted them to think we were normal. I was already the only Italian girl in our year and, apart from the abuse, I had a different life at home. I had to juggle two cultures. Keep them separated. At only twelve, I realised the two identities could not cohabit. My mother had never socialised with other mothers. The latter knew each other, talked about their children, and also knew each other's children. Mine didn't. Because of that I was more or less ignored by my friends' mothers. For me, speaking about my parents was difficult. I tried to avoid it. In essence, I was ashamed of my mother; of the way she looked, dark and broody; of the way she spoke, always shouting; and the way she behaved, gesticulating uncontrollably.

In those days, kids played in the streets. I went out to play when my mother was still at work. When I used to see her coming down the road on her way back from work, I would feel a stab in my heart. I'd be afraid, and I'd be sad. Sometimes I played in other kids' gardens. One afternoon a little group, Sandra, Theresa and me found ourselves in Karen's garden. Karen lived across the road. Sandra and Theresa a few doors down. We got Karen's rubber swimming-pool out and filled it up with water. We all sat in it and took turns putting our heads under water. Karen's mother kept an eye on us from a window.

When she thought we'd had enough she said we were to come out of the pool. I remember this as if it had happened only yesterday. The elastic had gone around the middle of my bathing costume, so it sagged. My inferiority was apparent. Karen's mother went to get towels and helped pat the three girls dry. I was left there dripping and took a towel when one of the others discarded theirs on the ground. Karen's mother ignored me. She said there was orange squash in the kitchen. Not being sure if there were any for me, I left in my wet costume, walked across the street to our house, and unlocked the front door with the key hanging on some string round my neck.

They had been talking about Sandra's birthday party. She'd sent out handmade invitation cards. I didn't get one. I was the only kid in the street not to go. I sat behind the wrought-iron gate, and watched my friends having fun. Auntie Marge saw me sitting on the pavement looking on with my face between the railings. She was livid. Red-faced from anger, she came, took me by the hand and walked me to her house.

She said she'd give Sandra's mother a piece of her mind. I don't remember if she ever did. But I do know that the women in the street called my mother: The Sicilian Woman. And they called me: The Sicilian Woman's Daughter. I heard them.

TEN

Wednesday 23rd August – evening

As I am dishing up the lasagne for supper, Humps comes in the kitchen, hugs and kisses me. "Have you had a nice day, darling?"

I am so pleased to see him. "Let's say it hasn't been boring."

"We wouldn't want our Mary getting bored, would we?

"No, we wouldn't. Come on, darling, it's ready. Zia made lasagne this morning and gave me some to bring home. Isn't that lovely of her?"

"Jolly nice of her. She's doing takeaways now, is she?"

"I think lasagne are only for family," I say.

"Probably cooks all the time to keep ennui at bay."

"I don't think so. She has lots of friends, they keep her occupied. She just delights in feeding all and sundry."

"From what you tell me, she certainly has a lot of coming and going, to and from her house."

"Yes, she does," I say. "Buon appetito."

"Buon appetito. Spaghetti bolognese for lunch and lasagne for dinner. I'm spoilt. This is carbohydrate heaven," he says.

"Not going to be heaven for our waistlines. Tomorrow we'll have salads for both lunch and dinner to compensate."

"Then, there's the barbecue on Sunday."

"That's right. I'm going to Zia's again on Saturday to get the desserts. We're having cassata Siciliana ice-cream."

"Excellent choice. Anything you and Zia do is fine by me."

"And what did you do today, darling?" I ask.

"Oh, I've been busy editing that talk I'm giving. It's far too long. I need to shorten it by at least a quarter."

"Well, you've ample time to work on it before the meeting."

After dinner, I phone our children. I haven't spoken to them for a while. Emma says that little Benjamin is getting over a mild virus which he caught from a friend's baby. Her husband Mark is well and has been busy mopping up water. The people upstairs had gone off on holiday, hadn't turned the washbasin tap off properly, and water seeped through the ceiling down to their flat. On the other front, my other daughter, Clara, is moving to be nearer her workplace to cut down on tedious commuting. It's a bedsit the size of a handkerchief, in a chic area, that's been done up stylishly, state of the art. She can't afford more although she works long hours. She says she is buying a few pieces of second-hand furniture. The two girls have always got on well together. But they now seem to be drifting apart because Emma always talks about her family and Clara finds her a bore.

The evening seems quite mundane after Giusy's story and after talk of educating Giulio in some way. Although, I am no longer a spring chicken, I glory in having a mother-figure in Zia. It is something I've envied Susi for.

ELEVEN

Friday 25th August

Thinking back to the day before, I decide to go and take a look around Alberto's Amusement Arcade. After all, they don't know who I am and anybody can go in. I need to get out at least once a day, and can pick up some shopping and a copy of the *Evening Standard* on my way back. Thought I'd just go and put my toe in the water and take it from there. Have a look round.

When entering the arcade, the place seems exciting and vulgar at the same time. It brings back memories of when we went to the fair as a child: the bright lights, the ding, ping sounds, the loud music. There are well-seasoned adults in Alberto's arcade. I look at one man, who must be about my age, oohing and ahhing because he isn't getting three pieces of fruit of the same suit on his one-armed bandit. An expensive hobby, I would think. He doesn't look well off. Broken shoes and dirty trousers.

He notices I am looking, turns to me and says: "Come here, luv, bring us a bit of luck, will ya?"

I move closer to him and, what do you know, some coins come clanging down. "Ya, see, you're me lucky star, ain't ya? Do ya wanna put some coins in for me?" he says, holding out the money he has just won.

I dig around in the deepest recesses of my mind and make my thickest cockney accent surface: "Yeah, why not, let's give't a go. I gotta bit of dough here meself. Try mine first."

I keep feeding the machine and win absolutely nothing. The machine has 'Lucky Slot' written on it. Yes, it is lucky for Alberto, no doubt.

"No good at gamin' me. Ain't ever been lucky," I say, "that's enough, innit?"

"Nah," he says, "gotta keep going now me luck's turned."

"Well, I ain't putting any more in," I say.

Then I see a machine with a grabbing metal claw hanging down, in a large glass cabinet, and a lot of teddy bears stacked up randomly underneath.

"Oh, I like the look of them. I'm gonna see if I can get me one for me grandson," I say.

"How old is he?"

"One."

"He'll like one of them, then."

"Won't he just."

After a few attempts, and a few 'Oh, Gawds,' I manage to grip a yellow and white teddy bear, and carefully hoist it out. In the meantime, a woman joins us.

"This is Belle," the man says, "she's me better half. Me name's Jack, by the way."

"Hi, Belle. Ya old man's been showing me the ropes. I never been in here before."

"Ain't ya," she says, looking at me as if to say 'you haven't lived.' "What's your name, then?"

"Mary."

A well-dressed man, about forty, in an impeccable suit, black hair, handsome, goes past in an I'm-irresistible swagger. He makes a bee-line for an attractive blonde woman in a short black dress and black tights, about the same age as him.

Belle says: "That's the owner. Eyetie he is."

So that's him. He walks up to the blonde whispers something in her ear, and she giggles out loud, smacking his wandering hand.

"She's the manageress," Jack says.

"Yeah, she manages his dick," Belle says, "that's why she's the manageress, here and all." Belle and Jack laugh, they think that is hilarious. I join in.

"I gotta go now. Me old man'll be wondering where I got off to," I say.

"Ya don't want him to think ya been manageressing, do ya?" Belle says.

I leave while they are splitting themselves at the seams.

That is interesting, I think. He's got another one on the go. How does he do it? Now I'll go to Giusy Hairstylist. Curious to see what her shop is like. I can have my hair cut and styled there. Get an appointment. She'll recognise me, no doubt. I put the teddy bear in a Waitrose 'Bag for Life,' so Giusy won't know I've come from the arcade.

The place looks smart. It has been done up nicely, though it is a bit kitsch for my liking. A young girl with bright pink sun-strokes in her hair says: "Hiya."

"Hi," I say, giving my speech a slight cockney accent. I couldn't speak too differently from the day I met Giusy at Zia's.

"Can I have an appointment for tomorrow, please?"

"We ain't got time tomorrow. It's Saturday. We're full."

Giusy sees me, says "Sorry, luv, be back in a tick," to her customer, and comes over.

"Hiya." She recognises me.

"We can find time for the lady," Giusy says to the girl, who must have been her trainee.

"No, we're full," the girl says.

"Erm, let's have a look," Giusy is getting irritated with the girl and grabs the appointment book from her. "Is it cut and style?" Giusy looks at my hair. "Can you come at six, or is it too late?"

"We close at six," the drip says.

"That's why I'm asking if she can come at six." Giusy sighs.

"Yeah, that's fine," I say, "see you at six tomorrow."

How's that for killing two birds with one stone? I get my hair done for the barbecue, get to speak to Giusy and find out more about the Alberto-Giusy-Olga-manageress quartet.

TWELVE

Saturday 26th August

Silvio is at Zia's on Saturday afternoon when I arrive to pick up the ice-creams. He is the oldest of Zia's children. I've always been intrigued that all their Christian names begin with an S – Silvio, Stefano and Susanna. Age wise, I am between Stefano and Susi. The ice-creams are ready, Silvio has just brought them round. They are individually wrapped in the most beautiful pearly paper depicting Etna, the Sicilian volcano, in a frame of oranges and lemons. At the bottom are little yellow labels in case I want to personalise them by writing names on them. In the ice-box there is also a syringe filled with liquid. Zia sees I've noticed it and says: "You just give one or two squirt. Maybe three if you want big diarrhoea."

"These are going to be a big hit. I am delighted with the result," I say.

"Cuppa tea?"

Silvio's mobile rings, he goes to the other room. As Zia is making tea and bringing out some bakewell tarts she has made, I tell her I've been to Alberto's Amusement Arcade.

"Zia, Alberto was flirting with his manageress. They might be having an affair."

"Ah, she lunchtime tart."

"Are you saying you knew about her, Zia?"

"Yeah, I know. Olga tell me."

So Alberto's wife, Olga, knows about her.

"Olga say she no problem. Olga no love Alberto. Olga want money."

Zia goes over to the sideboard drawer and pulls out a piece of paper. "Name manageress family on this paper. She have two children; three and six year old. I get from Olga."

"But Giusy doesn't know about the manageress, does she?

She didn't mention her the other day."

"No, she no know. She no say she want potion for rid manageress."

"I'm going to Giusy's to get my hair done this evening. Should I say something, hint at it?"

"No, you say no thing, you hint no thing. She expect baby. She need stay calm."

"Fine, Zia. I won't say a thing."

Silvio has finished his call and is back with us, drinking tea and eating bakewells. He talks about his ice-cream factory, how things are going well, and how his wife, Franca, is good at Sales and Marketing. One of his daughters, Nadia, works with them. She helps Franca and also does the accounts. The other, Anna, didn't want to work for the family business and went off to work for some furniture company. But she would be going to work for the ice-cream factory in the near future, given that both Silvio and Franca were thinking of retiring. I tell them about my children and about my adorable grandson, showing them pictures on my phone.

Then Silvio says he has to get going and can give me a lift home, if I want. The ice-creams will melt by the time I get home otherwise, although Zia has packed them in a sturdy ice-box.

In the car, Silvio tells me more about his business and family. And, of course, we speak about Zia, too. Silvio has always had a kind character, unlike his brother Stefano. Stefano went to live up north when he married Romina, a young woman from Newcastle whose family had emigrated there from Sicily.

My mother got on well with Stefano and Silvio. She bent over backwards to be nice to them when they visited us, there were drinks and food galore. In contrast she had no time for Susi at all. The three siblings often came to our house, with Zia when they were small, and on their own when they were older. Silvio was the best-looking boy I knew. He was simply stunning. He had this James Dean aura about him, talked with a cigarette hanging out of his mouth, threw his head back, while pouting his lips and puffing smoke out vertically, or in circles.

Girls flocked. He told me about them, who he was going out with, and how it was difficult to manage them. At a certain point he'd had three on the go at once. Got terribly muddled up. He couldn't remember what he'd said to each, and what film he'd seen with which girl. He managed to buy an ice-cream van. After a couple of years, he'd bought himself a second-hand red Triumph Spitfire, in good shape, and sometimes took me for a spin around London. I imagined we were Liz Taylor and Richard Burton, especially when I wore a headscarf on sunny days and the car's roof was rolled back. I adored him. He was six years older than me.

The last thing I wanted was for him to find a serious girlfriend and get married. That would have been the end of my special relationship with him. Whenever he said something about leaving a certain girl, I would encourage him to do so elaborating on the negative points he'd told me about: "She suffocates me." And I'd say something like: "You don't want to be with someone who suffocates you, takes away your freedom and ruins your life."

We used to laugh about Zia saying it was a stupid car because you could only get two people in it. "Where you put you shopping?" she'd say. And she kept that stick propped up against the front door. When girls rang the doorbell looking for him, she'd show them the stick and, if need be, she'd chase them off, waving it about shouting "You no touch my boy." He was the young male presence in my life when I was a teenager – my 'big brother.' I had no boyfriends, wasn't allowed out, he knew that. And I wasn't going to meet any boys at my girls' school.

I tried to tell him about the abuse my mother was inflicting on me. He said something about Sicilian mothers being hot-headed. In truth, he hadn't realised how serious it was, I didn't press the issue. It had already been hard for me to externalise it, stuttering it out to him. In essence, he was the ray of light in the darkness of my youth. But when Humps came into my life, he supplanted everyone who had gone before in my affections.

Humps isn't at home when I arrive. I put the ice-creams in the freezer. Start doing some dusting and hoovering. I haven't done much housework in the last few days.

THIRTEEN

Saturday 26th August – early evening

Time to go to Giusy's. The last customer is about to leave as I walk in. Giusy is giving the lady her change and a few sachets of something or other. Free samples? The customer gives me a sharp look and leaves without saying anything. Giusy and I are the only two left in the shop. Locking up Giusy says: "How much are we cutting off?"

"We could have an inch off, I suppose." Then looking around me, I say: "You've done up this place nicely."

"Yeah, I'm happy with the way it's turned out. There's lots of hairdressers round here, you know, I gotta fight for me customers. You've gotta be a better stylist, listen to the ladies, give 'em what they want."

"Never easy when you're dealing with the public. People can be difficult," I say.

"Think I told ya Alberto paid for a big part of the decoration. I'm giving him a percentage of the profits back. If it wasn't for him I wouldn't be making as much. It was old and scruffy before. Even if you're the best stylist in town, women think you're no good if the shop looks miserable. Now I got more customers 'cos they think I earned all the money used in doing the place up."

We laugh about it.

"How do you feel?"

"Not so bad. That stuff Zia gave me's a bit sickly and that's on top of morning sickness! But if I can get what I want, it's worth it. I'm not giving Alberto up. I tried before I got pregnant, but I always took him back. Now I've got this far, nothing's gonna stop me. When I see him I melt like butter. I can't resist him. He's just the perfect guy for me."

She dries my hair with a warm towel. As she pulls, trying to get the tangles out, she says: "I went round his house last night. I think what done it for me was seeing you in here yesterday. You're fighting for me so I thought I should fight meself, for what I want. On top of that I was fired up by Zia's potion."

"Oh, God. You shouldn't have gone to his house. What happened when you got there?"

"Alberto wasn't in. His wife said I didn't have no right to be there. She said I was trying to destroy her family, and Alberto couldn't care less about me. She says he's had loads of women, but I was the only one stupid enough to get meself pregnant. And that he's having an affair with the manageress in his arcade."

"Oh, I'm so sorry," I say. "I'm afraid, the manageress bit seems to be true. I went in there yesterday, and he was whispering sweet things in her ear. It was obvious something's going on there..."

"I couldn't give a fig. I'm not getting rid of the baby like that bitch of his wife told me to."

By now Giusy had raised her voice, while angrily snipping away at my hair. I was hoping I'd have some hair left before going home!

"Erm, you've cut enough off now, Giusy."

She didn't hear me. And went on.

"Anyway, I'd never have an abortion. I'm Catholic."

But not Catholic enough not to have an affair with a married man, it seems.

"And I'm gonna make him leave that manageress bitch, an' all. She don't know what she's got coming to her."

"I know it's difficult for you but you really shouldn't get so wound up in your condition. It won't do the baby any good."

Giusy won't be budged.

"Alberto's gonna give me baby his name. He says he's never loved any one like he loves me, and can't wait for the baby to be born. He says in a few more months we're gonna do the baby room up in me flat. He's gonna marry me, mark me words. Manageress ain't such a big problem. I'll scratch her eyes out if I have to."

"I don't think that's a good idea, Giusy. You need to calm down. You can't think straight when you're as angry as you are. I came here to say I want to help you."

"Yeah, but I need to help meself as well. I can't just sit back."

"I'll go and speak to Alberto if you agree. Find out what his intentions are. You can trust me, I was a teacher for years. I'm used to trying to solve issues between warring factions. I'll come back and tell you what he says. He's probably not aware of how stressed out you are."

"I'll do anything to have Alberto to meself," she says. "Anything."

"In the meantime, you do nothing. Agreed? You don't approach his wife, you don't approach the manageress. And you don't argue with Alberto. You behave with him as you did the first day you met him. Understood?"

"Understood."

She finishes styling my hair. Shorter than I wanted, but it

looks quite good. The style suits me. Although I insist profusely, she does not take any money from me.

"You and Zia are me friends. You're helping me. Friends don't pay."

"I'll be back soon," I say as I leave.

FOURTEEN

Saturday 26th August – evening

Humps has already got dinner ready. He always cooks at weekends. On Saturday evenings, after his afternoons playing tennis, it is cold meat, salad and boiled potatoes. What has changed is the time, eight o'clock, way past his Englishman's habit of dining at six-thirty.

"Your hair looks nice."

"Thanks, darling, I'm glad you like it. New hairdresser."

He isn't bothered.

"Got the ice-creams for tomorrow from Zia. They're in the freezer."

"Cassata, isn't it? I'm looking forward to that," he says.

"Darling, I was just thinking, about Brexit, could we please keep off the subject tomorrow?"

"I'll try, but if others bring it up, I'm not backing down. I'll say what I think. It's not good for banking, and it's our livelihood we're talking about."

"But you'll be retiring in a few years. And the government's not going to be influenced by anything that's said in the garden tomorrow – even though you're right," I slip in quickly.

"I know but that won't stop me airing my views. And, I'm not retiring for a long time."

"If it makes you happy, you just go on working until your heart's content. The cottage and chalet will have to wait."

Now that I've started enjoying my retirement, I don't want him making demands on my time. I have space. Other women have told me they hate having their husbands moping around the house.

"I hope you're not going to bring up that bike-story tomorrow," he says.

"I might have to."

"It looks like I'll be arguing with them about Brexit, and you'll be getting up their noses about those bikes," he says.

"Nothing more probable. We're going to be really popular, aren't we?"

We laugh.

"I noticed a teddy bear on your dressing-table, did you buy it for Benjamin?"

"Oh, yes... No. I won it."

"Oh. Where?"

"At an amusement arcade. We'll be seeing little Benjamin next weekend."

"You're a bundle of surprises. Can't imagine you in an amusement arcade. Don't know what Shakespeare'd say about that."

"He'd say, 'For I can raise no money by vile means,'" I say, lifting my arm and bringing it down again in an arching movement.

"You raised no money, but you got a bear." He laughs.

"Not a good deal, it would have cost me a tenth, if I'd bought it in John Lewis."

"John Lewis wouldn't sell a tacky bear like that."

"Gee, thanks. And how did your tennis go?" I ask.

"I lost as usual. Can't run around any more like those young ones snapping at my heels."

"Never mind," I say, "we'll win tomorrow!"

FIFTEEN

Sunday 27th August

The Sunday papers are full of the Labour Party coming out for Soft Brexit. No hope now that Brexit isn't going to cause friction during the barbecue. "Come on, let's go down and see what's happening," I say.

"Ah, Humphrey old chap," Richard says, fiddling about with spare ribs and sausages, when he sees us coming.

Don't mind me, I think, who am I to be taken notice of?

"Nice sunny day for our yearly jaunt, what?" Humps says.

Soon others come down, including jolly-hockey-sticks Barbara – Richard's wife. She sees Sarah and shouts with glee, "Oh, Sarah, darling, aren't we simply lucky, such a sunny day." They kiss each other on both cheeks, like continentals. Barbara looks over at me and says hello.

By then, Ruth and Ian, from the first floor, have appeared, too. Barbara walks over to them. Humps is talking to Charlie, so I think I'll go and keep Richard company.

"Those spare ribs and skewers look delicious," I say, "but on a hot day like this they shouldn't be exposed to the sun."

Barbara looks around at us to see what is going on.

"On a jolly hot day like this, meat shouldn't be exposed to the sun. Salmonella." I say. Upon hearing that last word a few heads turn round, including Humps's: "What?" Humps says.

"Salmonella," I repeat, in a louder voice, smiling.

Richard says something about the meat marinating and being covered, and the fire not being ready.

I put on my most severe serious teacher face, lift my chin slightly, cross my arms and stand with my feet apart. The telling-off position. "Richard, do you know anything about the writing on the wall in the bike-store above Humphrey's bike?" I tilt my head to the left a little, arch my eyebrows *meaning:* I am waiting for an answer. No reply. Richard goes red and concentrates on the marinating ribs.

"Richard, I know it was you. I'm not too fussed about being called an arsehole. You should have heard what some kids called me when I was teaching at grotty comprehensives. Oh, they were vicious, those kids. Hadn't been taught how to behave properly. But I will not, repeat WILL NOT, have you calling Humphrey an arsehole. Do you understand that, Richard?"

He doesn't answer, just scoffs. Says he has to get on with the grill and can't talk to me. "Dash it!" he says as a greasy rib slips from his hand.

"I expect that writing to be removed by the time I visit the bike-store again!"

That will do for the time being. Give him time to soak up what I've said to him.

So I saunter over to Barbara and Sarah. "Such a jolly day," I say, mimicking Barbara. "Excellent," Sarah says.

"Just been talking to Richard about his scribbling arsehole on the bike-store wall," I say, looking Barbara straight in the eye and smiling.

I always found that exposure, recounting events, helped when I was dealing with children at school.

"Oh," Barbara says.

"Oh, yes," I say.

"By the way, where are the Spanish couple from the fifth floor? Aren't they coming?"

"I don't think they could make it," Sarah says.

"That's a great pity," I say. "But never mind, if they can't, they can't. Oh, I must go and check up on the dessert."

"What is it?" Sarah asks.

"Ice-cream. But it's special ice-cream. Needs attention." By now they must think me bonkers. I could just hear them: "That mad Italian woman..." They whisper together about me as I storm off. Yes, they don't like plain speaking, especially at a social occasion. Everything has to always be hunky-dory – shove it under the carpet if it's unsettling.

The Spanish couple are in. I tell them the Riverside residents are having the yearly barbecue today in the garden. We'd be delighted if they cared to join us. "What now?" they ask (I knew they hadn't been invited). "Yes, right now." Pablo goes briefly and comes back with a bottle of red wine in his hand, then he and Consuelo come down with me. What an absolutely spiffing party this is going to be.

The young Spanish couple haven't been at the residence long. This is their first August. I take them to meet Richard. "Do you know Richard?" I ask the couple.

"Not very well," Pablo says, "we have seen each other from a distance."

"Richard, this is Consuelo, and this is Pablo."

I believe it is the done thing to introduce from the low to the high. The couple's arrival closes off Brexit talk, such a relief. I overheard Humps saying "It's all a bloody shambles." Humps is getting hot under his shirt collar.

"Maybe we should put off talking about foreigners until there aren't any around," I say, "though that won't be easy. Too many of us here now."

It is soon time to get the ice-creams. I give Sarah's portion one squirt, Barbara's two, and Richard's three. Then I give Richard's an extra squirt for the Spanish couple. I'm sure they'd agree if they knew. Taking the ice-creams out of the box, I am careful to give everyone their correct portion. Sarah asks if she can help. "No, it's fine. Why don't you top up glasses?" I say. Sarah's children want to give out the plates. We start a game of 'this is for Ruth, this is for Ian' etc. They love it. "...and this one's for Richard."

Compliments soon fly around about just how jolly delicious the ice-creams are.

SIXTEEN

Monday 28th August

Bank holiday Monday begins with heaps of housework. I am running around the house all morning. In contrast to my recent past, I am quite energetic. That's because I want to get as much done as I can, before going to Zia's in the afternoon to take back her ice-box and syringe. I don't want Humps to see that syringe. He might put two and two together. Also, I know Angelina and Provvi are going to Zia's this afternoon, and I want to hear about what's happening on that front.

After lunch, I leave Humps to load the dishwasher, as usual. He tells me he needs peace because he has to catch up on computer work. I tell him I won't be in the way as I am going out.

"Zia's, I suppose."

"Yes, that's right."

"Do compliment her about the dessert."

"Yes, I will. They loved it. Sarah's kids had second helpings, even though those ice-creams were more for the adult palate than children's," I say.

Humps disappears into his office.

While walking along the Thames, and seeing children with ice-creams, memories came back to me about eating Wall's dairy ice-cream in wafers sitting on a wooden bench in Auntie Marge's garden, when I was a child. Her cats would silently circle around us, or they'd lazily stretch out on the lawn. She taught me the names of flowers, what was weed and what wasn't. She had apple, pear and plum trees. We'd pick the fruit and bake it into cakes together. My favourite was apple crumble. I loved plunging my hands into the mixture, the soft feel of flour, and rubbing the melting butter between my fingers.

Sometimes we'd go for walks along the river bank, much as I am doing today on my own. We'd sit on benches under the willows and watch the boats go by. Auntie would often bring a picnic, little pork pies, cocktail sausages, crisps, nuts, and fruit. When the weather was hot she took me swimming at what were then called 'The Baths,' which have long since been dismantled and covered in concrete to make way for a slip road. Occasionally, I was allowed to bring a school friend along. But Auntie didn't like the girls from the council estate. She thought them common, and wouldn't abide girls smoking. Although I loved her to bits, she could be a grumpy old so-and-so – it surfaced frequently. Apart from me, she had no friends at all. I don't remember anyone going to her house, except for her two sisters, when they came down from the north. And a man, Charlie, who used to appear on Sundays for lunch. I never did understand his connection.

She'd tell me stories about the war, how she loved dancing. I distinctly remember her saying that she couldn't care less what a boy looked like, as long as he was a good dancer like her. She must have been very pretty when young, because she was still attractive even then when she was about sixty.

We moved in next door to her when I was four. She told me how she'd often heard me crying. But one evening it got so bad that she felt obliged to knock on our door. There was no answer. She went round to the back door, which was unlocked, let herself in and walked in the direction of my screaming. She said I was in a desperate state "weeping my heart out." It was about some medicine I wouldn't take. And I was being hit because of it. I was lying on my bed kicking my feet. My cheeks, Auntie said, were bright red from slaps. She was horrified. She wiped my tears and my nose.

When I was four-and-a-half I started school. I remember lagging behind my mother when walking along the pavement. She was holding my hand and yanking my arm hard as she raced in front of me because she was in a hurry. On my first day, I felt an atmosphere I'd never known at home. Relaxed. The grown-ups were nice to me. Made sure I felt at ease. Though I was wary at first. Also, I couldn't understand anything that was being said.

On the second day, Miss Sergeant stood at the front of the classroom, held up a bright green mitten and asked if one of us had lost it. I recognised it straight away but was too scared to admit it was mine. Probably because I didn't have the language skills to own up to it or, more likely, I thought I'd be punished for losing it. At first, I would hide in the store-cupboard. When Miss Sergeant found me there crying during playtime, she told me, in a kind voice, not to worry that my mother would soon come and take me home. Gradually, I got used to the kindness and school became my refuge. There, I could stop treading on eggshells.

Looking even further back, I now realise my mother had been knocking me about since I was very small. I still have two little scars on my head. They come out of my hairline and onto my forehead. Once when I asked my mother how I'd got them, she said it happened when she was combing my hair as a baby; she'd pressed too hard on the corner of the comb. It bled quite a lot, she said. They must have been deep cuts. And she must have done it on purpose. If you'd cut a baby's head once and it started bleeding, you wouldn't carry on and do the same thing again unless it was deliberate. Did she look down at the baby in her arms, at her head of fine dark hair, and say "I hate you." If she'd left me in a shoe-box on the church steps, she'd have done me a favour.

From what I can remember, I hid my mother's violence towards me, even from Auntie. I don't know what made me do it. An instinct that came from God knows where. When my mother tied me up and belted me, I tried not to scream too much, Auntie was only next door, though we didn't share common walls. The dread of people finding out was excruciating. I so wanted to be normal, from a normal family. If I had sought help, I think she would have inflicted even more violence on me. I was terrified into submission. It was our secret. A secret my mother shared only with me. And I with her and my broken dolls, who were my only consolation.

I had heard of Barnardo's homes for children. But I had parents. Would they take me? I had daydreams about turning up at their gates, telling them what I was going through. They'd offer me milk and say "You poor girl. You've been so brave. Why didn't you tell us before?" They'd let me in, and I'd be safe from my mother's clutches for good. I wished that I could live among other children who, had also been unlucky, then we could at least offer each other comfort, share our pain.

But, what if they turned me away?

SEVENTEEN

Monday 28th August

I am still shaken by the recent thoughts about my childhood when I arrive at Zia's clutching the ice-box. Angelina and Provvi are there. They look as sad as can be. Zia has laid out some cannoli Siciliani cakes filled with ricotta, and decorated with candied lemons. They look delicious. "Cuppa tea?"

"Yes, please, Zia. I'd love one."

Provvi now has a dark yellowish stain on her neck. Did the brute clutch her by the throat? Zia's right. That Giulio definitely needs some education. Provvi is looking down at her feet and is in the middle of telling Zia how her husband, Giulio, purposely ran into her with a shopping trolley, bruising the back of one of her ankles badly, on Saturday when they were doing the family shopping at Tesco's. Provvi keeps going through intervals of sobbing, blowing her nose, and sitting quietly gripping her hankie, when anyone else speaks.

Angelina has come up with an idea to get Giulio to The Village in Sicily. It would be her 60th birthday at the end of September, on Wednesday 27th to be precise. She says how a joint birthday party with her twin, Beatrice, seems plausible given that it is a special birthday. Beatrice and her family certainly can't afford flights to England. Also, the twins have a large extended family in Sicily who will all be invited making for a lively party. And anyway, in The Village, anyone can go to any party, invited or not.

Angelina says that it will be easy to persuade Giulio to go. "He likes showing off to the people he grew up with in The Village," Angelina says, "especially to his old schoolmates. He makes out he's been so successful in England and is well-off. What do they know?"

"You need tell Giulio he go to Sicily. We arrange rest," Zia says. "But you no need know detail. We think about."

She made it clear it was really up to Zia's contacts in The Village to decide. Maybe they would frighten him, give him a good talking to, maybe hit him, or worse. I don't know what was said before I arrived. And I don't ask. The fewer people know about what's going to happen, the less risk there is. People were careless and let out information, even unintentionally.

"What you have to say? You can no go on that way," Zia says to Provvi.

"I've come to the decision it's either me or him," Provvi says.

"It'll also be good for the children," Angelina says. "They're suffering, as well. Giulio doesn't worry whether the boys are there or not, he just lashes out."

"At the end of the last school year, their form teachers told me the boys are aggressive," Provvi says. "They hit other children, grab their toys, crayons or whatever, from them. They break toys by stamping on them, before giving them back. Or they throw toys at other children aiming for their heads."

"You know the boys would be better off as well, don't you?" Angelina says.

"Yes, I know," Provvi says.

"You come back, tell me when you book flight," Zia says.

They leave.

Zia picks up her knitting, and pulls at the ball of wool. She's nearly finished Humps's second bed sock. "I finish rib, then I make cord with crochet hook." For a few seconds the only sound in the room is the click-clacking of the needles. "When I finish you bed sock, I crochet blanket put on my leg when watch television."

"Do you think this will work, Zia?"

"I crochet squares, then I sew together."

"No, Zia, I was talking about taking Giulio to Sicily to get an education."

"Oh, you no worry. Not first time we give men education. Peppina find help. She know what to do. No problem."

"Zia, so you've done this before?"

"I tell you. You my sister daughter. Yes, done before. Why you think many Sicilian women no husband? Some Siciliani men too maliducati."

"When my father remarried and sent me away from our house, I was so angry I would certainly have wanted to give him some education."

"Ah, you father another minghiuni. But you no come to tell Zia. We rough him up a bit for you," Zia says.

"Yes, well I got that wrong, didn't I? Anyway, he's dead now."

"He no rest in peace," Zia says. "I tell cemetery people in The Village put him long way from you mother. He on cemetery edge in cassuni. You mother have nice marble tomb for herself in middle of cemetery. Megliu suli chi mal accompagnati" *meaning:* better on your own than with bad company.

In all honesty, I'd never been to the cemetery to see where my father's buried. I didn't go to his funeral when a cousin phoned me to say he'd died. I was quite gutted, but not enough to make the journey to Sicily to accompany him to his last resting place. I knew where my mother was buried because I went to Sicily with Zia and Susi to accompany my mother's body from England to Sicily. We had another funeral in The Village before she was buried, after the one in London for the Sicilian community.

"Neither Angelina nor her twin, Beatrice, have husbands," I say. "They died in an accident. That can happen to anyone, surely." This is a little tongue in cheek to find out what Zia knows. I'm quite sure they were killed.

"You innocent Englishwoman. You no know a thing. In England accident happen, in Sicily accident organised."

"You mean to say that their husbands were killed?"

"No. I mean say no thing. You say that. Anyway, Angelina husband and Beatrice husband, one more bastardo than the other one."

Zia doesn't want to say it outright. But it is clear that the two men had been done away with. She has made it as plain as she can without actually saying they were killed. I try to push the boundary a little further.

"What about your husband, Zia? What about Uncle Tony?"

"Ah, you want know much. You curious look in you eye. Curious no good."

She won't say.

"How did he die?"

"You want know much. I tell you. Heart stop, he die. My husband rest in peace."

"Sorry, Zia. It's just that I don't know what happened to Uncle Tony, given that he died years ago."

"He rest in peace, I tell you," she grits her teeth and knits faster.

I am making her nervous, but I have to ask, "You're not going to have Giulio killed, are you?"

"No, no. We give him education he deserve. If he behave good, we give him only little education," then she looks up from her knitting and says: "You want know too much. I tell you." Now wagging her finger at me: "Curious no good."

Maybe it's time to change the subject. Zia's getting quite worked up. So I tell Zia about my visit to Alberto's and Giusy's. Given that he's having an affair with the manageress, it means that he's not in love with Giusy. He's messing her around, too. It's not as if he found the love of his life in Giusy after he married Olga. He's simply sleeping around, using these women. He has no respect for any of them.

"He put in every woman say yes. All men try."

"But if you marry, you're not supposed to even try putting it into other women, Zia."

"You tell me name of man who put it only in wife all the life."

"Humphrey."

"Ah, you silly girl. Not possible. You believe love song."

"Of course, it's possible, Zia. People who marry for love stay together and don't go looking elsewhere."

Zia has calmed down now. She continues to give me nuggets of truth.

"You silly girl. When you marry man because he have nice house, you stay because house last long time. When you marry man you love, love change and he put it in other women. Love change, house no change."

God, she is so cynical. Though there is a germ of truth in Zia's philosophy.

"I married Humphrey because I loved him, still do, and want to be with him."

"Why did you marry Uncle Tony, Zia?"

"In old day, girl marry young. I no pretty like you mother. I find no man. Uncle Tony thirty, he want girl. No girl want him. He short. He no house. He no job, he want go England. We marry, and we go England. In old day, woman servant for husband. Hard life for wife. We smile. We suffer."

Uncle Tony was as much a Prince Charming as he was a tycoon. I remember my mother saying that Zia had come over to England with one pair of shoes, and they were already quite worn. When she finally threw them out, she took to wearing Uncle Tony's, filling them out by wearing two pairs of socks. They had one pair of shoes between them which meant they couldn't go out together. That's how well off they were. In that moment, I look at her and think Zia must have suffered a lot. Now she is totally void of romanticism. Not one crumb of it in her whole body. Was she born so rational? Or did she grow into it as a cause of life's hardships?

"You go speak with Alberto." Zia says abruptly. "I no go. I too old."

"Maybe, I don't know," I say.

As I go out, Zia accompanies me to the door. We see two women walking on the pavement towards us. I saw them at Zia's the week before: the sisters Rosa and Bella, Zia's nieces, on her husband's side. I don't know what their case is about. And I don't want to know. Before they are within earshot, Zia turns to me, gives me a wicked look, and says: "Blackmail."

"Zia, look, I really am not interested in their problems. I think I've already heard enough. I'll go and speak to Alberto on Giusy's behalf, see if I can get him to disclose what his position is and help her out."

"You do good job," Zia says. "Next time I give you bed sock for you husband."

EIGHTEEN

Monday 28th August

When it is raining, like today, I sometimes get morose although I adore rain when walking along the riverside: the pitter-patter on my umbrella, the luxurious green of trees and grass, the clean crisp air. But, as I walk back home on the glistening path, I can't help thinking about Uncle Tony and Zia. She was very young when they married. Being quite a bit older meant he took control over her, I suppose.

I remember Uncle Tony being vicious with Susi, when we were children. Strangely enough, I don't have any recollection at all about him hitting either Silvio or Stefano. Not only was Susi his only daughter, she was also the youngest out of the three siblings. She was two years younger than me; chubby, very pretty face, sparky. In short, she was the sister I never had. And, like sisters, we'd argue over silly things, most of the time because she took up too much of the single bed we had to share. Of course, I used to go to theirs, too. But never to sleep. My mother wouldn't let me, she eventually became irritated by Susi and stopped her staying with us.

Once when I went to their house, Susi was having lunch with her father. She refused to eat her vegetables. Uncle Tony took off his belt and slashed it hard across Susi's face. I distinctly remember the satisfaction in his face as he did this. Tears came running down her cheeks. She didn't squeal, like I tried not to when my mother belted me, she sobbed quietly, ate her food, while tears dropped down into her plate. Seeing her being mistreated was more traumatic for me than being beaten myself. This poor powerless child had to take what was being inflicted on her.

Even now we are around sixty years old, she'll say something about his violence, she doesn't show anger. I do. I have taken my anger around with me all my life – held its hand and nurtured it. But Susi did say she didn't feel much sorrow when her father died. Relief. If my mother had lived longer, I would have wanted some kind of revenge. Maybe that would have appeased my anger. Even though she'd tortured me, instead of loving me, I couldn't inflict anything bad on her. She suffered enough. Instead I looked after her. Catered to her every whim. Accompanied her to doctors, and ran round getting anything she needed, including medication at the chemist. My father did none of this. And when she died, I was sad.

Going back to Uncle Tony, I admit he could be nice, if he wanted. He had a great sense of humour and made us laugh. We cousins had great fun treading grapes in their bath to make his home-made wine. I used to take my wellies to their house and take part in the crushing. Silvio and Stefano, the show-offs, would stamp grapes in their bare feet. Susi and I wore rubber boots. Once Susi lost her balance, grabbed me to break her fall, we toppled over and ended up sitting on the grapes. Uncle Tony laughed and said that was the ideal way to press grapes and, that while we were sitting there, we may as well start throwing the stalks out of the bath. Silvio and Stefano would carry the squashed grapes out to the garden shed, in buckets, where fermentation would take place in a couple of wooden barrels.

On the other hand, I remember another two occasions which showed his vile side. Uncle Tony used to do odd jobs, for us and for Auntie Marge. Both my mother and Auntie

Marge thought he was considerate, a hard-worker, a good man. My mother used to compare him to my father saying the latter was a good-for-nothing lazy lout, while Uncle Tony was enterprising and easy to get on with. Beyond our gardens, there were fields and a disused railway line. Sometimes, Auntie Marge and I went for walks there, by climbing through a hole in her fence at the bottom of her garden. We had a similar hole in our fence, too.

One afternoon, when I was tending to my pet tortoise, giving it grass and talking to it, Uncle Tony came to look at it in its box. He said they were filthy animals. I defended my tortoise and carried on talking to it. He said talking to a tortoise was ridiculous, grabbed hold of it, took it to the bottom of the garden, leaned on the fence and flung my tortoise into the air, across the railway line, as hard and fast as he could. The poor creature landed in the field beyond, amongst the undergrowth. I yelled out. I tried to get through the fence to see what had happened to it. Its shell must have cracked to bits when it landed. But he grabbed hold of me, while I was still kicking and screaming, he wouldn't let me go. My mother came out to see what the noise was about. Uncle Tony told her I was having some kind of screaming fit. My mother slapped my face, then kicked me while I was trying to run away, shouting after me: "That'll give her something to cry about."

The next day, after school, when my mother was still at work, I went to look for my tortoise. I never found it. To this day I don't know whether it lived or died.

Yet another time, when Uncle Tony showed his ugly side, was when I went to play with Susi at her house. We were throwing and chasing a ball on the cemented passageway that led from their front gate to their garage. It was my ball. Auntie Marge had bought it for me. I still remember it vividly. It was half green and half yellow. The green side had yellow stars on it, and vice versa. He came out of the house saying the noise was getting on his nerves. He tried to catch the ball while Susi and I were trying to stop him. We thought he'd joined in our game. But he was getting angry. Susi and I were laughing. After running backwards and forwards a few times, he finally caught it. Taking out a penknife from his pocket, he laughed and watched our reaction as he flicked the knife open, plunged it straight into my ball and cut it in half. He threw the two pieces on the ground and went back inside. And that was the end of my ball.

I never told Auntie Marge about Uncle Tony belting Susi, nor did I tell her about the ball, nor about the tortoise. In fact, I didn't tell anyone at all. What would they have thought about my family?

NINETEEN

Tuesday 29th August

Coming back to the present, I am going to the amusement arcade to see if I can find Alberto. It has occurred to me that in just over a week, I am still acting like a teacher. Dispensing justice, or trying to. Putting order into the disorder among people. Dealing with conflict between kids was an important part of my profession. I had just stepped it up somewhat, dealing with misbehaving adults instead of youngsters.

Jack and Belle are there again. Jack waves to me and Belle shouts over: "You're back again, are ya? Can't keep away." They laugh, so do I.

"Yeah," I shout back, "I wanna get another one of them teddies for me grand-kid," as I head over to the big glass-case with that grabbing claw hovering above the pile of teddy-bears. The lovely old couple follow me over. I am glad they have. Going back to my cockney accent feels good. I still have it in me.

"Did ya win anything on the old slots?" I ask.

"Nah, ain't me lucky day today," says Jack. "You got change for a tenner?"

"Nah," I say. I could give them ten quid, but not if they are going to waste it on the one-armed bandits. "Why don't ya just keep ya money instead of wasting it here?"

"Yeah, ya come back yourself, didn't ya?" Belle says.

"Yeah, but I want one of these here bears."

All the time we are talking, I am trying to haul one out. But, of course, the claw has a loose grip. It goes on for a while until, finally, I manage to get one by its head. This time it's purple and white. That's two teddies for little Benjamin.

"Yeah, you're right," I say. "Would of been cheaper to buy one in Tesco's."

"Yeah, this place gets ya. You'll be back. We'll be waiting for ya," she says.

God, how I love Londoners.

I see the manageress whizz past.

"Sorry, must love ya and leave ya," I say. "Gotta ask the manageress somefink."

"Excuse me, excuse me," I shout after her, while trying to catch her up.

"Hiya, can I help ya?" she asks.

"Yes, I'd like to talk to the owner."

"We don't trouble him unless we have to. You can tell me, I deal with queries."

"This is personal." Imposing yourself is better done in a posh accent. They take you more seriously. "I have to speak to him directly. She looks at me askance: "Alright I'll see if I can find him. Wait here, please."

Soon I see her coming towards me followed by the slick owner.

"Hello, madam, how can I help you?"

The manageress disappears and leaves us to it. She no doubt thinks she will hear all about what I say to him later.

"I need to talk to you in private. I can't do it here."

"I'm a busy man, madam. I have an appointment in ten minutes."

"Let's just make it ten minutes in your office, shall we? Otherwise we're wasting precious time."

He turns around and walks back from where he came. Asks me to sit in front of his desk. As they always do, he has the high, smart leather swing-around, and the visitor has the lower, cheaper chair. That's one way of patronising you. By putting themselves in a position where they can look down on you. I am adamant it won't work with me.

"Nice place you have here."

"Madam, I'm very busy these days."

"Yes, I know you're busy."

"Am I supposed to know you?" he asks.

"No, we've never met before. I remember this place when it belonged to your father. It was a pub before, wasn't it? Your father opened it. Later you bought the property next door and turned it into a gambling den."

I want to establish that I know about his family.

He looks at me, tightening his lips and lifting his eyebrows. "What is it you want?"

"I'm here because of Giusy. She's expecting your baby and is suffering because she hasn't got a clue where she stands with you."

He looked slightly embarrassed: "And, what business is it of yours?"

"Probably none. But I'm making it my business."

"Who are you?"

"My aunt asked me to come and speak to you." I don't need to explain who she is. Just her name will do. "She's known as Zia," I say. A cloud passes over his face. He nods slightly to signal he knows who she is.

This worried him. He was smart enough to realise that when someone looks at you with a serious face and tells you they're part of a notorious Sicilian family, you've been targeted by an entity you wouldn't want to have anything to do with.

"But really, you don't need to worry," I say. "We only want to know where she stands. What your intentions are."

He goes and shuts the door, puts his phone on silent.

"It's like this," I say. "I don't like you deceiving these women. Let's just say that I'm here because I don't like women being treated badly."

"You are not getting mixed up in my private life."

That's what he thinks. I look around and say: "Look, you wouldn't want this place smashed up, would you? Those poor teddies with that threatening claw hanging over them would have their fur ruined by shattered glass. Now, we wouldn't want that, would we? I ask you to be reasonable. It doesn't look good for the Italian community, does it? You're having an affair with the manageress, Giusy is pregnant and so is your wife. What a mess." I shake my head slowly for emphasis. "Do you think you're behaving like a decent man? No, of course not."

After all the years of tiptoeing around my mother and trying to be more English than the English, I finally felt the freedom of being direct and exercising power over adults who, quite frankly, got on my nerves. A mafioso, I don't remember his name, once said that power is more exhilarating than fucking. I'm starting to understand that now.

"What is it you want from me? Money?"

"No. Don't offend me," I say indignantly. "It's nothing to do with money as far as I'm concerned."

"I'm sorry," he says.

"Take my advice. Just co-operate."

So, what is it you want exactly?" he says losing his arrogant tone.

"I want you to end the affair with your manageress. What's her name...?"

"Nancy."

"Yes, Nancy. Finish your affair with her. We've had our feelers out. We know she's married, to a man called Jonathan, with two small children. We know their names and ages as well: a boy of three called Oliver and a girl, Amelia, aged six. It will save you, your family, your girlfriends, and Nancy's family a lot of trouble in the long run."

I felt like swiping him round his greasy head, but didn't.

"Are you asking me to fire her?"

"No."

He looked at me waiting for more.

"You tell Nancy that someone is threatening to tell her husband. You needn't tell her we're Sicilian."

"Is that it?"

"No. We want you to decide between your wife and Giusy. So who's it going to be?"

"I don't need to think about that. Olga's my wife. She's only interested in my money. Giusy makes me happy."

"That's done, then," I say. "Will you divorce from your wife and move in with Giusy full-time?"

"What about my daughter? And, the new baby?"

"The judge will decide that. You put yourself in this mess. All you've got to do now is to man up and put things straight. I'll keep in contact with Giusy."

I get up to go. He rushes to open the door for me.

TWENTY

Tuesday 29th August – evening

Humps comes in while I am getting dinner. "Just get yourself sorted, darling. Dinner'll be ready in a tick."

"Not until I've given you a good kiss and hug first," he says.

"Haven't lost any of your charm with age, have you?"

"Oh, no. If anything it's escalated," he playfully boasts.

"You're all bouncy this evening," I say to him.

"Yes, things are going very well. I won't bore you with the details. Suffice it to say that I managed to get on with my work without being hounded by awkward people. And you, darling? What did you do today?"

"I had a look round some shops. I bought some yellow wool. Zia is making us bed socks. Yours are mint-green with white pompoms. You're going to look really sexy in those."

"What? You're joking, right?"

"Never been so serious in all my life." We laugh and hug. "And I went to the amusement arcade again."

I don't like telling Humps lies. But I don't mind not telling him the whole truth. There's so much about my family I've kept from him.

"What again!"

"Yes, it's... well... amusing."

We both laugh again.

"That's the point of their existence," he says.

"I won another teddy. Purple and white this time. That's two teddies we can give little Benjamin when they come here on Sunday."

"I don't remember you telling me they are coming here on Sunday."

"Maybe I forgot. Anyway Clara's coming, too. They'll be here for lunch."

"I was saving Sunday. I haven't finished that computer work I started. But I suppose I'll have to do as I'm told," he says.

"You know it saves a lot of trouble when you agree with me."

He gives me one of his lovely cheeky grins.

"By the way, I saw Sarah when I was coming up the stairs this evening."

Humps had recently decided he would climb up the stairs rather than take the lift as part of his endeavour to keep himself fit.

"Oh, yes. Did you speak to her?"

"Yes, she said she had some kind of stomach problems on Sunday night after the barbecue."

"Oh, dear. What a shame."

"Can't have been that bad if she's out and about," he says. "Seems that Richard and Barbara got it, too. Sarah said Barbara and Richard were quite bad, especially Richard."

"It's strange, isn't it?" I say. "That three of them have been ill. Was it anything to do with the barbecue, do you think? I'll have to speak to Sarah about it."

We left it at that. Humps picked up the remote control "Let's see if there's any news on."

So it worked. Thank you, Zia. I feel so good about it that I shake my fists with glee when alone in the kitchen.

TWENTY-ONE

Wednesday 30th August – morning

The next day I am determined to bump into Sarah to find out what happened. I spend the morning doing housework, keeping an eye on the stairwell every now and then, in case Sarah, on the floor below, comes out. I even go to our car-park to see if her car is there. Yes, it is. She is still in. At about eleven o'clock, I hear her talking to the children outside her front door. I quickly put on my outdoor shoes and run downstairs.

"Hi, Sarah. I'm nipping out to get some horseradish sauce for Humphrey's steak this evening. Always something missing, isn't there?"

"We're going to town. The children are starting school on Friday. We need to get some last-minute things. It's never-ending..."

"Yes, back to school already. Pity their summer break is over. No more barbecues now that the rain's set in." That gets me onto the right subject. "Humphrey told me that you weren't well after the barbecue."

"Yes, it wasn't too bad, but I could have done without it."

"It must have been the meat," I say.

"You reckon?"

"Yes, of course. What else? You can't leave meat in the sun like Richard did without there being some dire consequences. Do you remember I pointed it out to him? It was already there in the sun when Humphrey and I came down, and we were early."

"Richard and Barbara were bad, too. That's three of us," Sarah says.

"Richard probably shouldn't be trusted with the meat again," I say. "I wish he'd listened."

"So do I," Sarah says, "having that upset tum in the evening spoilt my day. After such a lovely afternoon. So how come the others didn't get it?"

"Probably because you got the meat on top that the sun was beating directly down on? Or simply because the others have stronger stomachs. We're not all the same."

"He should have listened," she says.

"You know what men are like, especially when they're

cooking. They never want a woman's advice."

"He got the worst of it. Barbara said he was up all night running to the loo," Sarah says.

"Probably no worse than yours. Men make such a fuss. Anyway it's his own fault. Couldn't have been anything else. When did you hear about ice-cream being off? Never. It simply melts." I say.

"Yes, of course. It must have been the meat."

"The Spanish guy upstairs was telling me how good he is at grilling meat. Back home he's got a huge family, but he's the one at the grill when they have barbecues. He told me nobody even goes near the grill when he's around."

"Maybe we should ask him to do ours next year," Sarah says.

"Good idea! That would be wise, I think."

And with that, I go off to the shops. If Richard doesn't remove that insult soon, I'll have to step up the punishment. Give him a little more education. Maybe get one of Zia's picciotti to knock him about a little in a dark alley. He's been warned.

TWENTY-TWO

Wednesday 30th August – afternoon

After my quick lunch I set off for Zia's yet again. I need to tell her about the Richard news. I must admit, I felt more than a twinge of satisfaction, though revenge is a base instinct, they say. Turn the other cheek. Forgive and forget. That's what we are supposed to do as civilised beings. But what I came to feel after the bike episode was different. Being downtrodden, not getting up and fighting back, that's what makes you feel worthless. While you're down bullies will inflict more pain on you. Yes, I definitely feel better now.

Would Uncle Tony have killed my tortoise and cut my ball in half if I had been twice his size and vicious? I don't think so. Though Uncle Tony had died his traits seemed to have lived on in his son, Stefano. In sharp contrast to his brother Silvio, Stefano was a scumbag. He took pleasure in hurting others. And he always avenged any wrongdoings. Stefano was born nasty, he'd been like that since he was small. He'd cheat at cards, steal my marbles and even took some money out of my mother's purse, which I got blamed for. I'd never stolen anything. Auntie Marge would have been horrified. He used to twist my arm round to my back and turn it till I pleaded with him to stop. He'd take one of my cheeks between his index and middle fingers, like a vice, and twist it round till he could no more. Then the other cheek making my face red. According to him that was an affectionate gesture. When we grew up we'd get married, he said. I said we wouldn't. He repeated, "Yes, we will, you'll see."

When I was older, about sixteen, Stefano came to our house, with a cousin of his from the other side of his family, called Adriano. Bella and Rosa's brother. Uncle Tony's nephew. My mother was in the back garden hanging out the washing. They stood in the porch and asked if my mother was in. I said yes. Stefano said: "When your mother's not in, we're going to come back and rape you." I was gob-smacked, closed the door on them, and from then on was terrified to open the door to anyone. I didn't tell a soul about the episode, didn't do anything about it. I don't know what was wrong with me, why I never reacted. But I went into avoidance mode. I avoided anyone in our community when I could because it was clear that they were going to keep hurting me.

That threat terrified me, though Stefano and Adriano didn't come back to rape me. Stefano did come back on his own every now and then. When my mother wasn't in, I wouldn't open the door. He sensed I was there, and used to whistle through the letter box, after having banged on the door, and he'd keep repeating: "I'm going to marry you," in a singsong voice. I'd lock myself in my bedroom upstairs, drag furniture and stack it up against my door, just in case he managed to break into the house.

Susi came to see me a few weeks later. She was visibly shaken. She said: "I've got something to tell you, but you mustn't tell anyone. Cross your heart and hope to die." I crossed my heart and hoped to die, though secrecy was what I was best at. Adriano had offered to take her for a drive. He headed for the countryside and raped her in a field. She was fourteen. "It was a nightmare," she said. "First he kissed me on the mouth and said we were just messing about. The more I tried to get away the tighter he pulled me towards him telling me not to pretend I didn't like it. He called me a slut. I felt so much pain." He'd hit her again and again to make her succumb. My poor Susi. And it happened again after another two girls were in the car and had then been dropped off. For girls, maybe rape, or the threat of it, was part of growing up. That's what I thought at the time. And that's how a girl's childhood is taken away from her.

We never told anyone.

It was difficult for us to protect ourselves from our cousins. Much easier with other boys. Of course, I understood from an early age that our family was mafiosa. It had its advantages. A couple of burly men once made a nuisance of themselves on the top deck of a London bus. I was sitting near the front, they were a few seats behind me. We were the only ones upstairs on the bus. Before I knew what was happening one of them came to sit next to me and the other one behind me. I was trapped. I kept my cool. The bus was travelling out of town and nobody came upstairs. The driver could help me out, if need be, so I decided to stay on the bus, past my stop. If I got off, they'd follow me. The guy sitting behind me asked if I was game for some sex. I told him no. "We'll just sit here till you change your mind," the other said.

I told them that my family would be very distressed if anything happened to me. "I'm Sicilian. My family has contacts, clever people who'd soon find you. No hiding place. They will make you pay for anything bad you were to do." That did it. They scrammed. Got off at the next stop. And I used this technique a few more times. Because of my Mediterranean looks they have no hesitation in believing I am Sicilian.

TWENTY-THREE

Wednesday 30th August – afternoon

I ring Zia's bell. It seems to take a long time for her to answer. I ring again. She eventually appears.

"Oh, Zia, how are you?"

"Me have pain in back today. I clean my big tomato pignata in the garden this morning."

"I'm sorry to hear that, Zia. Have you taken anything for your back?"

"No, I take no thing. I no trust doctor."

"No wonder you have backache, Zia. Did you carry that heavy cauldron out to the garden yourself?"

"Yes, I roll pignata out to garden."

Zia had always been wary of doctors seeing them as a notch higher than the police for wanting to interfere in people's lives.

"Do you need help with your tomato jars?"

"Yes, I happy you here now."

Zia makes tomato sauce every year for winter. She boils tomatoes, in her huge cauldron, then strains them, places the sauce in jars, and screws the lids on. When that's all done, she puts the jars back in the cauldron, on a camp fire, and sterilises them by giving them a good boiling.

"You know, Napoli woman Gennara, next door, she copy me. She make tomato sauce in garden. She buy bigger pignata than my pignata."

"I wouldn't worry about that, Zia. If Gennara copies you, it's because you have a brilliant idea," I say, thinking of Oscar Wilde's 'Imitation is the sincerest form of flattery that mediocrity can pay to greatness.'

"I make over a hundred jar this year."

"That's brilliant," Zia, "it'll keep you well stocked up for winter." She likes that comment, and smiles at me. "Maria, now you bring empty jar to garden and I fill while you hold jar, then you put lid on, pass to me and I screw lid on tight." She doesn't trust me to twist on the lids properly.

When we've finished, Zia asks: "Cuppa tea?"

"I'd love one. Did you make any cakes today?"

"I make cuddureddi at six o'clock this morning. They quick to make."

"Cuddureddi?"

"Yeah, you remember Ziuzza. She make cuddureddi. I have old recipe."

I wasn't expecting this. That brought memories back alright.

"Yes, of course I remember her."

"Oh, she lovely lady. Pity big bastardi kill her. If she live to see Young Cushi today she be proud. So proud."

She brings out cuddureddi that look just like Ziuzza's all those years ago when I saw the gun in her apron. Zia has even sprinkled them with sugar.

"I've bought your ice-box back. The syringe is in there." She takes it. "The ice-creams were so good," I say. "Everyone at the barbecue thought they were simply delicious. Zia, they worked perfectly. The two women had tummy troubles and Richard..."

"I guess... he shit for one army!" she interrupts.

"Yes, exactly," I say, laughing.

"Minghiuni, pigliati chissu!" *meaning:* big prick, take that! She makes an arm and hand gesture suggesting that Richard get stuffed.

She rushes off to get Humps's bed socks, places them on the table, and irons them with her hands. "Beautiful," she says, as she cocks her head to one side to admire them.

"Oh, Humps'll be pleased. They're lovely. Thank you so much. Zia, I have some yellow wool here for my bed socks. I want yellow ones like Sicilian lemons."

"Ah, and like Sicilia sun."

"Yes," I say, "and I want yellow pompoms, too. A hundred percent Sicilia."

She is visibly moved. I think I see a tear.

"I make for you. You no worry. I start now."

She comes back with her knitting needles and a tray of cuddureddi. As she knits, and I eat cuddureddi, I tell her about Alberto.

"Zia, I went to see Alberto."

"You tell him where sun rise and where sun set?"

"Yes. I asked him to come clean with Giusy so that she knows where she stands."

"So what he say?"

"He said that he prefers Giusy."

"What you tell him do?"

"To give up Nancy, divorce his wife, and go and live with Giusy. I think he married young. Olga wasn't the right choice."

"So we give Giusy another potion. She have potion for part-time Alberto. Now Giusy need full-time-Alberto potion. He need me and you to tell him what to do."

We laugh together.

Then Zia tells me that she has spoken to Giulio. She sent for him and he'd been to her house that very morning. He works nights, so went to see her before going home. "I tell him where sun rise in the morning, and I tell him sun set in the evening at end of day." Zia likes comparing a day to the start and end of life.

"Are you sure he understood about the sunset?" I say.

"Yeah, he know the sun go down and night come at end of day. He big bastardo, I tell you," she says. Seemingly he wasn't going co-operate. He told her as much himself. Calling Zia a busybody and making clear to her she was to keep out of what was the business of his and his wife's only. "He hard head," Zia says.

"What's going to happen now?" I ask.

"Angelina and Provvi tell me they book plane ticket to Sicilia for all family."

"Oh, so they managed it."

"Now we book ticket."

"Are you going to Sicily? Who with?" I ask.

"With you, silly girl."

"With me!"

"With you. We go together. I no see Peppina long time."

Oh, my God. I was taken aback, I hadn't seen this coming my way. Also, Zia wants to see her sister, Peppina. That is the very person I hoped never to see again in my life. Never.

"No, sorry I can't leave Humphrey."

"Englishman, he cook. He no miss you."

"Yes, he will. We're very attached to one another."

"We only go for five day," she says.

"Oh, Jesus."

"You silly girl. You go holiday. You see you mother tomb."

"Let me think about it."

"You no think about. We go. And we invited birthday

party. 27 September," Zia says.

"I need to talk about this with Humps. Maybe Humps can come too. He's always wanted to go to The Village to see where my origins lie. It's our wedding anniversary that week. We could celebrate it in Sicily."

"We go 26, we come back 30. Angelina family go 25. They stay longer."

"Does Peppina know you're going?"

"Yeah, she know. I telephone yesterday. I tell we go holiday, stay with Peppina."

"Stay with Peppina!"

"Peppina have space."

"Does she know about Angelina and Provvi?"

"Yes. I hint we need help for young man education. You no worry. She no stupid, she understand."

"So you've spoken to her about it?"

"You silly girl. We no speak on telephone, no write computer about business. I just give her a clue. She understand I tell you before. We discuss education detail when we in Sicilia."

For a minute, only the clickety-clack of Zia's needles can be heard.

"Even if I did come to Sicily, I'm not staying with Peppina. I'd book myself into a hotel," I say.

"No hotel in The Village. Hotel forty-five minute in car."

"It doesn't matter. I'd hire a car at the airport and keep it for the whole holiday."

"Ah, you modern woman. You do what you want. I tell Peppina only me stay."

Zia thought for a bit. Then said:

"Tart niece Bella and Rosa – the du big bagascie – come back to my house. Blackmail problem."

"Zia, I'm sorry. I'm not really interested in their problems. I don't even want to hear about it."

"Yeah, I tell you next week. When you tell me you come to Sicilia."

"I can phone you. But just assume it's a no until then," I say.

"No. You no phone. You come back see me."

Luckily Humps is out at a business dinner this evening. I don't want to tell him about going to Sicily straight away – not without sleeping on it for a night.

TWENTY-FOUR

Thursday 31st August

At last, a day off. A Zia-free day. I catch up on all my housework in the morning and do some serious food shopping in the afternoon. I vacuum the carpets, polish the furniture, mop the floors, and even wash the windows. Later I read the papers and do some tweeting. Also, I have to answer Susi's email, maybe I will phone her later instead. My life is certainly busy now.

Another thing I want to do is to check out the bike-store. Anger sets in again as I unlock the door. I put my head around the door. To my complete surprise, all the walls have been whitewashed. Gone are the perennial cobwebs in the ceiling corners. So, who's done that, I wonder. I lift the bike-cover a little, to make sure it is actually Humps's old bike under there. And, yes, it is alright – same as it has been all along. So that's sorted out. No doubt I will soon hear the whole story about the whitewashing from some good soul. It looks like Richard won't be getting the bashing I hoped he'd receive.

After my shopping expedition, I am going into our building with my bags, when I meet Barbara coming out in the opposite direction.

"Good afternoon, Barbara. Nice day, isn't it?"

"Very nice," she says.

"Barbara, I heard from Sarah that you and Richard weren't well after the barbecue. I was sorry to hear that."

"Yes, we were quite poorly. Upset stomachs are terrible."

"I know," I say, "but I'm quite annoyed with Richard. He didn't take any notice of my warning about leaving the meat in the sun."

"I'm sorry," she says, red-faced. "I have had words with Richard and he's embarrassed about it."

"Oh, well the whole business is over? You are well now, I suppose."

"Yes, yes, we're quite well now." She smiles coldly. "By the way, "Richard's had the bike-store whitewashed. Have you seen that?"

"Yes, I have. It's so fresh and clean now. Look, Barbara, let's forget about the insulting graffiti incident as well."

I can see from the sour expression on her face that she doesn't like me bringing that up. They can do the deeds but don't like the consequences.

"Agreed," she says. And we shake hands.

For high and mighty, self-entitled, self-aggrandising, bigoted snobs, they have climbed down a peg or two.

During dinner I tell Humps about Richard whitewashing the bike-store, about Barbara's climbdown and about how energised I've been – doing an untold amount of housework. Then I get onto the subject of going to Sicily.

"Well, that's a bolt from the blue," he says. "You haven't been to Sicily for about four decades. What brought that on?"

"Zia wants to go and insists I go, too. To visit my mother's grave, she says. I argued against it. Zia said I could stay with her at Peppina's. That's definitely out of the question."

"Of course, it is. I don't like the idea of you going on your own. I'll see if I can come with you. What week would that be?"

"At the end of September. On the 26th, coming back on Saturday 30th."

"Darling, I don't see why you shouldn't go. The change will do you good."

That was typical of Humps. As long as I am happy so is he.

"I suppose I could get a few days off work. All that overtime I've done. They owe it to me. It shouldn't be a problem."

"As far as taking care of me is concerned, I think I might just be taking care of you, if you come to Sicily, too."

"I'm not staying here on my own. Who's going to hold my hand when I can't sleep?" he jokes.

"Oh, Humps. That would be great. What a surprise! We could go and stay by the sea. In a nice hotel. Far away from The Village. What do you think?"

"I'd love it," he says, "you know I've always wanted to go and you've not been keen."

"Well, maybe the time has come. We can drive to The Village when we want to go there."

"That sounds splendid," he says.

"I'll tell Zia next time I go."

I can't pretend I don't have any trepidation about this. I've always tried to keep my family at arm's length. I suppose I have to be positive about it all. Sicily is a beautiful island born of Greek Myth and ventilated by warm African winds. The land of limoncello and granita. Many tourists go there who are not slightly connected to the place. Why can't we just go there and enjoy this land of my origins? I keep swinging between being positive about it and then imagining horror stories. It could turn out to be a fine mess I've got myself into. Is there a chance that Humps and I could be associated with anything untoward? No, of course not. Giulio would be straightened out somehow and would then leave Provvi alone. They knew what they were doing in Sicily. They weren't some tuppenny, backstreet, east-end, unwary, petty criminals. They were part of an ingrained age-old tradition, razor-sharp, highly-organised.

"I'll clear up," Humps says.

"Thanks, darling. I need to phone Susi. She emailed me and I haven't answered."

I do care about Susi. She tells me everything she's been up to. She is an open book about her life. About her chaotic work life. About all the men she's been sleeping with, and how good or bad they are in bed, accompanying her accounts with all the fine details. We have some grand laughs together. Giggling like schoolgirls. Essentially, she's been rudderless since her divorce, about forty years ago. The only husbands she's wanted after that, belong to other women. Their wives can iron their shirts after I've crumpled them, she says. And she exploits the men for all they're worth. She turns the whole concept of married men using single women on it's head. She's the single woman wringing out married men and hanging them out to dry. Or so she believes.

Whenever she is going through a change in her life, she'll get in touch. As in the recurring times the current 'husband' has left her or she's left him, or if she's changing her job. I give her no end of advice. None of which she's ever taken. I've come to realise that under the guise of wanting advice, lies the simple need to tell me what she's doing. She needs to share it. She needs me to tell her she is being hard-done-by. That is her endgame. But, I still offer her advice.

She adds, how can I say? Some excitement in my life? Different from me. I am boring in comparison. In her professional life, she takes on jobs far too difficult for her, then she gets sacked. She finds jobs that are paid too little and then leaves as soon as she finds a better-paid one. So round and round it goes, every few months or so.

In her love-life she is totally uninhibited. A woman who goes out there, weaves relationships with men, has a wonderful time, gets hurt, and starts all over again. At times, she gets into new affairs before the old ones have fizzled out: "You've got to be forward looking, haven't you, Mary?" Where she gets all the men from is a mystery to me. "They grow on trees," she says. With some, she remains friends – occasionally meeting them, when 'the call from the jungle' occurs. Or, if she needs money, one or two will oblige. She never seems to have money of her own. Whenever we go out together, I pay. Zia gives her money too, when she goes to her mother and pleads with her. This has been happening for most of her adult life, even as she is approaching the age of sixty. Often some of the men she has been involved with help her find a job. With a few, she's started up small businesses which have ended up falling flat on their faces. And losing the little money she had.

Susi eventually answers her phone. She says she has some bad news. She's lost her job.

"Oh, no! How awful! Not again," I say.

She came to specialise in marketing and sales. And nobody is as good as Susi in marketing herself. Unashamed bull-shitter supremo. It's surprising how far she's come without qualifications. She left school to get married and never went back. Essentially, she's lied her way up. One day I arrived at her home when she'd finished printing her CV. Handing it over to me, she asked if I'd have a quick look-through, check it for typos. "Susi, you don't have these qualifications – a degree in Media? Honestly, they'll find out."

"Yeah, I know they could find out, Mary. But I get experience for as long as they keep me. Yeah, I learn on the job. I've only been chucked out once for lying."

"Yes, but word gets around."

"London's big," she says. "What's the choice? I look at the job ad, and tell them I've got what they are looking for. You've got to get an interview. If you don't, you don't get a job. I wouldn't bother sending them my CV if I told the truth. It's a no-brainer."

"But you haven't even worked for some of these places!" I said, as I scrolled my finger down the list under the heading 'experience.'"

"They hardly ever check up," she said, "and, oh, by the way, I gave an agency your mobile number."

"Why?"

"Sorry, I didn't ask your permission before, but they suddenly threw the question at me. They want a professional to give them a character reference. Don't tell them you're my cousin, will you?"

Sure enough, they phoned me. That very same day.

Now some bright and slick 35-year-old, even more silver-tongued than Susi, is replacing her. They asked Susi to collect her things, then they put her at the door, within one hour of telling her she'd been fired. She needn't work her notice out, they said.

"From tomorrow, Friday, 1st September 2017, I'll be without a job. But I have ideas about setting up a little business. Seba's the one to help me with that. We still see each other every now and then."

Sebastian and Susi's affair lasted a few months. But he comes back on the scene every now and then. He has a house in the country and a small flat in London, which I would describe as his playpen. Like others, he makes out he's left his wife, has moved out of the family home, and is shacked up in a little flat because the alimony is such that he can't afford anything bigger – not in London, anyway. As it turns out, he is going back home, and his wife knows nothing about his ever moving out of the family home. But Seba left Susi for his ex-lover, who'd come back on the scene, and back to his play-pen; although he swears, he still loves Susi. And because he still loves her, Susi phones him, and he agrees they could start up a little business together.

Every time Susi meets a new husband, she carries out a survey. She finds out where he lives, gets his home phone number or his wife's mobile (which Susi finds in his mobile when he's stupidly distracted for some reason) then Susi phones the wife. Susi pretends she's from an airline or some other big firm, depending on the husband's lifestyle, and finds out as much as she can about the family. "The information," she says, "can come in useful." Especially when the husband's lying to her. "Anyway," I've heard her say, "it's nice to know who you're sharing a man with. We usually have a lot in common."

"Can I treat you to lunch tomorrow, Susi? Come on, let's get ourselves a nice meal washed down by plenty of good Italian wine."

"Where? When?" She jumps at the offer.

TWENTY-FIVE

Friday 1st September

"Susi, darling, so sorry about your job," I say, as soon she arrives at the restaurant.

She is a little dejected. It looks as if she hasn't slept well the night before. Dark rings around her eyes, her hair isn't brushed properly. She doesn't look like her usual self. During the meal, I am not sure what I can say to get her spirits up.

"Come on, look on the bright side. You're going to start a new business with Sebastian soon."

"Yeah, Mary. Do you know how hard it is to set up a

business? Loads of work and you go months without any money coming in. If you make a bit of money, it goes straight back into the business."

"But you're resilient. Determined. You always bounce back."

I suppose when we're down like that, we have to go through a sad period and nothing can help except the passing of time. I decide that the best way forward is distraction. I tell her about going to Sicily. She is so surprised, her wine goes down the wrong way. "You! To Sicily!" At least that makes her laugh.

"Humps is coming, too."

"What, Humps as well?" she keeps on laughing.

"What's wrong with that?"

"You hate the place, Mary. You've always hated The Village."

"No, I haven't," I say. "True, I've tried to keep away from our family. That was because I wanted to protect myself. I'd been hurt enough. And look at what they did to you!"

"That's true. I've always thought you were more sensible than me. So why are you going there?"

"I suppose the time has come," I say, "Humps has never been, he's always wanted to go."

"You know what," she begins, "I could come as well. What's to stop me? I've got sweet F.A. to do right now, and it'll take my mind off things. My mum might pay my fare, and I'll ask if I can stay at Aunt Peppina's."

Now that would really be an interesting expedition.

"I wanted to talk to you about Adriano. You know, all you went through when you were a teenager." I wasn't sure if it was the right time to mention it, when she'd lost her job the day before, but I've had the issue on my mind and need to tell her.

"That's water under the bridge."

"Maybe. But it has had consequences on you for all your life, hasn't it? You went into a wrong marriage with Enzo, and he left you penniless when he absconded to Sicily. Don't tell me it wasn't difficult."

"I haven't been any good at getting into long-lasting relationships with men. I'm not sure it's Adriano's fault. But he did cause me a lot of anger, fear and pain, though. Everything about me is wrong. Look how I've messed everything up."

"No!" I answer, emphatically. "There's nothing wrong with you. It was the people around you who were wrong. Your dad was rotten to you, your cousin raped you, we've grown up without good role models. Though I had Auntie Marge. And you didn't get a proper education.

"And even if you're right, how's that going to change now?" she asks.

"I don't think it will change now. But you could get some money from him. He's got a thriving business," I say.

"What from Adriano?"

"Yes."

"You're kidding me," she says.

"No, I'm not. I've never been so serious. Here you are without a job, and God only knows when you'll get your pension now the Government have put up retirement age for women. How are you going to live?"

"It'll never work, Mary!"

"Maybe not. But you need to try. It's retribution. It's putting things right, then laying them to rest. There's an open wound there now. You need to heal it. To do that will take some effort, but it has to be done."

"What am I supposed to do? Phone him up and ask for money?" she says.

"Absolutely not," and now I feel like Zia, "It's best not to use phone or email for something like this."

"Not sure," she says. "You know, I've looked up to you since we were kids," she says.

"Now I've stopped work I have more time and can concentrate on doing what I believe in," I say.

"And what do you believe in?"

"I believe in helping women defend themselves. Sometimes they need help. Getting them the justice we didn't get," I say.

"You're not going to get bored, then, are you? There are no end of women being treated badly out there. Where are you going to start?"

"With you. With the women I come across. I can fix a small number of wrongdoings."

"We should have gone to the police at the time. The police wouldn't do anything about my case now. It happened over forty years ago," she says.

"You're right there. They'd probably laugh."

"Exactly. So it's up to us. Or, I'll go and talk to him myself, if you want," I say.

"No, no, I want to be in charge."

"Do you know what your mother gets up to?"

"She's got lots of friends. They go round during the day and they chat. She bakes, knits, watches TV in the evenings. I don't worry too much about her because she's not alone much. She's making me some pink bed socks when she's finished your yellow ones, she told me on the phone."

"So that's how she's using up that pink wool. Those bed socks will go down a treat with your lovers," I say.

We laugh.

"Susi, I wanted to ask you something else, that summer when your dad died in Sicily – he was alright when you left England, wasn't he? What I mean is: do you remember his having heart problems, or anything like that? Was he being treated by doctors?"

Susi has a shocked look on her face. Her voice quivers.

"I don't know, Mary, I really don't remember. I was a girl and had other things on my mind. Anyway, it's painful for me to talk about him. It happened years ago, like the rapes."

"Sorry, it must have been terrible for you."

"Yeah, like Luca was terrible for you," she says. "You know, even if he wasn't kind to me he was my dad."

"I've put the Luca episode away in a drawer in my memory," I say. "But your dad's death must have been such a shock for your mum then she had to go through getting a death certificate and making funeral arrangements in Sicily."

"Yeah, wasn't easy for her. But Peppina helped out," Susi says.

"You and your family were all staying with Peppina, weren't you?"

"Yeah. Why are you interested in him all of a sudden?"

"I was thinking about him the other day. How cruel he was to you, how he killed my tortoise, cut my ball in half... I suppose he wasn't nice to your mum either?"

"All his anger and violence were for me and mum. My brothers never got hit. When dad was taking it out on me I used to think that he'd get rid of his anger and hit mum less. That's not how it works though, is it?"

"Absolutely not. Cruelty is infinite."

"You used to get hit by your mum, didn't you?" she says.

"I certainly did. Why don't we change the subject before we get too sad?"

"What to?" she asks.

"Men. Tell me about all the men you've seen in the last year or so," I say.

She laughs.

"That'll keep us here until this evening," she says.

"That's OK. I can stay here till six. It's only three. Let's order some more wine."

Going back home, thoughts of Zia killing Uncle Tony bounce about in my head. She said that doctors in The Village (there was only one when I was a child) were not 'curious' like the 'busybody' English doctors. Uncle Tony was forty-six. No age to die. But he was on the chubby side and smoked like a trooper. Either he really did have a heart-attack, or she poisoned him, or something, and passed it off as a heart-attack. Zia said he died of 'heart-stop.' And Peppina would have had a hand in it, too.

Am I imagining things? To me there seems to be a pattern emerging. Women whose husbands have died young. Have these women murdered their husbands? Or had them murdered? And coupled to that, men readily killed each other as well because of some conflict. Has the violence been handed down from generation to generation? Do we have it in our blood? I don't know what happened in our family before my grandmother's time. But was this a family of women avengers? Did the isolation of The Village miles away from other inhabited places facilitate killers? But the same was now happening in London. Zia doesn't have a husband. Most of her women visitors don't have one. And the woman who still has a spouse, Provvi, would be better off without him.

TWENTY-SIX

What Happened in 1974

1974 was an incredible and tumultuous year. The year Auntie Marge died, and the year that was pivotal in my three cousins' and my life. Every one of the young generation in our family got hitched that year although we were so young. Three of us got married and one got engaged.

When Auntie Marge died, she left me exposed to my

family's claws. I lost my adult role model. Uncle Peter rushed to our house one late Sunday afternoon in February. Visibly shocked. In a panic. "Quick," he said, "Auntie's had a bad stroke." He could hardly talk, but managed to blurt out that I should run quickly to the phone-box, dial 999 for an ambulance. I ran as fast as I could, crying all the way. There was a young man in the phone-box. He saw my state of despair, interrupted his call, let me in. After the call, I came out of the box sobbing. He offered to walk me home. "No, please, I've got to run back. My neighbour is dying." I hurried back to Auntie Marge's house. The man followed me. He stood outside the back door.

Auntie Marge was lying on the kitchen floor. Part of her body was frozen. It was heart-breaking to see her trying to talk. Only a few grunts came out. I was at a loss as to what to do at first, so just stood there and looked on. Then I fell to my knees, held her hand and cried. She must have realised it was me because she tried to get some sounds out. It was while I was kneeling beside her on the kitchen mat that she took her last breath. Dead. I howled. The young man behind the door, Tommy, came in softly. He patted Uncle Peter's back and said how sorry he was. Then he placed a hand on my shoulder and squeezed it. When the ambulance arrived, the three of us stood there and watched. I kept crying and Tommy put his arm round my shoulder. The body was taken into the ambulance and Uncle Peter went with Auntie Marge.

My mother came out of the house when the ambulance arrived, though she understood that Auntie Marge was in a critical condition when Uncle Peter came round, she didn't bother to go to Auntie's house while I went to the phone box. She hadn't come to console me, though I didn't expect she would. Instead, she started harassing me about Tommy. Saying I must have had a secret boyfriend without telling her. She was livid. Tommy was gob-smacked when she went into one of her frenzies. He walked off, turning his head back occasionally, while she was hissing at me.

It was the second time I had seen a dead body. The first was Ziuzza's husband. Auntie Marge was cremated. Frightening. A sad affair. The curtain not far from where I sat, on my right, slowly opened revealing a fire. The coffin glided into the hatch, and the curtain closed again. Afterwards there was talk about ashes, but I was in a state of shock and couldn't take much in. Only four people attended the funeral: Uncle Peter, Auntie's sister Dorothy, Dorothy's daughter Belinda, and me. That's all.

Nobody else bothered.

Carrying on with my account of 1974, I'd become a bag of nerves, plus I had nausea and dizziness. Sometimes my hands seemed to tremble for no reason. One of my mother figures had died, and the other one, Zia, lived miles away. I was left with my real mother. In many ways she relied on me. She had only simple vocabulary even in her own language. She had only gone to school for three years. For the rest of the time, she was needed to work on the land. Never having learnt English, beyond the basics of asking for things in shops, I couldn't speak to her in English. My Sicilian wasn't that good. Though it is a nice colourful dialect, it sounded stupid with an English accent. It didn't help that I'd become overawed by the beautiful language of poetry when studying for A level English. I threw myself into the beauty of highbrow English. And relished it.

With the help of my English teacher, Miss Green, I had a place lined up at an excellent university to read English. It was the beacon of light that kept me going; that glimmer of future happiness. I would be surrounded by people who loved Literature, like me. That would be the saving of me. My mother didn't agree with my going on to further education. She said I should go and earn some money, stop reading books which had made my brain go soft. Her main argument was that I was lazy so used reading as an excuse to get out of doing housework. So I laboured to get the house clean and shining, then I went off to read. But even that didn't work at times because she'd still want to whip what I'd read out of me. I couldn't mention university to her without her going wild. My father was indifferent, as usual, and just brushed me off by saying that I should sort it out with my mother.

Another reason why I desperately wanted a degree in English was because I had set my mind on it when I'd been deeply offended by Auntie Marge's sister, Dorothy, a few years back. She, her husband Arthur, and their daughter Belinda had been invited to Sunday lunch one day. I carried out my usual tasks of setting the table and beating the Yorkshire pudding. Dorothy said to Auntie Marge: "I don't understand the attraction of having this little cockney-Sicilian urchin as company."

Auntie Marge was livid. She hardly talked to her sister during lunch, speaking to Belinda instead. Belinda was talking about university. She was reading English and hoped to become a teacher. She seemed very intelligent to me then and, above all, very lah-di-da. In fact, I don't remember Belinda ever speaking to me. I was totally in awe of her. She was this grown-up, in a flowery dress and leather shoes, living on a totally different planet from mine. I felt I was akin to a worm and simply didn't deserve to be spoken to by her, or her mother.

When they left, Auntie Marge sat me down and said: "Don't take any notice of my sister Dorothy. She's a stuck-up old woman who's set in her ways. Belinda is going to be important. Before long she'll have a degree in English. She's a lady. She went to a girls' boarding school and has learnt all the social graces. One day she will marry an important man and have a good position in society."

This admiration for Belinda struck me, especially because it came from Auntie Marge, the woman I adored. The closest I'd come to a mother.

"Do you think I could go to university and speak like that?"

"No, I don't think so, dear. You didn't get the right start in life. Your school's not good, either. It's all those girls from the council housing estate over the bridge. They bring the tone down. They're common."

Thinking back, they actually were 'common' as Auntie Marge put it. A couple got pregnant at fifteen and had to leave school. Nearly all of them smoked 'in the bogs,' their language was uncouth, most of them swore like troopers. Their parents were Labour Party supporters, but of the right-wing bigoted, racist kind. They were all for equality amongst themselves but spurned foreigners, taunted homosexuals, and believed a woman's place was in the home, while the men spent their money in pubs. Most of my schoolmates' fathers were unemployed. I couldn't get my head round that. My mother and father both worked full-time. How was it that my schoolmates' parents hadn't filled those jobs? The vacancies were there before my parents ever arrived in England.

If only Auntie Marge had known that I actually did get an excellent degree in English and learnt to 'speak like that.' And I had a good marriage. It was not only that I didn't get a good start, or that my school wasn't of the best. More importantly, hurdles had been placed all along the track of my life up to when my mother died. But I triumphed. It was hard, but I made it.

I wonder what happened to Belinda.

Susi's wedding was in March. She was only sixteen and had to have Zia's parental consent. Silvio accompanied her to the altar. Susi and her groom, Enzo, did all sorts of silly things during the reception but, to be fair, they were little more than children. Enzo was a boy from The Village, a sheep farmer, and was a year or two older than her. The scene most impressed on my mind was when she was sitting at the top table, in her white lacy dress, eating salt-and-vinegar crisps out of the packet, and drinking Coca-Cola straight from the can. She looked like a child. My opinion is that she married so that Adriano would stop raping her.

Between dances Stefano stared at me from a distance across the hall. If I didn't dance with him, he said he'd make a scene. He kept coming back for dances, and holding me tight making my dress creep up at the back. He said our wedding reception was going to be better than this one. I told him, again, that he could forget about that. He said I had no say in the matter. His brother Silvio, of course, was inundated by girls and totally ignored me. I danced my heart out with anyone available: other boys, relatives, and even other girls, just to keep Stefano at bay for a while.

In July, I went to Sicily with my mother. I was eighteen. Going to Sicily had never been good news for me. Little did I know what my mother had planned. My father stayed at home. He didn't want to go. Neither did I. My mother more or less blackmailed me into it. Because her illness was advancing, she said she needed me to look after her, get medication for her, do the food shopping. My mother also got one of her friends to bully me into going. It was only a month, after all. My ineffectual father did nothing to side with me. Silvio was already in Sicily. Zia had sent him over to look for 'a nice wife.' So, begrudgingly, I went to The Village. At least Silvio was there. My mother's illness, my father's indifference and my recent swotting for A levels had taken their toll on me.

Arriving in Sicily with my mother was devastating. I was grief stricken. All the women in the village seemed to be there – in my grandmother's house. Nearly all of them were shrouded in black. Some were relatives, the rest were childhood friends of my mother's, neighbours, and simple hangers-on. They came to see how my mother was, but also to see what I had grown up into. The ones who had known me from previous visits, didn't like me because they knew I didn't want to be one of them. They were disappointed when they saw me. I was wearing a yellow mini-skirt and a yellow matching top with crystal buttons running down the middle, emphasising my small waist and large bosom. My legs were shapely and my shiny black hair hung down past the bottom of my shoulder blades. They were livid because I looked good. One observed my straight legs, gave a toothless grin, and said they would be bandy in a few years.

A redeeming feature came in the form of a couple of girls my age in the neighbourhood who'd been to high school. Luckily some youngsters were chafing against the older generation and were planning to leave The Village. These girls, though, would not be going to university. The mindset still hadn't progressed enough to allow women to gain academic qualifications. The two girls were at the crossroads of their lives wondering what to do with themselves. Franca wanted to find a husband while Patrizia wanted to join her father who'd gone to Rome.

Patrizia was my kindred spirit. She hated everyone in The Village, including her mother, said she wouldn't get involved with anyone. She would leave as soon as she found out exactly where her father was. He left the family home without giving a forwarding address. Patrizia said she'd go to Rome and investigate her father's whereabouts. That was ridiculous because Patrizia didn't have a penny to her name.

She could hardly afford an ice-cream when we went out for our evening strolls. If she couldn't find her father, she said she'd turn up at her aunt's house in Palermo and beg her to let her live there in exchange for housework. Peppina didn't like me talking to Patrizia saying she was an evil influence. Whenever she saw us together she'd call me up to the house and give me an 'urgent' task to do.

Franca was more submissive and more content with life. She had the most beautiful blue eyes. And there in Sicily, where most people were dark, those eyes looked even more dramatic. Sometimes the three of us would go out walking together. That was as far as our adventures took us and, when we bought ice-creams we thought we were in heaven. Silvio was there with some friends of his one evening and came over to see who these two girls were. As soon as Franca caught his eye, it was clear he was smitten. Love at first sight does exist, I saw it strike the moment Franca and Silvio set eyes on each other.

Soon, the engagement party followed. Franca looked gorgeous and, of course, so did Silvio. They were truly a beautiful pair. Franca wore a glittery, pastel multi-coloured maxi dress – patchwork motif – her hair done up with a couple of ringlets cascading each side. I had lost my favourite cousin, no more car expeditions in his two-seater Triumph. My slice of him had gone, slipped out of my fingers. I pretended I was happy: clapped and smiled when everyone else did. Guests gawped. Tickled because she was a virgin, and he a big-time Don Giovanni quite a few years older. Patrizia and I sat in a corner moaning about everything: the heat, the noise, our weight, The Village, the loud women, the sleazy men... Life and soul of the party, we were not.

While I was in Sicily, Patrizia didn't have a boyfriend – and neither did she leave for Rome or Palermo. We spent our evenings getting dressed up and strutted slowly around The

Village like peacocks, as we complained about our lot. In all honesty, it was done to parade ourselves in front of the boys – only to tell them to take a running jump if any of them as much as showed interest in us, which most of them did. When I used to go to her house to call for Patrizia, she was nearly always ready. She'd engage in a shouting match with her mother about having a few lira for an ice-cream. I sincerely think that her mother simply didn't have any money. Patrizia seemed to think she did. But as a last rite, before leaving home, Patrizia would take a white, enamelled bowl with a chipped blue rim, fill it with water, wash her feet, dry them, then put her shoes on. There in their only room which served as kitchen, living room, and bedroom, for both her and her mother, and bathroom. Their toilets were chamberpots. And in the mornings, Patrizia's mother and other women would throw the contents into the middle of the courtyard. It smelt to high heaven when the sun shone on that urine.

The days passed and not much happened. I'd read the books I'd brought with me from England. Of course there were no bookshops in The Village, no library either. One of the two food shops also sold magazines. I was then reduced to reading romantic magazines, called foto-romanzi, showing photographs of men and women falling in love with each other and talking in speech bubbles. The endings were pretty predictable. Boredom even led me to do more housework than usual.

I came to love washing my clothes. By hand, of course. My grandmother had a huge stone sink in her garden, built up against the side of her house. It had a built-in, corrugated washboard. In the Sicilian heat, it was a joy to plunge my hands into the cool water and splash about. We used an orange jelly-like soap called Sole, which you scooped out from a big plastic container with your hand. Peppina would sometimes comment that I was ruining my clothes by rubbing them so harshly. She said that if I wanted my clothes to last, I should wash them as little as possible. My frustration and anger was taken out on my clothes.

I had to do something. And it had to be something at home. When you put your nose out of the front door, you had to be careful not to put a foot wrong. The villagers would always find something to criticise. And it made me feel uncomfortable. Some would ask direct questions like Where are you going? What's wrong with your mother? Have you got a boyfriend? Is there a boy in the village you like? I can act as go-between.

On one of those rare occasions when I was home alone, I got a bucketful of water and a mop and cleaned the kitchen floor. My thoughts went back to when I was twelve and saw the horrific killing of that lamb. After the kitchen, I started on the living room-cum-bedroom next door. The room doubled up as Peppina's bedroom, the single bed in the corner had cushions placed against the wall during the day to, unconvincingly, make it look like a sofa.

When I cleaned under the bed, the mop hit against something hard. I lifted the bedspread and saw a small metallic suitcase. What would Peppina do with a suitcase? She never went anywhere. I pulled it out. It had a lock on it. I realised straight away that I would be in trouble if I as much as let on that I knew about the case. I put it back and stopped mopping. Threw the dirty water away and hoped neither Peppina or my grandmother noticed the mop was wet. I even went in and out of the house and garden several times, so that the floor didn't look too clean. I hunted around for the key. I rifled through drawers. Nowhere to be found.

A few days later, Peppina whipped out a handkerchief from her dress pocket. A key tinkled to the floor. I pretended not to notice. Asked her what we were having for dinner that evening, 'Mangi chiddru chi trovi' *meaning:* 'You eat what you get.' I poked out my tongue when she wasn't looking. That key. I must get it. See what's in the case. Another afternoon, my grandmother sent Peppina out to get some shopping. My grandmother went to lie down in her bedroom for her daily siesta. The old dress Peppina wore around the house was over a chair in the living room. Yes, the key was there. I fiddled about with the lock a little. Rusty. At last, it clicked open. There was an old sheet or two, in there. Yellowish. Why would someone lock up old sheets? I unfolded the sheets carefully and the reason soon became clear – wrapped up in them were two guns. Imagine my dismay when I saw them. I'd never seen a gun before. Quickly, I locked the case, kicked it back under the bed, and placed the key back in the pocket.

One day my path crossed with a young soldier along a dusty street. He said ciao to me as we passed. It so happened that he was my mother's cousin – the son of one of another of my grandmother's sisters – but I didn't know him. He was a few years older than me. I thought no more of it, until a few days later, his father came to my grandmother's house asking to speak to my mother. He asked if his son, Luca, could have my hand in marriage. The father would come back the following week for an answer.

When my mother told me, I felt a mixture of horror, incredulity and disgust. "No. I'm not marrying him or anyone. I want to go home." I felt despair, like I had done when I was twelve and threatened to be left in The Village. We started arguing, and it transpired my mother hadn't booked a flight back to England for us. It was all so ridiculous. How could I marry a man I didn't even know? He spoke Sicilian, I spoke English. My knowledge of the Sicilian dialect was not good enough for complicated conversations.

Peppina cornered me the following day when I was coming down from the attic. She stood in my way. She flashed a mean look at me and began by saying that I knew full well my mother didn't have long to live, and what a wretched girl I was not to please my mother. "No. No. And no. I won't," I said. "Yes, you will because if you don't get engaged to him, you are not leaving The Village. That is guaranteed," she said in Sicilian. "There is no way out. They are watching you." Whoever 'they' were. She proceeded in saying what a nice man Luca was and what an ungrateful wretch I was.

"You think you're beautiful, don't you? You're nothing compared to your mother's beauty when she was young," she said, repeating what she had said to me when I was twelve.

"I can't go through with it," I said, trembling.

She got hold of my neck and slammed my head against the wall behind me, the thump reverberated in my skull. Squeezing my throat she growled "There's no such thing as can't." As much as I tried, not a sound came out of my mouth, she was still clutching my throat. "Teach you to wear mini-skirts, what did you expect? You want to go back and tart about with those Englishmen, don't you?" My mother came in, sat down and watched as Peppina knocked me over and tried to kick the living-daylight out of me. I turned on my side in agony, and she stamped on me repeatedly at the height of my waist.

Added to that, one day when I was getting my underwear out of a drawer, I noticed a small plastic bag. I didn't remember putting it there. As I started opening it to look inside a most foul stench reached my nose. When I opened the bag I was greeted by the most horrendous sight. Bloodied animal innards. Probably chicken: slimy liver, lungs, kidneys, heart... what organs were they exactly? Without thinking, I took the bag to the bottom of the garden and threw it down the slope over the fence. I knew enough about my family to realise this was a threat. It meant, if you don't marry Luca, your innards will be extracted from you. Though, I don't think they would have done this to me. As usual, I absorbed the blow. Didn't mention it. Pretended it never happened. To this day, I still don't know if it was Peppina, my mother, my grandmother, or someone else.

This was one of the most terrible moments in my life. The realisation, when it dawned on me, I was going to marry a man I hardly knew. That I couldn't go to university. That I would never get out of this place unless I accepted. Maybe I could talk to him in my broken Sicilian. Put him off, see if he'd have pity on me, if he'd understand.

It seemed to be a Catch-22 situation. If Luca was called over to the house to speak to me, it meant I had accepted. There was no way I could go to his house. That was unheard of. Unknown to me, Peppina and my mother had accepted the marriage proposal. Luca turned up one evening at my grandmother's. I still distinctly remember him coming up the long flight of stone stairs leading up from the ground-floor stables.

He sat there on one of my grandmother's sunken raffia chairs. We others were seated on mismatching chairs and nobody spoke. My mother got out a bottle of Marsala from the glass-doored cabinet, put five little glasses on a plastic-flowered tray and poured out the liquor. She went round offering us a glass each, starting with Luca and finishing with me – I refused mine. Luca looked at me and smiled. My mother would have loved to slap me in the face, but couldn't in the circumstances. Instead she threw me an evil look.

My mother asked Luca about his mother, father and two sisters. One sister was married so she asked about her children as well. Peppina and my grandmother joined in and they chatted for a while in Sicilian, complimenting his beautiful and intelligent nieces. I simply sat there looking at my shoes. Then he spoke to me. He asked if I liked Sicily. I said I didn't. I wanted to go back to England. It seemed that he was thinking of emigrating and England sounded nice. He'd have to find a job, he said. My mother declared that we didn't know when we'd be going back. It all depended on 'circumstances.'

After that episode, the scene was repeated, more or less to the letter every evening. I had nothing in common with him. The only thing I figured out he liked was football. Something I knew absolutely nothing about, and neither did I want to. After the umpteenth time of sitting there getting frustrated, I turned to him and said: "When are we getting married?" He was taken aback by the suddenness of it, my mother was surprised because of my 'change of heart.' I'd realised that I was in a stalemate, these evening sessions could simply go on and on for months, so I had to do something to move things forward. He was actually not bad looking and physically attractive, slim and tall. My plan was to marry him, take him back to England with me, then dump him.

The next afternoon his clapped-out car came along the narrow street that led up to the dark courtyard where my grandmother's house stood in the corner. Luca drove my mother, Peppina, and me to a bigger village about thirty minutes away where we bought rings. I asked about the prices and chose the cheapest for myself: an engagement (dress) ring and a simple gold band. Peppina shot me a wicked glance, and I stroked Luca's arm in response.

Next we went to buy my wedding dress. My mother and Peppina were with me. Luca waited in the car. Again, I chose the cheapest one. High neck, long sleeves, and quite loose. I didn't want the wedding guests gawping at my body. By then, I was quite thin. I had practically stopped eating.

Luckily, I wasn't as curvy as before. Hopefully, I wasn't as appealing. When I tried the dress on, my head started spinning, I broke out into a cold sweat. I nearly fainted. My knees turned to jelly, so I sat down on the chair in the claustrophobic cubicle. As I sat there in my wedding dress I thought about how everything had contrived against me, and how lonely I felt. How I had always been on the wrong end of everything. But, I managed to pick myself up, get myself together, and go through with it. I had to. I had to get back to London.

The wedding was at the end of October, after which the newly-weds, accompanied by my mother, went to England for their honeymoon and stayed there. The wedding reception preparations began. I was nice to Luca realising he was my ticket back to England. I did feel a little sorry for him but thought that, on the other hand, I was going to help him settle in England and he'd have a job and future. He was none too bright, though he was fit and sporty, and he'd make a life for himself without me. Moreover, he wasn't aggressive, he was besotted, and I could twist him around my little finger.

Before getting married, we were required to meet the village priest, just the future bride and bridegroom. The priest was some cousin of ours, a few times removed. He ended his inquisition by asking us why we wanted to get married. Note that I was only eighteen. Luca said that he had fallen in love, wanted to spend the rest of his days with me, and have lots of children. That answer provoked a sickening feeling in my stomach working its way up to my throat. A long deep breath stopped me from vomiting. The priest then gaped at me, with a sort of lascivious expression, and said: "Maria, why do you wish to embark into matrimony with Luca?" I couldn't answer, I sat there, stared at him, opened my mouth slightly but no sound came out. "You are too modest to answer. You want to marry him because you love him, don't you?" I was still speechless. The priest got up and showed us the door.

Everything went according to my mother's plan, we were married in late October. It was all organised fast in case I changed my mind. Like in that film, the reception was big, fat and greasy. My father came over to give me away – which at least got him out of his torpor. I hardly knew anyone there. They were all my mother's, father's, and Luca's family and friends. The bride played her part because she was glad to be going back home: smiling at guests, thanking them for presents, dancing, clapping, though inside she was shattered, and feeling faint. I am his property now. I will have to rely on his clemency.

In the evening, the day after the wedding reception, Luca's mother and sister came to Peppina's house, where my family and I were staying. Including Luca. Peppina kindly gave us newly-weds the attic. We, actually, didn't have sex until we got to London. I spurned him because I felt rotten. At the moment of my new in-laws arrival, neither my father nor Luca were in. They'd gone to the bar to meet with Luca's father and offer drinks to all the men there as a celebration of our marriage. Maybe a custom, I don't know, and I'm not bothered, either.

Already wailing on their way up the stairs, my new in-laws reckoned that my family had swindled them. They had counted the number of bottles of alcoholic drinks – worked it out – and found that their share of financing the drinks had come to way too much. Which was perfectly possible. My mother sustained that so many bottles of drink had been consumed, Luca's highly-strung sister got so worked up that she insulted my mother calling her a thief and a liar, and asking her to produce the empty bottles. Peppina pounced on my sister-in-law, slapped and kicked her, told the two women to get the hell out of her house, otherwise she'd make them regret the day they were born. Though Peppina was older and weaker than Luca's sister, the latter knew it was for the best not to hit her back. Going down the stairs, Luca's sister started insulting me, saying I was far inferior to her brother, and I was a slut to boot. They didn't get any money back. Not a lira. Their protests were all in vain.

So, on that happy note, after another two days, the time finally came when we left Sicily. We went to say goodbye to his family, where the minibus that would take us to the airport was waiting. As Luca got in the bus his mother had a fit of active sadness. She kept hitting her own legs to the beat of "Figliu mio unni va?" *meaning:* "Son of mine where are you going?" The sister answered "Se ne va co' sta zoccula," *meaning:* "He's going off with this slut." There are many words for slut in Sicilian. Lucky for her, Peppina wasn't there, otherwise she'd have given the sister what-for. At last, the bus moved off. I smiled at Luca and said: "You'll love England" in Sicilian.

We lived with my parents at first, until we had enough income to pay for a place of our own. It was easy. Luca simply shacked up in my bedroom with me. I had a big single bed, and that had to do for both of us. For the time-being. And, it was in this bed that we first had sex.

Weakened, I still had to reassemble myself after the trauma in Sicily. Get my head together. Get some strength back. Start eating more. But being back in England was fantastic. Everything looked gorgeous to me. Everything: the leaves swaying in the crisp wind, the rain, the cracked pavement slabs, the daily newspapers hanging on a rack outside dingy newsagents, the smell wafting out of the greasy-spoon cafes, and even the broken litter bins. Not even a pure thoroughbred English person could love the place as much as me. I can guarantee that.

School had begun. I went to my old college to see if I could speak to Miss Green and was told to wait until her lessons were over. She was so pleased to see me. After telling her about my marriage, I said I'd decided to put off going to university until the following academic year. It was already November by then, and I was in no mindset for studying. Also, I needed to help Luca out. Get us both out of my parents' house for starters. He couldn't go on living with them after we split up. And, with three words of English and without a job, how was he supposed to survive on his own?

Life is full of surprises. It turned out I was the one to be jilted. Luca couldn't adapt to England. And wasn't even prepared to try. Quite frankly, we had nothing in common. On top of that he hated the miserable weather, missed the sunshine, missed those wild beasts of his mother and sister, missed sitting out in the balmy piazza in the evenings, watching his favourite football team on TV every Sunday at the bar. And he missed playing football for The Village team. The new goalkeeper was pretty useless, so his mates wanted Luca back. They were losing just about every game.

Going back was the only option, he made that clear. Staying in England was my only option, I made that clear. I asked him to be patient for however long it took me to find a job and a cheap place to live. Only then should he return home, after I had sorted myself out and away from my mother. Once we moved out to a bedsit, we saved up for his flight. I had found him work as a waiter in an Italian restaurant and had got myself an easy office job.

But I had to take time off work because I was becoming increasingly pale and tired. My doctor took a blood sample and discovered that I was severely anaemic, and I had an awful pain in my lower back. He sent me for an X-ray, one of my kidneys was seriously damaged. "Have you had an accident? Or a big fall?" he asked. "Your kidney is in a terrible condition. The damage is stopping iron getting to your blood. I'm afraid you will have to have it removed." I told him that I'd had a fall down a rocky slope in Sicily. "Unless it was a very long slope, I do not think that could be the cause," he said.

"It was a very long slope, indeed," I argued.

Of course, it was Peppina's stamping on the kidney that brought this about. My hatred for her was immense. I will get my revenge one day, I thought. But later I settled into a happy, comfortable lifestyle with Humps and, with time, revenge went to the back burner of my mind.

Luca looked after me while I recovered from my operation.

Stefano got married at the beginning of December 1974. A shotgun wedding in two senses of the expression. Stefano told me himself that he'd be getting married. He also said that when he'd heard the news about my engagement to Luca, his relationship with Romina, his future wife, was well on its way. Stefano's pride had been hurt, so he had to make it clear that it was he who'd left me, and not the other way round.

I'll never forget their wedding and it deserves to be related in some length. My parents, and Luca and I, went to Zia's house in the morning of Stefano's big day. Luca was still in London for three more weeks. Zia, Silvio and Stefano were at home. Everyone else was in church, including Susi, with her new husband Enzo, who later told me what happened there.

Zia and Silvio seemed worried when we arrived. Essentially, Stefano had changed his mind. He locked himself in his bedroom and refused to come out. He didn't answer his family's loud shouting and swearing, disgraziatu bastardo, going on behind his door. Smartly dressed, complete with carnations in button holes, we were in despair as to how to get Stefano to the church. He had found himself another woman, an Englishwoman, who had by far overshadowed the love Stefano had for Romina. Stefano hadn't had the guts to tell his future bride, and now he was adamant he wouldn't go through with the marriage. That's what he thought. But think again. You don't mess with Sicilian women. He had a choice of: his wedding today, or his funeral in a few days' time. He had to be at that altar dead or alive.

The priest was getting restless. Looked at his watch. Five minutes overdue. Grooms were always supposed to be there early. This one was nowhere to be seen. The bride would soon arrive. There was whispering between the church benches. A young man, one of the bride's relatives, hurriedly went to look for a phone-box and warn the bride not to set out. Too late. He came face to face with her Rolls on his way to the phone-box. He ran into the middle of the road in front of the car and insisted it stop. Having been told that the bridegroom hadn't put in an appearance, the driver, one of the bride's cousins, parked at the side of the road. They all discussed animatedly whether they should wait there, or take the bride back home. If he didn't appear soon, then the male relatives of the bride would go to Zia's house and totally beat the shit out of Stefano. That was unanimous. One of the young men had a gun and said not to let Stefano go anywhere near him because he wouldn't be able to stop himself shooting the minghiuni. And, with that he fired a warning shot up in the air outside the church. The shooter went into the church and hid the gun under the robe of a Saint Anthony's statue.

On a street, near the church, red-faced with fury, the bride's father got out of the Rolls, started kicking a tyre while shouting to Susi, standing on the kerb across the road with Enzo, "I'll kill that stra-minghiuni fittente of your brother with my own hands. God is my witness." A couple of passers-by stopped briefly to watch. "Whacha looking at, fuck off!"

Enzo was about to cross the road and give the bride's father a good hiding for insulting his brother-in-law. Susi managed to drag her husband back to the pavement.

Having heard that the bride's car was round the corner, Romina's mother ran out of the church to the car to console her daughter. She yelled at her husband telling him to calm down: "Maybe his car's broken down." As an answer, her husband kicked her in the behind. Romina yelled "pig" through the car window to her father. Then she locked herself in the Rolls. Through the window, the father threatened to hit her too, for wanting to marry such a minghiuni. "I'll kill you and him." The bride unfolded a lace hankie from her clutch bag, wiped her tears. Then she howled into her bouquet.

Meanwhile at Stefano's house, we watched while Silvio tried to break the bedroom door down. Zia, who was holding the self-same big stick she used to chase off Silvio's girlfriends, shouted: "Big bastardo son just like you father. God in heaven rest my Tony soul," as she made the sign of the cross. Next she ran outside round the house to make sure he didn't flee from the window, followed by Luca. The door caved in. Zia had been right. Stefano was climbing down the drainpipe. Zia was waiting for him at the bottom. His feet hadn't touched the ground when she started beating him for all she was worth with the stick. Luca tried to stop her. Stefano couldn't go back up because Silvio was showing him his fists from the window.

Zia threw her head back, lost her hat, looked up at Silvio and said, "Come down, put my big bastardo son in car." Then she made a gesture of anger typical of Sicilian women: she put her own right hand in her mouth and bit it hard leaving a semi-circle teeth sign on her hand. Silvio ran out and, together with Luca and my father, forced Stefano into the back of the green Volvo. Zia and Luca sandwiched Stefano between them, locking the doors in case he tried to escape. Silvio jumped into the driver's seat, while I sat in the front passenger seat next to him. My parents followed in their car. Zia shouted at Stefano all the way to the church. Calling him names while she repeatedly spat on her right hand and tried to tidy up his unkempt hair. "You get married, you look like tramp." When she finished tidying his hair, she slapped him in the face for good measure.

Our car, containing the precious groom, overtook the bride's. Romina's family sighed with relief.

But when Stefano arrived at the church, two policemen where standing at the entrance. Someone had phoned the police. It couldn't have been one of the wedding guests because Sicilians sort things out amongst themselves so never call the police. It must have been one of the residents living nearby who heard the shot. The police asked for everyone to come out of the church. They searched a few men, but no incriminating weapon was found on any of them. One woman told the police that it had been a firecracker to celebrate the wedding.

The police disappeared and Stefano was marched to the altar by Zia and Silvio. A couple of young men, on Romina's side of the family, moved in to stand behind Stefano in case he tried to run off. When the bride appeared at the door, linking arms with her father, the organist put all his zest into piping up the wedding march filling the church with joy as the whole congregation stood up ready to partake in Romina and Stefano's best day of their lives.

Two highlights stuck in my mind about the wedding reception. The first was the cutting of the cake, and the second was the band.

When it was time for the happy couple to cut the cake,

Melina, the bride's mother got there first. She was still smarting about the wedding farce. The humiliation he'd brought upon her daughter in front of her friends and family. Now she needed to make a statement.

Melina held the cake-knife straight into Stefano's face, the tip resting right between his eyes. One of the disco balls, glittering above, caught the light and made the knife glint. Silence. All the guests watched. Even a baby, who'd been exasperating everyone, stopped crying. It was a dramatic moment. After the suspense, Melina eventually said to Stefano, "You see this knife?" Stefano nodded backwards trying not go get his face cut. "If you as much as harm a hair on Romina's head, this is what you'll get in your stomach." Melina handed the knife to her daughter and said, "Congratulations." As the bride held the knife on the cake, Stefano lay his hand on hers. And the knife sank into the soft cream and sponge, making a clean cut through the white icing.

Zia would not seek revenge for Melina's outburst. This time it didn't need setting right. Stefano deserved it.

The band struck up the Sicilian song "La luna amenzu 'o mari, Mamma mia m'ha maritare." Which loosely translated means "The moon is in the middle of the sea, Mamma mia, I'm going to get married." The tenor, Leonardino, little Leonard, appeared on the stage a couple of minutes later to sing the song. An Elvis look-alike. Hair, parting on the left and greased right over. Little Leonard was famous, and admired in the community, for three reasons:

The first was that he had a most beautiful voice. That's why he was invited to every Italian wedding in the area. He'd sing his heart out. But he had a technique that made him even more popular. Guests would crowd around his feet near the stage and implore him to sing. He let the music play on and didn't start singing until the cheering was loud enough. After that he went on singing long into the night.

The second was that he'd never done a day's work in his life. He was blighted by perennial backache. Not when dancing though. He jumped up and down like a spring. His tarantella couldn't be matched by anyone.

And the third was that he was living in a household with two sisters. Leonardino had it all organised. One sister went out to work while the other stayed at home to look after the house and their four children: two girls by one of the women, and two boys by the other. The children, all short like him, had inherited his musical skills: they played instruments, sang like angels, and danced like professionals. The family broke out into singing and dancing whenever they could, delighting visitors to their house who were always welcome. This commune must be nearing its golden anniversary by now.

The cake was delicious.

Luca flew off, back to his native land just before Christmas so he could spend the festivities with his family. I accompanied him to Heathrow. Though there was no future in our relationship, I was sad to see him go. He had been my nurse and my friend. I didn't tell my parents he'd gone and spent Christmas alone. It was great. But my mother found out from Peppina between Christmas and the New Year. With the new academic year getting closer, I had to save money. Next autumn, I started my university course and changed to working part-time in Sainsbury's, so I had time left for my studies. I lived on my own in the bedsit right through university, until I married Humps.

TWENTY-SEVEN

Sunday 3rd September

And now, back to the present. It is always a special day when we see our children. Clara arrives first, then Emma, Mark with little Benjamin, soon follow. Benjamin, of course, is the star – and he knows it. He is thirteen months old, not walking yet, but is standing on his own.

"Hey, I've got two little bears for you," I say, picking Benjamin up in my arms and taking him to the bedroom to get them. He is thrilled, shakes one by the arm and throws it to the floor. We take the bears into the living room and join the others.

Humps is in the kitchen cooking Sunday lunch. Nobody's Sunday roasts come anywhere near Humps's. He learnt to cook from his mother, Penelope. That's something she is really good at. I've already set the table. Clara tells us about her move, how she still has a lot to do to finish furnishing her new flat, and how it is made difficult by her being busy at work as well. She graduated from Oxford in History of Art and worked for the Uffizi in Florence for two years. She is more similar to me than to Humps, with dark features. Whereas Emma has Humps's green eyes and light complexion. Emma and her husband were on the same PPE – Philosophy, Politics and Economics – degree course in Oxford. We managed to get our daughters into Humps's Alma mater. Both Emma and Mark work for the government. But they don't talk about their work, they talk about Benjamin all the time. He is now saying 'Thank you' when anyone gives him anything. He also says 'grazie.' Emma speaks to him in Italian because she thinks he should grow up speaking a second European language. My daughters are both fluent in Italian, we spent our summers in the Dolomites when they were girls, where they also went to Italian language classes. As for the rest, they are as English as they come. They have as little idea about Sicily as Humps has.

The kids want to know how I am getting on. Am I enjoying my retirement? "Yes, I am, very much."

"Mummy, what do you do all day?" Clara asks.

"All the usual humdrum stuff like housework, shopping, cooking..."

"And she spends an awful lot of time at Zia's as well, don't you, darling?" Humps shouts out from our open-plan kitchen. Emma looks at me askance.

"She's elderly," I say, "so I pop in and say hello. Nice walk along the river, before the underground. Gets me out. Some fresh air."

"And we're going to Sicily at the end of the month," Humps again, instead of concentrating on his cooking.

The kids want to know all about this. Mark says he's never been to Sicily and would love to go. Before he has time to suggest that they come with us, I say: "Wouldn't it be lovely to go on a tour of the whole island in spring when the almonds blossom?" I go on to point out how it is still very hot in the south, far too hot for Benjamin. That seems to have put them off.

Lunch is ready so we all go to our places. Benjamin joins us in his high chair, still the centre of attraction. We talk, laugh and have a great time. I love my family. Then, when the time comes for dessert, I fish out the cassata ice-creams left over from last week's barbecue. There are five – exactly right.

"Mary's been going to the amusement arcade as well," Humps says.

Thanks, Humps, I think. The kids want to know all about that too, of course. I play along with the idea that I am going a bit doolally in my old age. Then, to take the attention off me and into the public arena, I make a remark about Brexit.

That gets them all going. While they get animated about politics, I take Benjamin over to my favourite armchair, and we play at throwing teddies onto the floor.

TWENTY-EIGHT

Monday 4th September

Back to another trip to Zia's. It is one of those great English days when the weather hasn't made up its mind what it wants to do. Zia is on her own when I arrive.

"Cuppa tea?"

"Yes, please. What delights have you baked up today?"

"Cup cakes," she says, "white icing on top."

She brings them into the living room. "They look tasty. Only good ingredients in them, eh, Zia? No nasty e-numbers?"

"These only for friends," she says.

"Zia, I was thinking of going back to see Alberto tomorrow. See if he's told his wife. What do you think?"

"Ah, good idea you go see what big bastardo decide."

She takes a key out of her blouse pocket then opens the padlock on the pantry door. That key is on her all the time, in some place or other. She goes into the pantry, pulling the door to behind her, then tugs on the string hanging from the ceiling to turn the light-bulb on.

"It's pretty spooky in there, Zia." She has to go down three steps to get to the shelves, and it is pitch black at the bottom. "Can I come in?"

"No, you no come in."

"Why not?"

"Keep my things in here," she says.

"Yes, but why so secretive? It's only oil, vinegar, salt, sugar and pickles, for God's sake."

"You no come in!" she raises her voice.

Of course, that sets me off wondering what she is hiding in there, right down the bottom where the light doesn't shine. In any case it must be a playground for cockroaches and similar creepy-crawlies.

She came out with a little bottle, "I put on table, you take when you go. Give new potion to Giusy."

"Zia, can't you give it to Giusy. I don't believe in all this potion malarkey, I'd feel stupid taking it."

"Ah, but I no believe. People need to believe. People need help."

"OK, Zia, but I'm not taking it."

"So you no take. I give when she come here."

"Zia, Humphrey has agreed to go to Sicily on holiday. We'll be there when you are."

"I think, good idea he see Sicilia. The island of his wife."

"Zia, I am not from Sicily, it's my parents' island, not mine. I don't want Humphrey involved in anything bad."

"He no involved. We just teach Giulio lesson. Humphrey nothing to do with Giulio. You nothing to do with Giulio."

"I think it's best if we don't all go together. After all, Humphrey and I are staying in a hotel. You and Susi are staying with Peppina. We'll go on different flights."

"No problem you go when you like."

"We're going a few days early on 23rd September. It's the Saturday before. We'd like to go and visit some archaeological sites and spend time on the beach. Enjoy ourselves."

"We go see you mother grave," she says.

This is a fixture in Zia's brain.

"Maybe. And Uncle Tony's," I say. "Is he buried near my mother?"

"No. He not near mother," she says. "Susi coming to Sicilia. She no job, no money, no man."

Zia is trying to change the subject away from Uncle Tony.

Something isn't right. Maybe I am getting obsessed with killings, my imagination is stretching a little too far.

"I know. I'm so sorry about Susi losing her job. Won't be easy to get another one. Not like when we were young," I say.

The doorbell rings. It is Bella and Rosa again. "Blackmail," Zia says when she sees them behind her door. Again, I say to Zia: "I don't even want to hear about it. You'll have to sort it out." As soon as Bella and Rosa come into the house. I say: "I'm sorry, I really must go as I have so much to do. I hope to catch you next time." They simply look at me, turn round and go down the corridor to Zia's living room. Oh, well, I think, if they're going to be so obnoxious, I'll definitely not get involved in helping them.

TWENTY-NINE

Tuesday 5th September

Back in Alberto's Amusement Arcade, Nancy disappears as soon as she sees me. A few moments later Alberto is heading in my direction. He smiles, greets me: "Ah, signora Maria!" and leads me to his office.

He is in a good mood.

"Hello Alberto. How are you?"

"Fine, fine. I have to thank you."

"For what?" I ask.

"For making my life easier. I can see the direction it's going in and feel much better for it."

"Really? What direction exactly?"

"I'm living with Giusy, and I will leave my wife. I have already given Nancy up."

Seems too good to be true to me. "Have you spoken to your wife about this?"

"Yes, I've asked her for a divorce. She already knew about Giusy and Nancy, even if I didn't tell her."

How naïve can men be?

"What did she say?"

"She wants the house, the children and half a mil lump sum."

"Can you afford half a million?"

"Yes, but she also wants maintenance."

"Women don't come cheap, do they? You got yourself into this, it's going to be expensive to get out," I say, not helping matters. "The judge'll decide."

"And Giusy is determined she wants me. She adores me, not like my wife who only wants my money."

"Well, you give your wife her money and start a better life with Giusy."

Unbelievable. Can it be that easy to convince someone that they need to resolve their family dispute? I'd have to make sure he practises what he preaches. I go to Giusy's Hairstylist straight away to see what she has to say about this new development.

It is nearly the end of her working day when I arrive. She sees me and says: "I'll be with you soon, luv, when I've finished me lady." I sit in the waiting area and pick up a magazine. I don't recognise any of the celebrities. In the seventies it was important to be 'with it,' and I was. Now I can definitely say I'm 'without it.' Out of the corner of my eye, I see the customer paying and being handed sachets of free samples.

"You can go over and make yourself comfy," Giusy says pointing to one of the black leather chairs in front of the mirrors. She comes over to me after she has locked the shop door. Brushing my hair, she says: "How are you and how's Zia?"

"We're well, thanks. I've popped in to talk to you, it wasn't to get my hair done."

"Yeah, might as well give ya hair a bit of shape while we talk. I like to keep me hands busy."

She takes me over to the washing basins.

"Well, the whole question has been solved," I say. "We've triumphed. That potion Zia gave you, you can stop taking it."

"I've already stopped," she says.

"Good."

"I thought if you want something you've got to go get it yourself. I had it out with him," she says.

"Did you? How did you go about that?"

She takes me back to the black leather chair in front of the mirrors.

"Last week, Thursday, I think it was, we were messing around. He was lying on the floor, and I sit meself over him, like I was riding a horse, with me knees firmly on his hands. I flicked me penknife at him and said to him: "Al, no kidding, one night when you're sleeping, I'm gonna cut your throat with this, as sure as me name's Giuseppina, if you don't divorce your wife and marry me."

"What?" I say.

"Yeah. I dunno what it is, I think it might be me pregnancy, y'know me hormones, but I'm ever so brave lately. I saw how brave you and Zia are, and I'm fired by me love for Al. I told him he's gonna be mine or nobody's. I told him I don't care if I die, but he's gonna die before me or with me. He hasn't spent another night with his wife since then. Over the weekend, him and his wife had it out and they're divorcing. When that's sorted, we're gonna get married."

"Well done you," I say.

"But I'm still taking the other potion cos I wanna boy."

How could she still believe in all that hoky-poky?

"I wanna boy so he can take over the arcade when he's big. We're gonna call him Alberto junior. Then it'll still be

Alberto's Amusement Arcade."

"A girl could run the arcade, too," I say. "Alberta?"

"Ah, ya know how much we Sicilians like our traditions. We stick men's names up in lights and let them think they're in charge. But I'm gonna be running that joint. It's all about determination, innit? An' I tell you something else. That Nancy bitch'll have to go. I'm not having her swanning around teasing Al's prick all day. I know a little, fat, hairy Sicilian woman who's eager for the job. That's the way it is with a man, you gotta keep tabs on him. You see him. You want him. You get him. Then you have to make fucking sure you keep him," she says sounding like Julius Caesar. Only Giusy was one step ahead of Caesar. Julius Caesar missed a trick: he didn't say anything about how to keep hold of what he'd conquered.

Giusy keeps back-combing my hair. "Sorry, Giusy, I think my hair's got enough volume now," I say. I've got an enormous head of hair. All this talk about Alberto is very well and good, but I need to stop her from taking her emotions out on my hair, making me look like I've just had an electric shock. I'll have to wash it again when I get home. I just hope I don't bump into anyone I know on the way.

The mystery now remains as to who actually clinched the deal. Was it Giusy or was it me? Admittedly, Alberto was between a sinister Maria-rock, and an alarming Giusy-hard-place. I reckon that the knife is mightier than the word. But maybe I can take some credit for this. I feel I am getting better at making idiots see sense, after my first success when giving a Brexiter a bollocking. I'm getting quite a liking for giving people an education. Now isn't that a more exhilarating activity than going to a book club, or making aimless small talk at coffee mornings? It's just occurred to me, how boring other women are compared to Sicilian women. I'm now ready to take on Bella and Rosa. See what I can do for them.

And, as for Alberto, he's going to have his hands full for the rest of his life. His Don Giovanni days are well and truly over – finished, finito.

THIRTY

Wednesday 6th September

Susi phones me. Says she's going ahead with the start-up project. "I know starting a business isn't easy but I've loads of experience in Human Resources. I'm going freelance working for small businesses that want to outsource their HR work. I have contacts."

"I thought you were in Sales and Marketing, and that you were going into business with Sebastian?"

"I am. But I got lots of HR experience in three of my jobs. So I'm starting two projects."

"Brilliant idea, if one doesn't work, the other might."

She hasn't been any good at working for herself in the past. But she needs support. No way she wants the truth. Been there, done that, got the message.

"That's not all I'm going to do." Susi says she's also going to be involved in running a new women's helpline. Not only for victims of violence, but for whatever problem they may have like money problems, not having anyone to babysit, to sort out their taxes, welfare benefits for them and, of course, to help them find work...

At the other end of the scale, they will recruit women who are ready to help other women. Co-ordinate it all. "Like, you know, pensioners who have time on their hands, who can act as grandparents to kids if they don't have any," she says.

Is she trying to recruit me?

"I'm interested in helping out," I say.

"That won't be until November at the earliest, maybe it'll even be in the new year. I have meetings with the others involved in this project. We've got to iron out some challenges, so keep it on the back boiler for a mo.'"

"Fine," I say, "Why don't you keep me updated, and we'll see how it pans out?"

"Yeah, will do. By the way, I've given up on men for the time being. I've got these projects to work on, and they'll only get in the way. You know what men are like, they take up so much time."

"I think you know more about them than I do," I say.

We laugh.

"Now the real reason why I'm phoning is that my mum wants to see you urgently."

"I was thinking of not going for a while. I've been there almost every day lately. I need a break. What's it about?"

"You know what she's like, Mary. She wouldn't tell me."

"Why doesn't she phone me herself?"

"She hates phones. She thinks someone's always listening in," Susi gives a chuckle.

"Whatever it is, can't you go and help her out? You are her daughter after all."

"I know, but she thinks you're more sensible. You'd do me a favour if you went."

"OK. I'll go tomorrow. I've set my mind on staying at home today."

I tried second guessing why Zia wants to see me. Probably about Provvi. Oh, my God, I hope that husband of hers hasn't killed or maimed her. Or has he decided not to go to Sicily? I am going to worry all night about this. But, even so, it'll have to wait until tomorrow.

THIRTY-ONE

Thursday 7th September

When I arrive, I can see Zia is pale with worry. I try to defuse her anxious state by distraction. I ramble on about the Giusy-Alberto affair, how it is all sorted by Giusy taking the situation into her own hands. Zia doesn't comment. Other times, she'd have been all too ready to sit down and gossip about it. It is clear she has to get something out of her system.

"What is it, Zia? What's wrong?"

"I tell you something top secret. Bella and Rosa."

"What about them? Have they been causing you grief again? You needn't worry about them. Zia, you're elderly and need a nice peaceful life. Why don't we go out for a walk? You hardly ever go out. Some fresh air will do you good."

"I no go out. I safe in my house."

Then she says something that makes my bones go cold.

"Bella and Rosa blackmail me."

"Blackmailing you?! Zia, what have you done?"

"I done nothing."

"Are you sure?"

"I sure. I sure."

"So how can they blackmail you? Just don't open the door when they come here."

She looks at me as if to say I'm naïve, it will not solve anything.

"Zia, whether you did anything bad or not, you'd better tell me what they are accusing you of." I put my arm round her shoulders. "Don't worry we'll sort it, whatever it is." I try to keep her spirits up promising something I probably won't be able to deliver.

"Bella and Rosa, they two sister. They Tony niece. They daughter of his brother, Teodoro."

"I know. And..."

"They say I kill my husband."

I knew it. I've suspected the same. Now the knots are coming to the comb, as an Italian proverb has it.

"Zia, you've got to tell me if you did kill him. I can't help you if you don't tell me the truth. I promise I won't tell anyone. I won't go running to the police. I'll pretend I don't know, like I haven't known for all these years." I am rambling on again, because of the shock revelation.

"I help kill him," she says, "But I no kill him."

"Oh, my God. Who did then, you must know?"

What she says then knocks me for six.

"Susi."

"No! No, Zia, you're confused. Susi was only a teenager when Uncle Tony died. She couldn't have done that. She was little more than a child – and a sweet child at that. Susi doesn't harbour anger like me. She just couldn't have done it."

"She kill Tony. I see with my eyes," Zia says.

Jesus, Mary and Joseph.

"Where did it happen?"

"Here in this room."

"Here?! But he's buried in Sicily," I say.

"He no buried in Sicilia. He buried here."

"Where? Which cemetery?"

Looking towards the pantry door, she doesn't answer my questions. Instead she goes on to describe how it happened.

Zia was in her living room one morning in summer when Uncle Tony came in from the garden and began hitting her on some pretext or other. Zia was screaming, she was lying on the floor while Uncle Tony was kicking her. Then he got hold of her and tried to stand her up. But she fell back down again. While Uncle Tony was bending over her, Susi came in and planted the biggest kitchen knife they had into his back and, at the same time, Susi threw Zia another knife. Susi stabbed her father again. He turned round to grab Susi's arms and while he had his back to her, Zia managed to hold his arms to stop him harming Susi. Susi seemed possessed by the devil, Zia tells me, and kept stabbing him even when he was lying in a pool of blood, even when it was obvious he was dead.

"So you buried him in the pantry, didn't you, Zia?"

"Yes, Susi and me bury in pantry."

I had a feeling about that pantry. Uncle Tony had been there all along, buried in that dingy, damp, dark, creepy pantry. They couldn't have disposed of the body all by themselves. Zia has a lot more to tell me. If she wants my help she is going to have to reveal everything.

The devil is in the detail.

THIRTY-TWO

Thursday 7th September

We sit and drink some tea. I have to let these unbelievable revelations sink in. After a while I ask her about the crime scene.

"Who helped you, Zia?"

"When Tony die I panic I call Old Cushi."

Oh, yes, Old Cushi. He had contacts alright. Old Cushi arrived shortly afterwards. Uncle Tony was still on the living room floor. In this very same room we are sitting in. Old Cushi gave orders. Told Zia and Susi to fetch buckets and start cleaning the blood up. He called some builders. Four men, in overalls, arrived in a van. They thought of dumping the body on a construction site they were working on. But that might have turned out to be risky. Old Cushi decided Uncle Tony should be buried in the pantry. They were sure he'd fit in there. If he didn't they'd have to cut off his limbs.

"But, he fit," Zia says. Old Cushi told Zia and Susi to go upstairs and clean themselves up: "Have a bath, put your clothes in the washing-machine," he said. The four men dug a hole, laid Uncle Tony in it, and cemented it over. He's been lying there for about four decades.

I ask Zia to let me into the pantry. I want to see it for myself. She unlocks the door, pulls the string so as to switch the light on. The pantry looks like any other pantry would. Shelves fitted to the walls, holding pots, vases, bottles and little boxes. Its floor looks like any other floor would. But right at the bottom against the far wall is a vase with plastic flowers in it, and a plastic statue of the Madonna. Pitiful. All those years. I can't get over it. I'm totally gob-smacked. Why have I, of all people, been dragged into this?

"Bella and Rosa come tomorrow," she says.

"Zia, you still have a lot of things to tell me."

"You no tell police," she says.

"No, of course, I won't. We'll figure something out. What do Bella and Rosa want from you exactly?"

"Money."

"How much money do they want?"

"Want £400,000. Want £200,000 each."

"But you don't have that kind of money, do you?"

"I have some money. But if not have, they want I sell house."

"Do they, now?" I say. "How did they find out about Uncle Tony?"

"They no know Susi and me kill Tony," she says. "They only suspect."

Essentially, it was guesswork. But they've guessed right. Bella and Rosa knew their Uncle Tony was violent. They'd seen Zia with black eyes. When his death was announced suddenly, their family couldn't believe it was a natural death. It seemed strange to them at the time, but thought nothing of it for years. Now they have both grown older, have been widowed, and have more time, they decide to see what they can get. They think blackmailing Zia is win-win for them. They reckon that if Zia killed her husband, she'll pay up; if she hasn't, then she will have nothing against their having Uncle Tony's grave dug up in Sicily and have a DNA test carried out.

"Whose body is in Uncle Tony's grave, then?" I ask.

"I no know him. Old Cushi organise."

Zia tells me that the day after the murder, Old Cushi flew to The Village on Uncle Tony's passport. Uncle Tony was off work for three weeks for the summer break. When Silvio and Stefano came back home in the evening, from their summer job, fruit-picking, they were told that their father had had to leave for Sicily – urgently – given that his mother had been taken ill suddenly.

When in Sicily, on his way to the village, Old Cushi met up with two of his men, who arrived with a third man. This third man was shot in the woods near the roadside, wrapped up in a blanket and hidden in the woods for a day. Word was put around that Tony, travelling from England, had had a heart-attack on the road to The Village. They said Tony had been taken to the hospital in the next town.

His elderly mother was told his body had been embalmed straight away because of the heat. The next day the body arrived in The Village already sealed up in a coffin. Tony's mother insisted on seeing her son's body. She was told that by now the body would smell, and it was best to leave well alone. The mother wouldn't take no for an answer, so Old Cushi called two men to weld the coffin lid off. The body had been bandaged up, including his head, and only part of his face was visible. His mother wailed when she saw the face. She was taken away and sedated. She lived the following days in a state of confusion – at times saying it wasn't her son, but at the same time wearing mourning clothes and accepting condolences and visitors at home, telling them what a wonderful person her son was.

A death certificate was issued and, soon after, when Zia, Susi and her brothers arrived, the funeral and burial were carried out.

Neatly finished off.

THIRTY-THREE

Friday 8th September

Now Bella and Rosa are planning on having 'Uncle Tony's' body exhumed in Sicily. And for this reason they are going to The Village in a week to organise it. Today is ultimatum day. The day the sisters deliver their last warning to Zia: pay up or be exposed as a killer. Not being related to me, I don't know them that well. They are part of the community though. Therefore, I have vague memories of their being a couple of dullards – went about in twos. Reminded me of Rosencrantz and Guildenstern – each a half, making up one person together. But, I can certainly recollect who their brother is: Adriano. The scumbag who threatened to rape me, along with my cousin, Stefano; but who ultimately raped Susi repeatedly instead. I suggested Susi and I blackmailed Adriano into giving Susi recompense for his violence, while here are his sisters blackmailing Zia.

When the doorbell rings, Zia's face is as white as a ghost's, her hands trembling: "Bella and Rosa," she utters.

I usher Zia upstairs. "You're going to bed, Zia. You're in no fit state to confront these two airheads. I'll do it."

"What you do now?"

"To tell you the truth, I don't know, but I'll think of something. You just go on up now."

"They take my money, my house..."

"They'll take nothing."

Opening the outer door, I tell them Zia isn't well and had to go to bed. In their matching purplish and green flowery dresses they look quite innocuous. "I like your dresses," I say. "Did you make them yourselves?" They look at each other. This is a gesture they will repeat again and again, just about every time I say something. It seems as if they need some kind of constant consent from each other. Well, I am going to give them plenty to confer about.

"Come in, come in," I say. "I've always been in a rush when our paths have crossed here at Zia's. Contrastingly, I have all afternoon today so we can sit down and have a nice little chat," I smile. "Cuppa tea?"

Coming out of the kitchen with a tray of tea and lemon cupcakes, I catch them confabulating. They stop and stare at me. "Oh," I say, "Zia made some lemon cupcakes this morning. Aren't we the lucky ones?" They nervously take one each when I offer them the cakes on little plates.

"Nice day, isn't it?" I say. "Sun's been shining all day. Rain coming in the next few days. You know, when it starts raining it never stops. I'll bet it's going to be a long cold winter..." This is getting tiresome. There I am talking and talking to fill in the empty silence. I am also doing it so that they feel at ease. Well, what the hell, they'll just have to feel awkward. I stop my gush of words and look out of the window. We sit there for a while longer drinking tea.

"We came to talk to Zia," Bella says. Rosa nods.

"I'm afraid you can't talk to her today. You do know she's eighty-seven, don't you? She's been getting quite feeble lately. Too much worry. She told me you were coming here today, and I volunteered to meet you. You can tell me whatever you wanted to tell Zia."

"It's not easy for us to talk about it with someone else,"

Rosa says. "It's nothing to do with you."

"Why? I have Zia's full consent to discuss the delicate issue you came here to talk about today. Just tell me as if I were Zia. It has everything to do with me. I'm representing her."

It is easy for them to bully a little old lady. It is going to be a bit more difficult with me. They know that. They look at each other again before plunging into the heart of the matter.

"We think," Bella begins, "that Zia killed our Uncle Tony."

"And what makes you think that?" I say.

"There was rumours when we was kids that she killed him. My mum and friends talked about it." Bella nods her consent to Rosa's statement.

"So it's not all guesswork, then?" Like I had to at school with the children, I would have to explain the situation to them to make them understand where we were at. "In other words, I thought you were only guessing at it. But now you bring forward evidence. Your evidence is that your mother talked about it to others. It's only hearsay. No evidence whatsoever. If I remember correctly your mother, Signora Carmela, was a choice gossip. Anything she said cannot, for one moment, be thought of as reliable."

"Other people was saying so, as well," Rosa says.

"Yes, because your mother had put the thought into their heads," I lean forward towards them, then say slowly: "Your mother was a liar."

That didn't go down well. They didn't like it and got quite irate. Rosa opens her mouth as if to say something, but Bella answers instead. "How dare you call my mum a liar?"

"How dare you call my Zia a murderer?" I say. "Which is worse?"

They look at each other. Say nothing.

"Do you think your Uncle Tony was a nice man?" I ask.

"We knew he was hitting Zia. Mum talked about Zia's

black eyes and bruises. That's why we think she did it. She had a reason to kill Uncle Tony. And mum said he went off to Sicily without saying anything to my dad. We was in Sicily at the same time, on holiday. Then we was told, Uncle Tony was dead. Even my grandmother said she didn't think the body in the coffin was Uncle Tony."

"So why didn't your father go to The Village sooner to support your grandmother's doubts?"

"I told you. All our family was already in Sicily," Bella says. "We was staying with my mum's family in another province in Sicily."

"Our gran didn't have our mum's parents' address to send us a telegram," Rosa says, "my gran couldn't read or write. The telegram came late and our dad got to The Village after the funeral."

I lean forward towards them again, slowly put my elbow on the table to prop up my face, squint my eyes and say slowly and gravely: "Then maybe your dad killed Uncle Tony in Sicily?"

They are horrified, start shaking their heads. Get cross. Their dad, they say was a gentle man. He didn't have it in him to kill someone.

"I'll tell you what he did," I say. "It's obvious, isn't it? It's just dawned on me – clear as daylight. He knew Uncle Tony was going to Sicily, he found an excuse to get away from his family, killed Uncle Tony and then went back to his family at your grandmother's. As if nothing had happened."

They are gob-smacked. "Our dad didn't have a reason to kill Uncle Tony. Our dad and Uncle Tony loved each other," Bella says.

"Are you sure?"

"Yeah, we're sure," Rosa says.

"I'm not." I say. "I think they sorely hated each other."

"No, they didn't," Bella says.

"They put on a show of affection," I say. "I heard rumours as well as a kid. Uncle Tony was a philanderer."

Confused, they turn and look at each other.

"It means that Uncle Tony went with other women. He had affairs. One of the reasons he kept hitting Zia was because she opposed his extramarital escapades."

"We never heard anyone say Uncle Tony had affairs," Bella says.

"Of course you didn't hear about it. Those involved, like your father, are the last to know, aren't they?"

By now they are totally confused.

"Yes," I say. "Uncle Tony's longest lasting affair was with your mother, Signora Carmela."

They are open-mouthed with shock. Bella breathes out and says: "You're making it up."

"No, I'm not. Everyone knew, it was the talk of the community. It was also rumoured that your father was homosexual."

They gasp.

I have nothing against homosexuals, in fact I like them very much. When I first went to university my best friends were two gay blokes. They made the curtains for my bedsit. I only had one window. The best drapery in town – beautiful! You should have seen the flounces. In Bella and Rosa's small minds, homosexuality must have been the worst sin a man could commit.

"Another lemon cake anyone?" I went over to them with the tray, but they refused. "You know, these lemon cakes are delicious. I must get the recipe from Zia," I say.

"Your mother probably wasn't getting much sex. So Uncle Tony took advantage of the situation. Your father knew about it and tried to stop the encounters. Signora Carmela and Uncle Tony got a jolly good liking for each other and wouldn't stop. Now do you see why your mother was telling all-and-sundry that Zia had murdered her husband? Distraction, my dear ladies, distraction. 'Shine the spotlight over there, on Zia; and not on me. I'll keep myself hidden in the wings, thank you very much,' Signora Carmela would have said."

"We don't believe any of it. It can't be true," one says, while the other nods.

"It's true. True as I'm sitting here. I'll wager that if you did exhume his body, your father's DNA would be all over it," I say. "Well, ladies, I need to be getting on."

They stand up.

"Oh, and another thing," I say, "I wouldn't go to Sicily if I were your good selves. If you do go, buy a one-way ticket. Neither of you would come back. You'd be cemented up in your family tomb, probably next to your Uncle Tony, or he could be your father for all you know. Mark my words, if you go to Sicily, now or at any time in the future, you will not come back. Let the dead rest in peace. Give up ideas about exhuming bodies." They stare at me. I show them the way out. "Just don't go," I say, shutting them out.

I tip-toe upstairs to see how Zia is getting on. She is sleeping like a baby under her pink velvet bedspread. On her dressing table are various objects: a jar of Pond's cream, a black hairpin, crochet hook entangled in my yellow wool, a couple of terracotta pots, and a sea-shell jewellery box. I go back downstairs to tidy up. There is a big tin on the kitchen table. I pull it open to see what is inside. It is full of lemon cupcakes. She lives on her own and makes cakes for an army. Tears come to my eyes, thinking of Zia's lonely life. What life has it been? Shut up in this house with a cadaver for company – always afraid someone will discover the body. And living in fear that the public might discover that Susi, her precious daughter, is a murderer. Zia's life has rotated around that pantry. What will happen to the house when she dies? Susi will have to come and live here. On the other hand, would anyone know there was a body there? No, they wouldn't. But Zia has to get rid of that little altar down there: the bunch of artificial flowers, and the plastic Virgin Mary statue.

"Zia," I call, "wakey, wakey. Cuppa tea? Lemon cupcake?"

She opens her eyes and yawns. "What time?"

"It's 4.30." I put the tray before her. Sit on her bed. Rain is patting on the windows.

"Cosy. Tea in bed," she says. "What happen with two sister?"

"I don't think you need to worry about them any more, Zia. To cut a long story short, I've asked them not to go to The Village."

"They say yes?" she asks.

"Well, I don't think you'll see them again, nor will they go to Sicily. But I can't be sure of that. They're pretty thick."

"They no dig up body?"

"Not if they've got a granule of sense. But, Zia, we have to sort out your pantry. You can't have that altar down there, if anyone were to see it they'd find it odd. It might set them off thinking all sorts of strange things."

"They no see."

"Let's suppose, now it's not going to happen, but let's just suppose that you were taken ill suddenly. Someone could find the altar. They might get ideas of digging the floor up."

She thinks about it.

"I'll tell you what we'll do," I say. "We'll get a nice photo of Uncle Tony put it on a table and you can place the Virgin Mary, flowers and even a candle around it. What do you think of that?"

"I think good idea. I put on table near phone."

"Yes, and the pantry door must be unlocked at all times. You draw attention to it by locking it. Throw away that lock and key."

She says she will leave the door unlocked, but she'll keep the lock and key in case she needs it for some other reason.

"You do all that this evening, please, Zia. I need to go now."

I can't find the light switch when I walk out of her bedroom, so go slowly down the dark, narrow staircase, feeling my way. The carpet is lighter along the edges of each stair. Worn out.

On the underground, I manage to contain myself. But when I get to the Thames towpath, I let it all out. I cry. I cry like a child. I cry for Zia – a wasted life. I cry for Susi, raped in her youth and having to go round with a killing on her conscience. Maybe I even cry for myself, for my past that has raised its ugly head into my present, even though I have put up airtight barriers. It has seeped through anyway.

When I see Humps in the evening, I feel immediately uplifted. He is my fixed star, reference point, my north, my south, my east, my west. And he has been so for nearly thirty-five years. No nonsense and let's get on with it, kind of thing. No time for feeling sorry for yourself. He pulls me up when I think too much.

"Hello, darling. Had a nice day?"

"Bloody awful. Stock markets are all over the place. Clients phoning wanting miracles."

"Well, you're home now. We'll have a lovely relaxing weekend, plan our Sicily trip and book it. We're going to have a wonderful time. Think of lovely beaches, great food and chilled wine."

"We certainly need to have a break. Get away from it all," he says.

"You're telling me."

THIRTY-FOUR

Sunday 10th September

We are in for a quiet day. On Sundays, if we don't get to see the kids, I phone them, then tell Humps their news. We have a tendency to think they get things wrong, but we let them get on with it. Humps is against interfering in their lives. If it hadn't been for him, I think I would have waded in with unwanted advice and probably ruined our relationship with them. News was mostly the progress of little Benjamin. How he's added new words to his vocabulary. He is saying 'mama' and 'dada,' and pointing with determination when he wants something.

After the Bella-Rosa episode, I feel I need to speak to Susi, too. I'll phone her and see when we can meet. I don't want to discuss this on the phone with Humps in the house.

"Hi, Mary."

"Hi, Susi. How are you getting on with your new little business?"

"Oh, it's OK. I've contacted a few people. If it works, it's going to be much better than working for the Americans. In the end, they might have done me a favour."

"That really is good news. I was phoning to see if we could meet up for a drink."

"I don't have much time right now. Not during the week anyway. I could do this evening, if you want."

"Fine, done."

We set the time and place.

"Humps, I'm going out for a drink with Susi this evening. I'll have to leave you on your own." Before he could say he wants to come too, I say: "Woman-to-woman talk. You know how it is."

"Sounds like I'm staying here," he says.

"You can catch up on your reading. Have you finished this

week's *Economist*?"

"No, but I suppose I'll finish it this evening."

We meet at the pub. Susi comes in and finds me. She takes her jacket off and puts it over the back of a chair. I go to the bar and come back with two lagers and two packets of crisps.

"You're looking good," she says to me.

"Am I? I didn't put much effort into doing myself up."

"You don't have to," she says.

"Well, look at yourself. You're always tip-top."

"I try," she says.

"I went round your mum's yesterday. She's been through a harrowing time."

"Why's that? She didn't say anything to me."

"She wouldn't, would she? She's trying to protect you."

"From what?"

"Your cousins Bella and Rosa have been blackmailing her for God knows how long."

"Oh, those two. They're weird. They won't get far."

"I know. They're strange. They don't talk much, but when they do it's poison," I say. "When you were kids, did they know about what their brother was doing to you?"

"No, I haven't told anyone, except you. I don't think he'd have told them."

"I'm sorry, I wasn't much help."

"You had your own problems," she says.

"And so did you have other problems. Big time, huge ones. Your mum told me about your dad's death."

Susi blushes. I have visions of little sweet fat-faced Susi sitting at the dining table being belted.

"Look, Susi," I say. "I completely sympathise with you. You were a kid. You'd been through so much and so had your mum. Don't worry. No one'll find out."

Tears well up in her eyes. "My dad has haunted me all my life. Whatever I do, wherever I go, I take this round with me."

"I know what you mean. My mother's been the backdrop of my life. It's like I'm living my life out on a stage and what she did to me is there, engraved behind me. All this forgive and forget crap doesn't work. At least it doesn't work for me. I'm still angry. If you haven't forgotten, then you haven't forgiven."

"What exactly did mum tell you?"

"Everything, I believe. She told me about how you and she fought against your dad, how he was buried in your house by Old Cushi's men, and how someone else was buried in your dad's place in Sicily. Is there anything else to know?"

"Not really. That's about it."

"I've been asking myself who's buried in your dad's place in Sicily. Your mum didn't tell me that. Do you know?"

"I heard talk about it."

"What did you hear?"

"He was an illegal immigrant."

"Oh, no. Poor man."

This just got worse and worse. I put my head in my hands.

"Was he simply picked on because it was easy to hide his disappearance?" I ask.

"There's that as well, I guess. The main reason was he was taking advantage of a young mentally disturbed girl in The Village. She got pregnant. Her mother organised an abortion for her."

"Oh, my God!"

"So they decided he had to pay for that. He had to be killed."

"They were waiting for the right moment to dispose of him, weren't they? And it presented itself when your dad died?"

"Yeah, that's more or less it, Mary. They spread the word around that he'd gone back to his country. Old Cushi was powerful both over here and over there. Now his son's taken that role over. 'Young Cushi' mum calls him although he's just a bit younger than us."

"Well, if he's under sixty that would seem young to your mum. Like a thirty-year-old looks young to me," I say. "Would Young Cushi know all about your dad's disappearance?"

"Yeah, I'm sure he does," Susi says. "He worked with his dad, Old Cushi, for years. Must've known."

"Keep the business in the family, eh?" I say.

"Were Bella and Rosa blackmailing my mum about my dad's death?"

"Yes, they said they'd heard their mum, your aunt Carmela, say that your mum had killed their Uncle Tony. They were trying to get your mum to sell her house and give them the money."

"Oh, God. She'd rather die than sell that house. That was never going to work though, was it?" Susi says.

"I don't know but they are pressing heavily on your mum to do just that. They want to get 'your dad's body' exhumed to prove your mother killed him. That would have all sorts of knock-on effects. If they find out it isn't your dad in that grave, then they will try to discover where he is actually buried. A big bloody mess would follow."

"Mum didn't say anything about this blackmailing," Susi repeats.

"She doesn't want to upset you."

"I know. Sad, isn't it?" Susi says.

"It sure is. We're catapulted into this community, and through no fault of our own, we take the consequences. We try to figure out how to confront the dark side of life from childhood and through our teens when we don't have the instruments to deal with it. And when you're an adult, it leaves you with a painful black hole inside; and you're forever trying not to go to that dark centre, moving around the perimeters and trying not to get swallowed up by it."

"You're sure good at philosophising. Must've been all those books you've read," Susi says.

"I'm not sure whether that was a compliment or not. Whatever. I know my mind's hyperactive and a bit abnormal."

"You said it."

We laugh.

Then Susi goes serious again:

"What happened in the end? Have they given up on getting the body dug up?"

"Yes, I'm pretty sure they have."

"Don't be too sure of it. Bella and Rosa are both false and stupid."

"A bomb of a mixture," I say, "and bombs explode. It seems to me that those two have a way of getting themselves into things they can't handle. Fools rush in where angels fear to tread."

"Yeah, OK, don't start off again," Susi says, and smiles.

"So are you still planning on coming to Sicily, even though you're busy now?" I ask.

"Yeah, why not? Some sunshine'll do me good. I think if I have a break, I'll be readier to work harder when I get back."

"Another thing, Susi. I know you're busy – maybe you could find just a little time to go and see your mum. The other day when I was there, I felt she was lonely."

"I keep meaning to but things gets in the way. I'll see what I can do."

"And, a huge tin of lemon cupcakes are sitting in her kitchen in need of being eaten up."

THIRTY-FIVE

Tuesday 12th September

Zia phones me. Something she hardly ever does. Moreover, it is morning. Whatever it is she wants, it has to be serious. She is in a panic. "Maria you come my house quick."

Susi is there when I arrive. "What is it? You two look as if you've seen a ghost," I say.

"It's Bella and Rosa. Bella phoned mum this morning to say goodbye. They're flying to Palermo on Thursday morning as planned. We only have today and tomorrow to decide what to do. I mean, even if they dig the immigrant's body up, after all these years, there's not going to be much left of him to analyse, is there?" Susi says.

"Believe me. There'll be more than enough," I say.

Zia has created an altar for Uncle Tony exactly as she said she would, on a little table next to the phone. His photo is in the middle, and around it are two candles, the Virgin Mary statue, and the plastic flowers. The pantry door isn't locked. In fact, it is ajar. Small consolation now we have this news.

"We can't stop them going," Susi says.

"That's right. We can't," I say, "but we can stop them arriving. They need to disappear shortly after they arrive at Palermo airport.

"What we do? We send picciotti?" Zia asks."

"Yes, it's the only way," I say.

"Are we going to have them killed?" Susi asks.

"I'm afraid it's the only way," I say. "Can you think of any other way to solve this?"

"We could give them some money, maybe a deposit," Susi says.

"No, that would be like admitting the crime. They'd come back for more and more money," I say.

"Young Cushi send picciotti," Zia says.

"Yes, Young Cushi has to send picciotti to Palermo to meet them. I've got it! Taxi driver. Yes, they meet the sisters, or stop them on the way. They do the deed and take them to some construction works."

Zia agrees that would be good.

"Why don't we let them go and see what happens?" Susi says.

"No, we no see what happen. We make happen what we want," Zia says.

"You can't do that," I say to Susi. "And do you realise how far-reaching the consequences could be for you two? They've got to be stopped. Well, we can hardly invite them over tomorrow and kill them here, can we?"

Zia and Susi look at each other.

"One moment, I have poison in pantry. I make jam tart, I put poison in tart."

"Why do you keep poison?" I ask.

"For rat."

"No, Zia," I say. "You can't poison two people in one go. We'd soon get found out. It's not like causing diarrhoea."

"We give diarrhoea, they no go."

"They'll only put it off. They'll still be a threat," I say. "No, it's got to be picciotti waiting for them when they arrive."

"Picciotti taxi-driver. We organise," Zia says.

"They were warned," I say.

"I tell silly bagascie many time."

"It's their choice," I say.

"I telephone Peppina," Zia says.

"You need to tell her what they look like and what flight they're on," I say.

"You silly girl," Zia says. "Name enough. Young Cushi have men in airport. They see name on passport."

Zia dials the number on an old Nokia mobile. She says it's an Italian mobile. The conversation with Peppina took place in Sicilian along the lines of:

"I have depression. I've been having problems like those I had when I was forty. It's come back again. Old Cushi treated it for me. Now I need some more treatment. Maybe I've been depressed because I've been thinking about when my poor husband **died on his way to The Village,**" she emphasised the last phrase. And then: "There are two packages arriving this Thursday morning by plane in the capital. Can you ask Young Cushi to send someone to pick them up? I'll call again when I feel a bit better."

Zia finished the phone call and whipped out another mobile. This time she dialled another number in Sicily – it belongs to Peppina's neighbour, Zia says. "Hello. I'm your neighbour's sister. Remember me?"

What Zia meant here was you know who I am without telling you. Zia, Peppina, and my mother grew up with this neighbour.

"Can you tell my sister that these two women are coming to Sicilia, please?" Zia gives this woman names, ages, and a brief description of the two to give to Peppina.

Zia waited about thirty minutes and, with the same phone she used to call the neighbour, she calls Peppina again. After some small talk, Zia tells Peppina she's been attacked by two vicious female dogs, and that she'd like to get them put down but she needs some help. When she finishes the call Zia says she'll throw the mobiles in the Thames. "I no like use phone. But this emergency."

"I was sure they wouldn't go," I say. "It's like teaching really. All that time and effort in explaining concepts to pupils, you think they've understood, then you give them an exercise, and they get it all wrong."

"I don't know how you could have taught all those years," Susi says. "I couldn't do it. Those sisters are plain thick."

"Well, I agree with all that," I say. "But, after all, it's their choice."

"Ah, I finish you bed sock," Zia says.

"Yes, I saw them on your dressing table the day the two sisters came here. You were working on the cord," I say.

"You wait moment before you go. I go get," she goes upstairs to get them and is soon back. I take these symbols of lemons and the hot Sicilian sun home with me.

THIRTY-SIX

Tuesday 19th September

It's now a week since I went to Zia's last time, when Susi phones me in a panic. Bella and Rosa left for Sicily five days ago. I have been wondering when I would hear about them again. I decided I wasn't going to inquire.

"Mary, you must go to my mum's house tomorrow!"

"Calm down, Susi. Just take a deep breath then tell me what's happened."

I knew Zia had inculcated Susi with fear of talking over the phone, so she wasn't going to tell me everything she knew.

"All I can say is that you must go to my mum's tomorrow afternoon," she repeats.

"Look, sorry, but I can't just go running round at your mum's beck and call. I've got my own life to live."

"Mary, Adriano's going to my mum's tomorrow afternoon. You know, his parents are both dead and he sees my mum as a mother figure."

Don't we all. Zia is a mother figure for umpteen people, and counting.

"She doesn't want to meet him on her own," Susi says. "She's scared of him. He's hot-headed, though he's always been good to my mum. He goes off into a fury if you say something he doesn't like. I can't go, what with all he did to me when I was a girl. I never ever want to set eyes on him again."

I sigh. "Yes, I understand your position. I'd react in the same way, if I were you. I'll go. Do you know what time he'll be there?"

"He said he'll go sometime after three. He'll see if he can finish work early."

THIRTY-SEVEN

Wednesday 20th September

I arrive at Zia's a few minutes after three. No sign of Adriano. But Provvi and Angelina are there already drinking tea and tucking into strawberry jam tarts. It is clear that Provvi has been knocked about again. She is talking about a big gash above her eye. She tells us that she thought she needed some stitches, but she hadn't gone to A&E otherwise they'd have started asking questions. Poking their noses into her business. Making things worse for her. Instead she called a nurse, loosely related to her, who went to Provvi's home, when her husband wasn't in. The nurse didn't ask questions and did her job of sewing in a few stitches.

Provvi is at her wit's end. She is worried about her children. Giulio has also threatened to kill her. Something he hasn't done before. "It is getting worse. It's a terrible thing to live in fear in your own home..." I say.

"I can't take it any more," her mother, Angelina, interrupts. "I'm not well and I don't need all this worry about my daughter. Every minute I curse the day she married that scumbag. He's ruined our lives."

"I'm sorry about this," I say. "It must be a living hell, awful for both of you. You really need some peace."

"Peace, peace! What is it?!" Angelina wails. "I've never had any. First my husband and now my son-in-law. What's wrong with these men?"

So it seems Angelina's husband had been violent, too. Angelina was at the end of her tether. Provvi took hold of her mother's hand, tried to soothe her saying: "Mum please calm down, it's not good for your heart."

I saw the stitches above Provvi's left eye when her sunglasses slipped a little as she bent her head.

"He no good shit," Zia says, then glances at Uncle Tony's photo, in the middle of the altar she's created.

We sat there in silence for what seemed a long time, but it was probably no more than a minute or two.

"Jam tart," Zia pipes up.

"No thanks," the two women say.

I take one. They are seriously delicious. "Is there any more tea in that pot, Zia?"

"You want tea, I get fresh for you."

When Zia was boiling water in the kitchen, Provvi whispers to me: "You don't know how lucky you are. I so wish I hadn't married a man from The Village." That's when I decide to turn the conversation to the trip to Sicily.

"Still Sicily will be a break, won't it?"

"While Giulio is treating my daughter like this, there will be no peace for us," Angelina says.

"He hates me being away from him," Provvi says. "That's another reason why he's coming with us."

"I hope he doesn't spoil your birthday party," I say to Angelina.

"The best thing you can do is not to think about it. Take things as they come," Angelina says.

"I've been doing that all my life," Provvi says.

Zia came back with a pot of tea.

"Lovely," I say.

It is a few minutes after four o'clock when the doorbell rings. Adriano has arrived. Zia goes pale, "What he want?" Angelina and Provvi understand that Zia's next guest might want to speak to her in private and leave as Adriano comes in.

Adriano is worried about his sisters. He tells us they have been reported missing. He wants Zia to know that. It isn't surprising that he has come to Zia for comfort. He seeks answers in her cosy living room, amid cakes and cuppas. Hospitable. That's what Zia is. And she is charming, has comforting words for anyone who needs them. And time? Time is no issue, she would never hurry anyone out. You can stay at her home for as long as you like. She makes you feel at home. Welcome.

Adriano tells us his sisters were last seen getting into a taxi after a bus, on the way to The Village, broke down. He's come to tell Zia that he is going to The Village to help search for them.

"I'm so sorry to hear this," I say to him. "Whatever could have happened? I'm sure they'll be found safe and sound. Maybe you should wait a little longer before panicking."

"I gotta go. I'll feel better if I'm there doing something. Better than staying here doing nothing. I've contacted the police in The Village, they said they are looking into it. They think my sisters have gone off to somewhere else."

"They could be right, you know," I say. "Surely the police will give you updates on their findings, even if you're here."

"No, it ain't the same. I gotta go."

Zia gives him a hot mug of tea.

"What can you do?" I ask him.

"I don't know right now. But God knows that I will find out what happened."

"Why did they go to Sicily?" I hazarded.

"On holiday. And to go to the cemetery to visit the graves

of our mum and dad, Uncle Tony... It was years since they went last time."

"They'll turn up somewhere. Maybe, on a whim, they decided to visit some other place first. Like Taormina, for example," I say.

"No, then why did they take the bus to The Village?"

"Maybe the bus driver made some recommendation, so they decided on the spot." What a feeble thing I've just said.

"Their mobiles ain't working. The batteries must've run down."

I can't answer that.

"We hope, we pray," Zia says.

Adriano stares at the floor in front of him. Instead of the wild bull Zia was expecting, he turns out to be as helpless as a lamb. He looks dejected. I could feel sorry for him if he hadn't raped Susi. And that was in the period when Susi and her mother were being beaten to a pulp by his sweet Uncle Tony.

Adriano has had a comfortable little life with his wife and children, and he has a successful window-cleaning company. Contrastingly, Susi has been haunted by demons and hasn't been able to establish a loving relationship with any man. It has all been sex for her. Thinking that's all she is good for. Being an object to be used and discarded. I'm not a psychologist, my view may be totally wrong, but that's what I think. The easiest thing is to agree with him, so that he goes to Sicily and gets an education as well. That would be excellent revenge for Susi. So I change my tune.

"Well, you might be able to track them down, if you go. One thing's for sure you'd be the most dedicated. The police have plenty of other cases to think about," I say.

He agrees with that.

"We're going to Sicily as well. My husband and I are leaving Saturday. Zia and Susi are flying out on Tuesday week. A friend's birthday party. You probably know them: Angelina, she's got a daughter called Provvidenza who married a chap from The Village called Giulio."

"Oh, yeah, I know Giulio. We've been out drinking with other mates. He's a nice guy."

Yes, of course, Adriano would know and like Giulio. Two of a kind. Well, they might actually get their comeuppance together.

"We stay with my sister Peppina," Zia says.

"If you need us you will find Zia there. Do let her know about any developments," I say. "We'll help if we can, won't we, Zia?"

"We hope, we pray."

Adriano leaves, thinking he has our full support and probably feels blessed because Zia will be there in Sicily at the same time to comfort and assist him.

Zia obviously doesn't know about the rapes. Susi swore as much. If Zia had had even an inkling, she would have hung Adriano up to dry by the cugliuna in her pantry. It was indeed lucky that I'd met Adriano at Zia's. Any thought of blackmailing him, for money to make amends for Susi being raped, was now out of the question. He'll pay a far higher price. Everything is coming together.

After Adriano leaves, Zia tells me that Provvi and Angelina are visiting on Wednesday afternoon at three o'clock. Would I be there? "I'm sorry, Zia. I can't make it. So much to do before we go." I stand up to leave, "See you in Sicily. Meeting point will be at Peppina's." I kiss Zia on both cheeks.

"Ah, you wear you bed sock in bed?"

"Yes, Zia," I lie, "they're fantastic. "

She is pleased. "I make pink bed sock for Susi, then I make blue bed sock for you Benjamin. I start blanket after that."

"That'll be great," I say. I kiss her on each cheek and say:

"Bye for now and have a good flight over. It's alright, Zia, I'll see myself out."

PART II

Sicily, 2017

THIRTY-EIGHT

Saturday 23rd September to Monday 25th September

"Come on, we'll miss the flight if you mess around any longer," Humps says.

"Alright, Grumps," I reply. "Don't get so worked up. We don't want to spoil the holiday before leaving the house, do we?"

"Bloody last-minute-itus. And how much more are you packing into that suitcase?"

"When you're looking for something on holiday, and I fish out what you need, you'll be glad I took it with us. Do you mind helping me close this thing, please, darling?"

We manage to get out of the door, on our train, only to get to Heathrow hours before we could even check in our suitcases. Humps likes to get there early. Sit in the business lounge, read all the papers while drinking white wine and eating anything from curry to chocolate cake. If we went back home now, Humps would have been more than satisfied with his 'holiday.'

When we land in Palermo, the first thing that knocks us back is the heat. "Bloody hot," Humps says, as we walk from the plane to the terminal.

"Come on, let's go and get an air-conditioned hire car, that'll take us to our air-conditioned hotel," I say.

As we are whizzing along the motorway, I couldn't help thinking about where exactly Giovanni Falcone, the judge and magistrate, his wife, Francesca Morvillo and their driver and two bodyguards, were blown up by the mafia. This must be the route. And then I see the tall brown monument erected in their memory with a high parched mountain acting as a backdrop. I ask Humps to stop at the next lay-by – to look at it properly and to take in the scenery. The landscape around us is dry, you could say scorched, with a few contorted trees here and there. They look as if they are groaning and, at the same time, they look hostile. A hot wind conjures up, out of nowhere, lifting dust and spinning it in concentric circles.

"It was here," I say to Humps, in front of the monument, "that Falcone was killed." I am moved. After a few minutes I say: "Shall we go?"

"Whatever madam desires," Humps says jovially, and opens the car door for me. Of course, Humps knows about the bombing of the bravest anti-mafia judge whose famous comment was that the mafia had a beginning, therefore it must have an end, like anything else. This must also be the area in which Rosa and Bella disappeared. I wonder where they are buried.

As soon as we set foot in the hotel, the tiredness of the journey disappears. It is so beautiful. Baroque with cream walls depicting figures from Ancient Greek mythology in stucco. We are welcomed with a glass of champagne at reception. Our room is tastefully decorated with a view over the beach to the Mediterranean – no road in between. Sea, sand and sky – no clouds.

"Look at that view, Humps. Isn't that better than sitting in the airport lounge?"

Dinner is on the hotel's veranda directly on the beach. A balmy evening. We eat to the sound of waves served by immaculately groomed waiters in pristine white uniforms. They recommend little plates of tasters for antipasto; they recommend ricotta and pistachio pesto pasta for our first course; they recommend fresh grilled sea-bass for our second course; they recommend a bottle of chilled Benanti Pietramarina white. Who are we to argue? We'll decide later if we can manage the ricotta cannoli dessert.

The next day is spent mostly on the beach: walking, reading, generally lolling around, swimming and eating ice-creams. And on Monday we have more of the same. We decide to give the archaeological sites a wide berth. Maybe we'll go and see them some other time.

Today, Monday, is also our wedding anniversary. Perhaps Humps has forgotten. He hasn't as much as hinted at it all day. I bought him a pair of silver cufflinks, had them engraved with an M and H entwined, they are not too showy, otherwise, I know, he wouldn't wear them. Evening comes and I get dressed up for dinner. Even if he has forgotten our thirty-fifth wedding anniversary, I am going to spend it in style anyway. We are led out to the veranda on the beach again.

Actually, Humps is dressed up to the nines as well. A young man comes towards us carrying a huge beautiful composition of flowers. It is Mark! What is he doing here? "Happy anniversary," he says. Clara appears too, and then comes Emma with little Benjamin. Wonderful! The waiters ask us to move to the bigger table in the corner. Emma and Clara have decorated the table with an assortment of little cards, place names, candles and flowers. They all knew about this surprise except for me.

Far from forgetting, Humps fishes a deep-blue box out of his jacket pocket. I gasp when I open it. Inside is a beautiful white-gold necklace with a mother-of-pearl oval-shaped pendant, and earrings to match.

THIRTY-NINE

Tuesday 26th September – morning

Luckily the kids show no sign of wanting to go to The Village when I tell them during breakfast that Humps and I are planning on going later that day.

"I want to see The Village, the place of your origin. You've kept me away from it long enough," says Humps.

"You've insisted so much that in the end I had to give in. Anyway, you know I like to make you happy, don't you?"

"Like I do with you," he says.

"OK," I say. "You drive?"

"I'll gladly be your chauffeur, madam."

"I need to warn you. Out there, it won't be anything like it is here. This is a smart tourist area. We're going out into the wild."

"I can take it as long as I'm with you," he says.

"You're incorrigible."

"Long may it last."

Then he proceeds to tell the kids about my new-found attachment to Zia. "Back in Blighty she's spending all her days at Zia's house, aren't you, darling?"

"Well, not all my days. I have been there quite a lot lately. I don't deny that. But now I'm no longer working, I don't have excuses not to go."

"You've made a point of not having contact with your family for years," Emma says. "We hardly know any of your relatives."

"And that's the way it should stay," I say. "Now wouldn't you rather enjoy the sea, than come with us to a backward medieval village?"

"I quite like the idea of a medieval village," says Clara. "We can spend tomorrow on the beach. If we don't come with you now, when will we have the chance again?"

"You've got a point there," Emma says. "Yes, let's all go."

"The car's big enough for all of us," Mark says. "Let's do it."

"We can't all pounce on Peppina," I say. "You don't understand. Once we leave this town, there are miles of barren countryside. Along the only road to The Village, all we'll go through are two separate hamlets. We have to wind our way over the undulating land. To say that it's at the back of beyond is a gross understatement."

"Is there a bar in The Village?" Clara asks.

"Yes, there is in the piazza."

"That's fine, then," Clara says. "We can get drinks and snacks at the bar and wait there, if all else fails. I can drive."

"No! No way," I say. "Daddy's driving and I'm sitting in the front passenger seat next to him. This isn't England, you know? None of you have any idea. When we go through the hamlets, or meet anyone along the country roads, we have to be careful. If there are people standing in the middle of the road, you don't ask them to move. No horn honking. You turn your engine off and wait until they've finished. When they move, we can go."

"What's that all about, then?" Emma asks.

"About power and control."

"What?" Mark says.

"Exactly, as I said before, none of you have any idea. If you want to come, you keep quiet and do as I ask. That's a non-negotiable condition."

And on that strict-teacher note, we get into the car and set off. I tell them: "This island is in a pincer and it trickles right down to the extent that it affects your everyday behaviour. For me, it's palpable, I can almost touch it, and I certainly feel it. It's so different from your safe cosy London world."

"Wow, is this place exciting, or what?" Clara says. "It's all new to me and needs to be explored. I want to understand it."

Shortly after leaving the seaside town behind us, the bumpy, dusty, winding road begins. We come across a shepherd with his flock. When he sees us he stands at the side of the road, instructs his dog to move his sheep to one side so we can get by. I wave and thank him. I say to Humps: "Please, just please, don't run over one of those sheep. Or cause one to fall over the ridge." We bump our way slowly, curving past the flock. We are so close to them that one or two of the sheep rub up against our car. Little Benjamin is ecstatic, jumps up and down, points to the sheep while oohing and aahing.

The landscape is desolate. Hard terrain parched by the unforgiving sun. It probably hasn't rained for months. No greenery in sight. On we drive slowly until we come to the first hamlet. People are sitting and standing along the road talking to each other. Mostly men. As we pass, they stop and stare at us. "Don't worry folks," I say, "they are simply curious. They do that with every passing car. Used to do it forty years ago, still doing it now."

"That's weird," Emma says, "they don't even pretend not to be looking."

Dogs are roaming around on their own. One of them stops in the middle of the road in front of us.

Humps looks at me: "What am I supposed to do now? Wait for it to display its power and control over us?"

"I don't know," I say. "Wait a moment and see if it budges."

A man steps down from the pavement. Gives the dog an almighty kick. The malnourished dog whimpers and runs off. The man doffs his cap and gestures to Humps that we can continue our journey.

"Poor dog," Clara says.

We go through the next hamlet, or should I say a ghost hamlet? Unfinished houses. All at different stages of construction. A few are only frameworks of a house. Sad brick skeletons on the horizon. Stray dogs roam around here, too; looking for food, looking for water, while cats laze in the shade of red oleanders. "I don't know how the bus ever gets to The Village," Humps says, "bloody difficult enough for a car."

"There's no bus route along this road. It comes from the opposite direction, then goes back the same way. If you want to go to the sea, you have to go by car."

The road widens. We come to a drinking trough for animals with clear water running into it from a tube. Little Benjamin loves water, he smiles and kicks while he plays with the water tinkling out of the tube. "This is drinking water," I say, "people from The Village come here to fill up containers of it to take home. Carrying water was something I helped out with. That was in contrast with my life in London where we had running water and plenty of food. You," I pause and look at my family one-by-one, "assume that my life's been like that as well. I've wanted a better life for you two," now I'm looking at my daughters, "I've kept you away from here where relatives actively seek to harm you, where there's danger at every corner. This is the place where I was so severely beaten that I had to have my kidney removed..." I stop. My daughters look at me in wonder as if they are seeing another side of their mother. "Sometimes," I say, "it annoys me when you take your easy lives for granted." I am near to tears. They don't comment.

There was complete silence all around. Nobody who lives in the area would venture here at this time of day. They'd come early morning or in the evening. Not a car, nor people, just the sound of water running into water, and a few flies buzzing around. Peace and tranquillity. We stand there and listen. Pointless talking would spoil the moment. A pleasant breeze wafts over us and creates ripples in the water. Behind us an empty boundless stretch of neglected land. Scattered sand-coloured boulders, shaped like kneeling nuns with their heads down to pray, looking closely at the spidery cracks in the terrain. The distant sharp sloping pathways and sinister mountains make the landscape look unforgiving.

After a few more kilometres, we enter The Village. Tall terraced houses painted orange, yellow, pink, with green or brown shutters. We drive up a narrow black slabbed road. Between the houses and the road are high narrow pavements on each side, also used as a step up to front doors. Scooters randomly parked along the sides of the road. We pass an altar dedicated to Mother Mary with dessicated flowers in vases, and a rusty candlestick clogged up with hardened wax. A little further down is a small shop selling religious framed pictures of Jesus and various saints, they are randomly pinned to the wall of the shop. Washing is hanging on curtain lines across the road from one house to the other, and also parallel to balconies. Kids play in the streets watched by grandparents on wicker chairs balanced on the pavements. A mother calls out from a balcony to her son below. Eyes follow us.

Soon we are in the main piazza. The village's only bar stands at the top of the piazza; men sit at tables on the pavement outside the bar and some are sitting in the middle of the piazza in a cluster. A few of the older men are wearing coppolas, flat caps typically worn by the older generation in Sicily. "The men in black coppolas are those whose wives have died. A sign of respect," I say. A group of younger men are playing cards on coloured plastic tables in the shade of old trees. Ours is the only car in the piazza and the men stop what they are doing to see who has come into the village. No doubt someone will follow us to find out which family we belong to. After they've seen us go into Peppina's house, they will leave us alone. A lot of emigrants come back to The Village from abroad. So they are used to these returning strangers.

We stop on a side street off the piazza. "Can we park here?" Humps asks.

"You can park anywhere you like," I say, not adding that my family are the bosses here, so we can do what we want.

"Do you want to go to the bar, or are you coming to meet Peppina?" I say to the kids. They decide they'd like to get a drink at the bar, have a quick look round The Village, then meet us at Peppina's.

"There's not much to see," I say. "But if that's what they want, why not?" The sun is beating down. "Let me take Benjamin, then; he'll suffer in this heat. He's better off indoors with us. Peppina's house is just up there. Take that first little alleyway on the right," I say pointing up the road, "you'll come to a courtyard. It's the house in the corner."

FORTY

Tuesday 26th September – afternoon

As we approach Peppina's house, we see that the front door is wide open as it always was, during the day, in my grandmother's time. We walk straight in and I repeatedly call Peppina as we climb up the uneven, stone stairs leading directly to the garden. No answer from Peppina, but Zia shouts out, "We here in garden." Zia and Angelina are talking animatedly. Provvi and her kids, who are tearing around, are here, too. The women sit in the shade of the house.

About halfway up the continuous two flights of stairs is another flight leading to the living quarters: on the right is a big bedroom-cum-living-room, where Peppina sleeps. Then, on the left, was my grandmother's bedroom. From that room another door opens up to yet another stone staircase that leads up to the attic. This is one open space, where the sisters slept as children. There is one toilet, no shower or bath – only a huge tin bath standing in the corner of the kitchen. I had a few baths in that tub as a youngster. Women would walk in and out when I was trying to wash myself. I'd wait for everyone to go, so that I could stand up and wrap myself up quickly in a bath towel before walking through Peppina's room, through my grandmother's bedroom, and up to the attic to get dressed.

You have to go through Peppina's room to get to the kitchen. From the kitchen you can step out into the beautiful garden. It is definitely the best feature of the house. The big stone oven, where Ziuzza used to come and bake, is still here. The bottom of the garden slopes downwards. The wide open views are in stark contrast to the suffocating, closed-in courtyard at the front of the house.

We walk towards the women from London. I ask if Peppina's in. "No, she out at moment," Zia says. She fetches a couple of chairs from the kitchen, "Asetta, asetta." They pay compliments to Humps and me about having such a lovely grandson. Little Benjamin coos and waves at them. Angelina and Provvi have never met Humps. Always the gentleman, even in his khaki Bermuda shorts and hairy legs, he shakes their hands and says: "How do you do?" They answer that they are well, thank you. Angelina looks taken aback by him. She probably didn't realise that I had such a scrumptious husband. She's intimidated by Humps – maybe by his clipped Oxford English. Humps can't do cockney like I can. He's the genuine article, to the manner born. Susi shoots right over abandoning her texting when she sees us, acting all flirty. She's intimidated by nobody. She'd better keep her paws off Humps. Men seem to be a rare commodity round here.

Zia brings out a terracotta amphora and pours fresh water from it onto the lemon at the bottom of glasses. "Biviti. Hot in Sicilia. You need water," she says handing them out, and then pours water into Benjamin's bottle. We quench our thirst.

"Come on. I show garden and lot of chicken," Zia says. Little Benjamin has already seen the chickens and is flapping his hands in their direction. Provvi's boys are pulling faces at them. Zia beckons to me to follow her inside while the others stay in the garden.

"What's the news," I ask Zia.

"Adriano think sister Bella and Rosa no alive any more."

"He's not going to get much information from the people here. What do they know, anyway? The sisters didn't get here," I say.

"He can no make problem. He no know where to start."

"Has he been to the police?"

"Ah, he get nothing from police. Nobody talk."

The police have spoken to the people on the bus. As witnesses none of them were of any help. They said they didn't remember a man getting on at a bus stop after the bus left the airport. The driver said he sold the man a ticket, but couldn't say what he was like. He hardly ever looked passengers in the face, unless they were pretty women. Anyway, he'd never been any good at guessing ages, which led to his upsetting women in his time. The man could have been twenty-five, could have been fifty-five for all he knew. Neither could the driver say how tall he was, or what his build was like. "I'm sitting in the driver's seat, one step up," he said, "how can I estimate anyone's height? And how can I see how fat they are? The safety glass between me and the passengers distorts body shapes."

The police didn't press him for more information. That's what the driver said and that's what the police wrote down in their report.

"How do you know all this?" I ask Zia.

"From Young Cushi man in police station. You no need know his name. I tell you rest when we in London."

"Have you seen Adriano?" I ask.

"No, I no see. I invite him come see me. Maybe he come in next day. Speak to me. I like mother for him."

"What's happening on the Giulio front?" I ask.

"Thursday morning early. In countryside. He go mangiare ricotta with Adriano. I no know more."

Mangiare ricotta in the early morning, when it is fresh, is something emigrants visiting The Village do as a way of getting an injection of nostalgia of their past lives, or that of their parents, before wholesale emigration opened up after World War II. At that time, about 90% of the villagers were peasants.

Now shepherds offer mangiare ricotta as a traditional tourist trip in the deepest countryside where their flocks roam. After the first milking of their sheep at dawn, the first batch of ricotta is made in their shacks.

"There are a couple of things I want to ask you, Zia."

Benjamin is getting restless so I give him my phone to play with.

"The first is: how come the front door's always open here. It's been like that since I can remember."

"So Peppina no go up-down stair every five minute, let women in when visit."

"Yes, but your house in England is like a fortress, and you have women coming and going there, too."

"You right. But in The Village people know Peppina. Nobody come rob. My sister can put cash in middle courtyard – nobody touch. Nobody take it."

Of course, it makes sense. Everyone in The Village knows about Peppina's network. How she is close to Young Cushi. They all know they'd pay a very high price if they slight Peppina, never mind take anything from her.

The second question is:

"Why does Peppina hate me so much?"

"I no know."

"Yes, you do know. There must be something."

"I tell you in England."

"No, Zia, I want to know. Please tell me now."

After a little more persuasion, she says:

"She say you and you father, kill you mother."

"What? My mother had a terrible illness. You know that!"

"I know. She say you evil. You mother ill because you evil like you father."

"Oh, please. For God's sake," I say.

"You want know. I tell you."

"And what about before my mother became ill? When I came here and was a child of twelve?"

"When Peppina young, she want marry you father."

"You're saying that my mother and her were love rivals?"

"She want marry you father. But you father want you mother."

Zia explained that Peppina had been engaged to my father. That meant my father would visit grandmother's house to see Peppina. And during those visits, he fell in love with my mother, who, in Zia's opinion was more beautiful and sparky than Peppina. However, Peppina didn't blame my mother. The three sisters had always seen themselves as one entity. It was my father Peppina hated. When my mother died, Peppina rekindled high hopes that my father would finally want to marry her. Instead he married someone else.

"How is that my fault?" I say.

"I no know. She have silly brain. She no marry other man."

"I still don't see that it's my fault."

"You problem, you look like you father."

She doesn't know any other reason Peppina could hate me for. I believe Zia. Peppina can't take it out on my father, the real culprit. So she lashed out at me instead, because I was my father, in part.

"Yes, but you can't blame an innocent child like that. A child cannot be evil. Anyway, my father also abandoned me when he remarried. You both know that," I say.

"You father no-good bastardo man."

"Uncle Tony wasn't any better," I say.

"He double no-good bastardo man."

"In that case, why did you dedicate that altar to him in your living room?"

"God forgive me. God save my soul."

"Have you confessed your role in his death to your priest?"

"No. I confess before I die. I no want go to hell."

"Zia you will go to hell, if you're not careful."

"I no go to hell, I tell you. You go to hell. You no believe, you godless woman."

FORTY-ONE

Tuesday 26th September – evening

Peppina's back. She comes into the room, looks me up and down, then ignores me. She's in awful shape, fat with unsightly varicose veins showing through her flesh-coloured pop socks. A maroon dress tight around her stomach and loose around her chest. And a pendant depicting Mother Mary on a gold chain round her neck. Her hair is pulled back and tied into a loose pony tail with a big, black slide.

The door is open, I can hear that my kids and Mark have also arrived. Zia and I follow Peppina into the garden. Peppina sits down and folds her arms as if she were in a huff. She turns her face to her left, bends her head down a little, and spits on the ground. "Vileno," she says.

"This is my Aunt Peppina," I say introducing her to my family.

Humps says he's pleased to meet her, and holds out his hand, but she doesn't take it. Clara smiles and says, "We've already met Peppina. We saw her in the piazza."

Peppina is staring at Benjamin. I feel a shudder, something sinister. To Humps and Emma I say in a low voice: "You mind Benjamin he could be in danger here, and I don't mean from the chickens. Aunt P could harm him." Emma asks Mark to hand Benjamin over to her and Humps keeps close by. They are beginning to understand how vicious this woman is. Peppina is probably wondering what we are saying. Problem for her is she doesn't understand a word of English. Without uttering a word, she goes indoors.

I call Clara over to a quiet spot near the chicken house. "Tell me, where did you meet Peppina, then?"

"Oh, mummy. You should have seen her. We'd just had a drink in the bar and then walked to the middle of the piazza. You remember that cluster of men we saw when we drove through the village? Well, they were all sitting round Peppina."

"What?"

"They were protecting her by sitting tightly around her. When they saw us approaching one of the men got up and stopped us from going any further. It was as if we were at a customs check. The man asked us what we wanted and, in the meantime, another three men circled us."

"Jesus. And, what did you say?"

"We said we were just looking around."

"He asked what family we belong to. I told them we are related to Peppina and explained where she lives. 'She's our great-aunt, my mother's aunt, her mother's sister, I said.'"

The black-coppola went to the middle of the group, asked Peppina if that was so. "Yes," she said, "they were supposed to arrive today. Let them through."

When she saw my kids she was quite unmoved, said they

were beautiful, that you could tell they had the same blood as her own, but that they had been contaminated by my blood. Luckily Mark doesn't understand Italian.

"Mum, I'm so in awe of Peppina," Clara says. "She was wielding power over all those men. All she had to do was to lift a finger and they obeyed. It's fascinating – you'd have thought she were Margaret Thatcher in the way that she bossed men around." Clara admired the Iron Lady for her tenacity and determination.

"Well, that's a turn-up for the books," I say. "Are you telling me you admire Peppina?"

"Yes, mum, she's powerful. She's mafiosa, isn't she?"

"Um, well, there's something about her."

"Mum, she's brilliant. I'm telling you, she's a boss," Clara says, hitting the nail right on the head. "I could tell by how the men addressed her with deference."

"That's no business of ours," I say, "just keep away from her."

"God, if I didn't have to go back to work, I'd stay here and find out more," Clara adds. She's so excited, "Mum, it's like being in a mafia film."

Angelina and Provvi come to us to say their goodbyes. "See you at my birthday party," Angelina says to me.

"Yes, of course, Humps and I will be there." The mother and daughter leave. Zia says she has to join the rosary, which has just started in the courtyard. Susi is messing about with her phone in the kitchen. We reckon we'd better be off as well.

As we go through the courtyard, we see Peppina leading the rosary, like she has done every evening for about sixty years. A group of eight women are huddled in a circle shrouded in black, each one holding a string of black beads in their hands, and a small cross, which they kiss. Holding the cross in their left hands, they make the sign of the cross with their right hands, first touching their forehead, then between their breasts, followed by left shoulder and right shoulder. Clara takes a picture of them with her phone. Luckily, they don't notice. "Put that phone away," I say. Emma and Mark roll their eyes and can't wait to get away. I don't think they'll want to come back to The Village. Once is enough. They don't see the folkloristic side of this like Clara does.

Out of the five mystery categories of the rosary, this evening must have been The Sorrowful Mysteries. They are probably at The Scourging at the Pillar judging by the singsong lament with Peppina invoking the Lamb of God offering his suffering to wash away the sins of humankind. The others seem to be in a muttering trance as they repeat Peppina's words verbatim, bowing their veiled heads into the circle. And then Peppina asks God for mercy for all sinners who are not worthy of living in His light. The black shrouds repeat. As we distance ourselves from the courtyard, "save us from the fires of hell" can still be heard.

As we are about to get into our car a scooter whizzes by with a big box balanced on the back wheel advertising a bakery. It makes a sharp U-turn, heads towards us and stops. Speaking in dialect the rider says: "Is that you, Maria?"

"Yes", I say, and at the same time realise who it is: "Luca! Oh, my God, Luca!"

"You haven't changed much," he says kindly.

His hair is littered with grey, he is somewhat thicker around the middle, but definitely recognisable. The man who nursed me and got me out of my mother's clutches.

"My family," I say to him making a sweeping gesture with my arm towards Humps and our children. "This is Luca, my first husband."

Mark laughs. He thinks I am joking. Emma nudges him.

He looks around bewildered. Clara says: "Oh, my God. I can't believe this." Although Humps and our kids know about Luca, they were still agog. Luca looks at them and smiles. Humps is somewhat fazed by Luca. I don't think Humps ever expected him to be so good-looking. He feels uneasy. Luca had been some haze in my memory for years, and suddenly he's materialised. The two men shake hands, then the others do the same. Luca compliments me on Benjamin saying he is a lovely baby, blonde hair, blue eyes. He holds up his hands and shows us six fingers; he has six grandchildren.

Then he insists we go to his home, just down the road. He won't take no for an answer, wants us to meet his family. We follow downhill until we come to a narrow cobblestone road. As we are approaching the end of the alley we see a bakery sign. A waft of freshly baked pizzas billows in the air. Pointing to a slat type plastic curtain at the entrance, he says: "This is my bakery. We took it over from my wife's family. My three children work with us." He pulls the curtain aside, we enter a huge room, with ovens on either side. A woman is standing in the middle leaning on a long-handled wooden paddle, supposedly used for getting bread out of big ovens. Children are darting all over the place. Little Benjamin joins the merry game and squeals too, adding to the general mayhem.

The woman leans the paddle against the counter, wipes her hands on her apron, and shakes our hands. "This is my wife," Luca says. He tells her who I am. Her smiling face becomes serious, she inspects me, glancing all over me, then does the same to Humps. She nods her head, satisfied. No threat from either of us. Luca lifts a red and white, chequered tablecloth covering pizzas in a large basket, from which he takes six of them, then places them in boxes. Humps offers to pay, Luca looks offended, turns and says to me: "Friends don't pay."

On our return journey we stop at the water trough again and eat our pizzas. Little Benjamin gets tomato sauce over his face and clothes, and even in his hair.

FORTY-TWO

Wednesday 27th September

The next day we spend mostly on the beach. In the late afternoon, Humps and I set off for The Village. It is Angelina and Beatrice's sixtieth birthday party that evening. Apart from weddings, parties are open to everyone in the village – hardly anyone receives an invitation, nearly everybody goes. Word of mouth says there is a party in that particular house on such-and-such an evening. The parties consist of music and dancing, cakes and alcoholic drinks. The success of the party is measured in litres of drink. And if the dancing space in the house isn't enough, dancing is extended to the street below where music blares through open windows. The street is blocked off by cars parked horizontally across the access roads. Nobody complains. Nobody asks the town hall for permission.

In the large living room of the house, I recognise a few faces. Provvi looks amazing. Her hair is shiny and curls bob up and down as she dances with Giulio. It is touching to watch her dance with that limp. A little clumsy, but she is enjoying herself. Has he stopped beating her since they've been in Sicily? Does having to stay with relatives stop him from lashing out at her? This place isn't as anonymous as London. The coward can probably restrain himself when he wants to. In my view, this makes his behaviour even less acceptable. He inflicts pain on his wife when he can get away with it – without any negative consequences for himself.

Provvi rushes over when she catches sight of me. "Nice to see you again. How are you?" She shakes Humps's hand.

"I'm fine," I say. "I've been worried about you. But you look wonderful."

"I feel wonderful."

I didn't want us to refer to her husband's behaviour with Humps standing there. It might embarrass her.

"I'll catch up with you later," I say, "I want to say hello to a few people."

With that Humps and I take our presents over to the twins. We've bought them a Sicilian terracotta vase each. They are thrilled with their gifts and Angelina, in particular, looks radiant. Once Humps and I have rid ourselves of the parcels, we have a waltz around the floor. All that spinning gives me a chance to see who else is there. People watch us. Not because we are good dancers, nothing of the sort. They will have whispered amongst themselves informing each other that we are related to Young Cushi. That I married a foreigner. Humps, as the typical Englishman, is overdressed. Lots of jeans and T-shirts here, on this hot evening, while Humps wears a suit, albeit a summer one, silk tie, and the cuff-links I gave him for our anniversary.

After the dance, we go over to Zia and Susi. "I need speak to you in private," Zia says.

"Susi," I say, "wouldn't you like to dance with Humps?" I trust Humps. They whirl off. I am anxious to hear what has happened on the Adriano front. Curving her way through dancers, Zia heads over to Beatrice. I follow her among the laughing and chatting in the smoke-filled room. She asks Beatrice if we can use her bedroom for a while for a private talk. Beatrice nods. I signal to Humps that I'm going out to speak to Zia, "Won't be long." I mouth to him from a distance. I sit down on the bed ready to listen to what Zia has to say.

Zia tells me that Adriano, Bella and Rosa's brother, has appointed a private detective to investigate his sisters' disappearance. A lead came from an article in a Sicilian newspaper that had published the photo of the bus driver. Adriano's detective tracked the driver down. Apparently, through the sleuth, Adriano offered the driver money in exchange for information. "I no know how much." The driver provided the number plate of the taxi Bella and Rosa had been bundled into, before they were driven to a road-construction site.

"Bella and Rosa have met their maker, and it looks like Adriano is also heading that way," I say.

Adriano took the car registration number to the police. One of Young Cushi's infiltrated men at the police station told Young Cushi.

"Young Cushi say taxi-car no problem. Stolen." Zia says. "But we kill him. He hard-head man. He no give up."

"So what's going to happen now?"

"One school friend of Giulio go ricotta mangiare in morning, with Adriano and Giulio. School friend is a Young Cushi man. Shepherd also Young Cushi man."

"So, are Adriano and Giulio going to be killed in the morning?" It was obvious they were. It was a stupid question. But I was saying it more to myself, to get my thoughts straight rather than asking Zia a question.

"We no talk about now. Friday I let you know if all OK. I tell you all about in London."

We go back to the party. Susi and Humps come and ask if we want a drink. I am still a little shaken. "Yes, of course. Thank you," I say, "I could really do with a drink." They have armed themselves with some iced-lemon-liquor cocktail. "I'll go and get Zia and you some," Humps says. When he is back with the drinks, Humps asks: "Are you OK, darling?"

"Yes, yes. I'm fine. I think the heat's getting at me, that's all." I sit and sip my drink trying to come to. Then I ask Humps to keep Zia company a moment as I want to speak to Susi.

"You know about tomorrow morning?" I say to her.

"No, what's happening?"

"I thought your mother would have told you."

"She doesn't tell me much. She trusts you more than me because she sees your mother in you. She told me that," Susi says.

"Well, maybe because I've been visiting her a lot lately, and we have stronger ties than before."

"So what's happening, then?" Susi asks again.

"I think Adriano's day has come."

"What do you mean?"

There you go. That's why Zia doesn't trust Susi. Proper Sicilians understand nuances. You don't have to spell these things out. Maybe that's why Zia is more inclined to confide in me. I change my mind. I don't want to tell her. Zia wouldn't like it anyway.

"Adriano's going to mangiare ricotta. I'll bet he hasn't done that for a while."

"And what's that to me?"

"Well, they're all excited about it..."

"I'm not," Susi says, "I couldn't care less about what he does."

From a distance I see a woman walking fast towards us with a big smile on her face.

"Maria!" she calls out as she approaches us. "Maria!"

I don't recognise her.

"Sono Patrizia. Remember!"

I try to lift my spirits.

"Oh, Patrizia! Oh, my God! How lovely to see you again. After all this time." We hugged and hugged.

"You look great. You're a lady," she says.

"And look at you! You look so lovely. You've changed so much, too. Tell me about yourself. So you never made it to Rome."

"No, I didn't go in the end."

That was mainly because her father hadn't shown signs of wanting her anywhere near him. Without a job or a place to live in the capital, she couldn't summon up the courage to go out into the big wide world alone. Especially as she had never left the village. Then, she met the love of her life, married him and stayed. She was quite the lady of the village because, to my huge dismay, she had married Cushi. Yes, Young Cushi!

I am speechless for a moment or two. Hoping my inner turmoil doesn't show on my face and become visible. I manage to blurt out: "Oh, how wonderful," in shock at this revelation. All the time Zia was talking about Young Cushi, I didn't realise that he'd married the best friend I'd had in Sicily. Patrizia and I have never kept in touch. I have no idea how much she knows of his affairs.

I don't want to call Humps, but Patrizia points to him: "Is that your husband?" When Humps realises we are talking about him, he makes a beeline to us, and I introduce them to each other. A little after, what must be Young Cushi himself appears. It is him! We all shake hands and Young Cushi invites us over to the bar. "What'll you have?" he says. Patrizia wants a Marsala, so we all go with that. Young Cushi is actually a distinguished looking man. Eloquent and softly spoken. Average build. He has his grandmother's sharp blue eyes. He says he remembers me from our teenage years, when I spent some time at The Village. He was even at the wedding reception when Luca and I married. In fact, he danced with Patrizia most of the time, he tells me. And Patrizia has always spoken highly of me, it seems.

A shiver runs down my spine. So, even in those days, unbeknown to me, I had 'a man of honour,' a mafioso, at my wedding – who knows how many more of them were there. It's not as if they have it written across their foreheads. At the time, I was so wrapped up in trying to get back to England that I hadn't taken much notice of what went on around me, at my own wedding reception, or in The Village.

Young Cushi takes my hand and leads me to the dance floor. I'm still in a daze. A cha-cha. Humps and Patrizia follow us and start dancing, too. Zia is intermittently watching us and talking to a little group of women. Susi is flirting with a couple of men. Young Cushi asks, "Are you enjoying your holiday?"

"Very much," I say. Lost for words.

"Does your husband like it here? I hear from Zia that it's the first time he's been," Young Cushi says with a hint of disdain.

"Well, I've always worked hard and didn't have much time for holidays." He knew I was fabricating.

"Such a pity," he says. "You are a thoroughbred Sicilian. Like me. Sicily flows in our veins. You should be proud. Marrying an Englishman doesn't dilute your blood."

They keep wanting to reclaim me back. I just smile at him. I don't know what to say. Thankfully, the dance is over. Patrizia and Humps join us. Young Cushi looks at Humps, "Humphrey, Patrizia and I would be delighted if you and your good lady came to our house for lunch on Friday. You can bring your children as well, if they want." He looks at Patrizia and asks: "We're free on Friday, aren't we?"

"Yes, we are," she says. "What a beautiful idea! Zia and Susi can come, too." Humps is pleased to accept. "Let's go over and invite Zia as well," Young Cushi says. We follow him like obedient poodles. I say to Patrizia that Clara would be happy to join us, but not to count on Emma and Mark because they had told me that they'd rather spend the rest of the holiday on the beach.

Zia had told me, when we were back in London, that Young Cushi is the only man in The Village that the Madonna bows down to. Once a year the Madonna statue is taken out of the local church and paraded through the streets. Women hang their best embroidered sheets over their balconies to decorate the streets along her route. As she passes, the villagers elbow their way to the statue to pin money to her dress to pay homage to her. But when the statue passes Young Cushi's house, it is the Madonna who pays homage to him by bowing down in front of his gate. He and his family watch from their balcony.

At the party, people keep coming over to pay their respects to Young Cushi, who is still sitting with us. I know hardly any of the villagers. But amongst them are Luca and his wife. They sit with us. And again we are taken to the dance floor – this time me waltzing with Luca, and Humps with Luca's wife.

After the dance I warn Humps that if we keep drinking like this, we won't be able to leave The Village this evening. I don't want to stay here. I don't want to be here when the Giulio and Adriano deed happens in the morning. Humps reckons Sicily is great fun. He's now taken off his jacket and tie and has rolled his shirt sleeves up. Still drinking. Ready for more. At that point, I realise I will have to drive him back. Then he blurts out a sentence that freezes me.

"I'd love to go to that ricotta experience with Adriano and Giulio tomorrow morning."

"What?" Someone must have told him about it. I wasn't expecting this.

"I want to go mangiare ricotta with Adriano and Giulio in the morning."

"You can't." My legs begin to tremble.

"Why not?"

"B-because we're going back to the hotel tonight."

"Can't we stay here?"

"Where?"

"At Peppina's," he says, "we can sleep in the attic."

"No! No, we can't. Don't be silly. She hasn't got room. Zia and Susi are staying there. You can't be the only man amongst women. It's not a done thing here. We need to go back to our hotel where our kids are."

"They won't miss us. It only takes a phone call."

"Please Humps. Please listen to me. You can't go, and that's the end of the story."

"Oh, I do love a bossy woman."

After more dancing and drinking, especially on Humps's behalf, we leave.

"Come on, get in the car," I say, holding open the front passenger door. He's tipsy.

"Are you driving?" he asks.

"Well, of course, you can't drive in that state. We'd finish up in some deep ravine."

"I love Sicily," Humps says, in his dazed stupor. "Why haven't we been here before?"

"Because it's not all as wonderful as you think. It has a very dangerous side to it."

"All I see are fun people, sun, sea, beautiful dark women, incredible food."

"Darling, this is the land of the mafia."

"Rubbish." he says. He's drunk. "Maybe it was once. It's not half as bad as you make out."

"It's double as bad as I make out," I say.

"They look nice enough to me. Take Luca, he couldn't have been more friendly."

Humps is falling asleep. But not quite there yet. I don't bother to explain that if Luca has a profitable bakery then he will be paying protection money. There is a short silence, then Humps begins again.

"You'd have six grandchildren if you'd stayed with Luca. I can imagine you with that wooden paddle in your hands. Threatening. That's what you'd be. Bloody dangerous woman."

"Alright, darling, see if you can nod off."

"Bloody dangerous woman," he repeats.

"Darling, now, can you get some shut-eye so I can concentrate on the road, please?"

FORTY-THREE

Thursday 28th September

Down for breakfast at 10 o'clock, just before it shut. The kids are still having breakfast. I tell them about Young Cushi's invitation. Emma and Mark turn their noses up. Clara says: "You bet I want to go. Just don't leave me behind." As we are enjoying our fresh croissants and cappuccino by the sea, thoughts of Adriano and Giulio flitter by in my mind. I keep trying to bring my focus back to us sitting under the sun amongst the sound of waves breaking, and seagulls squawking.

Giulio and Adriano's day has come. Brothers in death. Two men who've played their cards wrong. Who have hit above their height and tumbled down. Others might have got away with what they did, but these two operated under the shadow of an unforgiving and relentless justice, which is far bigger and powerful than they were. The Ancient Greeks called it hubris leading to tragedy. The Ancient Sicilians call it vendetta leading to justice, without any right to appeal.

After breakfast, we join the kids on the beach. And in the afternoon, mostly due to my insistence we, finally, manage to get around to visiting the archaeological site. The excavations. Needless to say, I spend most of the time thinking of Bella and Rosa. Underground. In their final resting place under a motorway. Would they be found in the distant future? Would archaeologists be thrilled to inspect their skeletons, lay them out on stainless steel worktops to scrutinise them? Study their earrings, necklaces, rings. Wonder why they weren't buried in sacred ground? Would they trace them back to England? How did they get there? Their fillings. Was the amalgam different from that used by dentists in Sicily? Would dental specialists discover that? And, what about Adriano and Giulio? Were they lying in some dry, sandy soil out in the back of beyond of the Sicilian campagna. Could these other two bodies be traced back to England in the far-flung future?

In the afternoon, Susi phones me. She asks if we can pop in to see Zia before going to Young Cushi's. "I don't think we'll have time."

"Oh, just a few minutes. Mum's made some cakes and wants you to take them to Cushi's. We're walking, we can't carry trays. The cakes'll go off in this heat, anyway."

"OK, I'll see what we can do."

FORTY-FOUR

Friday 29th September

So in the morning Humps, Clara, and I arrive at Peppina's again, to pick up Zia's cakes. "I so love this house," Clara says, "it's so Sicilian. It feels like Don Corleone is going to walk in any minute." She doesn't know what I went through here. Her life has been so easy. She simply hasn't a clue.

"Susi, you give Humphrey and Clara cake, make cuppa tea for them. I come back in minute. I speak to Maria in attic," Zia says.

She takes me by the arm and marches me upstairs.

"Zia, what's this. What are you doing?"

"I want tell you what happen to Giulio and Adriano yesterday. One minute. You my poor sister daughter. You like daughter to me."

"Yes, I was thinking about them yesterday. So what happened?"

Zia has received information from Young Cushi and his men.

All was still and dark when the two men were picked up yesterday at five o'clock in the morning by a trattorino, by Adriano's school friend, who is now part of Young Cushi's family. Family is of utmost importance in Sicily; with brothers and sisters in blood as the highest form of family.

The trattorino went to Giulio's first, then Adriano's. Literally translated, trattorino means 'little tractor.' Trattorini have replaced the mules of our grandfathers. Farmers now use a trattorino as a means of transport to their land because it climbs over the most rocky and hostile ground. They proceeded to travel through this barren moonscape-like land, until they reached the sheep farm in the middle of nowhere. Silence. Nothing stirred. Until the shepherd came to welcome them, interrupting milking his sheep.

Adriano and Giulio were encouraged to try their hand at milking without much success. Then they followed the farmer into his shack to take part in the ricotta-making process. They ate some of that pure white cheese washing it down with home-made white wine. Then they squeezed ricotta into little plastic colanders to take back with them, but that ricotta would never make it to The Village.

"Ah, you don't get this in England, do you?" said the shepherd.

"No, we have a very different life there, we're always indoors," said Giulio, "always working; house and work, that's what we have there."

"I couldn't live in London," said the shepherd, though he'd never been there. "All that traffic, noise and filthy air. Give me the Sicilian campagna any day."

"We emigrated for work. For money. This is a God-forsaken place," said Adriano. "I like my life in London and wouldn't want to come back here."

"Each to his own," said the shepherd.

The shepherd has this conversation with every emigrant visiting him, whether they come from Germany, Belgium, America or any other place he hasn't visited.

At about eight o'clock they set off for the return journey to The Village. After half-an-hour's bumping up and down, they could see a huge pile of rocks in the distance. What wasn't visible to them, behind the rudimentary wall, were four men, two had rifles. As the trattorino approached the rocks, the driver went full speed, jumping off just in time before it crashed. Adriano and Giulio were catapulted out by the impact, and landed heavily on the rugged ground. The four men ran to the scene, using rocks two of them bludgeoned Adriano and Giulio to death. Then they placed the bodies side by side, went over them with the trattorino, and overturned the trattorino on them. Adriano was placed near the driver's seat and Giulio at the back. They dismantled the impromptu wall, and scattered the rocks.

No mobile connection there. The alarm wasn't given until late afternoon. By Provvi. A search crew was sent out. All they could do was bring the bodies back to their families who'd have to start thinking about making funeral arrangements.

So, in a sense, Adriano had been luckier than his sisters. At least he would have a grave with his name on it, whereas his sisters have no memorial to commemorate their lives. The sisters started the ball rolling, and their deaths led to their brother's. And, added to that, it took a long time coming, but Susi's rapes have now been properly avenged.

By 12.30, we are already ringing the bell on Patrizia and Young Cushi's well-polished door, with a tray and a bag each in our hands. It is exactly the time they wanted us there. And we are punctual. A young maid in a black dress, and pristine white starched apron, opens the door. She welcomes us in. Patrizia appears at the top of the wide marble stairway and hurries down to greet us:

"Ciao, I'm glad you came," she shakes Humps's hand, then kisses Clara and me. "I can't believe you've come back after all these years. The times I've thought about you," Patrizia says to me.

"I know," I say, "I've thought about you so many times, too. Never would I have imagined you'd still be here in The Village. And you're so happy." This was actually true, I wasn't toadying up to her.

"Yes," she says, "I decided to stay, and I've come to love The Village. It's strange how we change."

"It certainly is," I reply.

"Oh, Clara, you must meet my daughter, Adele, she's the same age as you."

The maid is still standing behind us. Patrizia gestures to her to take the trays to the kitchen. We give Patrizia the flowers and bottle of wine we bought for them. She leads us into their magnificent dining-room. Baroque. Blue and white. Huge high windows which look out onto a garden lined with plants – red and pink oleander, lemon and olive trees, and other plants I don't recognise.

The whole place is filled with a light we don't have in England – so bright and clear – a light that sublime artists, like Turner, would love to have captured.

"What a beautiful house, you have," Humps says, Clara and I nod in agreement. I think Humps has now understood what I'd never told him: that my family is up to its neck in mafia.

"Thank you," she says. "We'll have our aperitif out on the veranda."

"Oh, how beautiful," I say.

Young Cushi with a young lady come out to join us and following them close behind is their maid with a tray of flute glasses full of sparkling white wine. "This is our daughter, Adele," Young Cushi says, introducing her to us.

A splendid young woman in her thirties, with strong Sicilian features like Patrizia's. With all this splendour: the house, the food and the women, how am I ever going to drag Humps away from Sicily? Adele can speak perfect English – an American accent. Turns out she graduated in law in the USA. Humps and Clara soon get talking to Adele, while Patrizia and Young Cushi are all over me. We are offered smoked salmon and shrimp antipasto with a cream called froth of champagne.

"How are you enjoying your stay in Sicily?" Young Cushi asks me again.

"Oh, it's brilliant! And Humps and Clara are in love with the island. It's going to be difficult to get them back home," I joke.

"Sicily certainly has its charm," he says.

"It does," I say, "A charm like no other." What on earth was I saying? I was still smarting from Young Cushi's rebuke while we were dancing.

Patrizia gets up "I need to go and talk to the cook for a moment."

I smile at her as she walks by.

"Zia has been telling me about your visits," Young Cushi

begins. "She holds a special place in my affections, like Peppina does, too. My father and your mother and aunts were more like sisters to my father than cousins. The three sisters have been part of my life since I was a toddler. First in London and then here."

"I know," I say, "Zia is special to me, too. I'm very fond of her." I didn't mention my mother or Peppina.

"And intelligent," he says.

Zia would not seem so to Londoners. Mostly down to her simplified English. A habit she got into and vehemently holds on to. A kind of endearing trademark. Patrizia, in the meantime, has come back. Sits with Adele, Clara, and Humps. Adele and Clara are laughing their heads off. Humps must be telling them his repertoire of corny jokes.

"Yes, Zia's very bright. And she's had a hard life," I say to Young Cushi.

"I remember my father telling me about her violent husband," he says.

"I know about that," I say. "I actually experienced some of the bad side of his character."

"My father put things right. He saw it as a mission. God on high required it from him. He was convinced of that. I inherited that belief from him, you know. Zia has the same family mindset. She does help me if need be: though, of course, I have men taking care of more important things in England. Zia is getting a little old now."

"Yes," I say.

"Susi is not quite like Zia. Don't get me wrong, she's a nice enough woman, but she hasn't got Zia's laser mind like you have."

Young Cushi has just offered me a position within the organisation in London. But I turn it down by ignoring his veiled offer. And instead I say: "Yes, Zia is much more rational." I can tell by the look on his face that he's disappointed.

"If you need any help," he says, "of any sort in the future, do let me know. We are family."

"Thank you," I say. That's generous of him given that I have just refused his proposition.

"Ah, our first course is ready," he says, "let's go to the table," he holds his hand out for me to take, and accompanies me over to my chair at the elaborately decorated table. He pulls the chair out for me to sit on.

Over lunch, speaking about Zia and Susi, Patrizia says: "They are joining us later for dessert. They'll be here at about half past two. Zia said she has a special diet and would rather cook for herself. These older ladies are so set in their ways."

"My mother and grandmother were like that, too," Young Cushi says, and my grandmother, I remember, was always baking, like Zia," he says talking about Ziuzza, my grandmother's mafiosa sister, shot in a road, "And she would only eat food she cooked herself. God bless her good soul, and my mother's."

Adele tells us about her adventures in America; where she went and what she did there. Young Cushi told us about Sicily, Patrizia about her house, and we proudly give them a quick talking tour of London. Clara talks about London galleries. Adele says she'll be visiting London soon and staying with Zia. "That'll be nice company for Zia. She gets lonely sometimes," I say.

"Yes, my wife has grown fond of Zia," Humps says, "she's often at her house."

Dessert waits for Zia and Susi to arrive. The two are promptly shown in by the maid. We get up to greet them. From then on Zia is the star of the dining-table, until Patrizia suggests that she show us around the garden and then view her collection of precious vases and her art collection.

Wandering around the luscious greenery, despite the eternal drought in Sicily, we meet two gardeners, who, to me, look more like bodyguards. Water in these parts is still rationed. Only mafiosi have access to ever running water. We go back in to view the vases. They are lined up against windows so that the light beams through them and shows up their true beauty in all its splendour – cut crystal, mother of pearl, silver, stone, terracotta, Chinese porcelain, enamel, gold inlay – you name the vase, Patrizia has it in her house.

Then we go up to another floor where Patrizia keeps her art collection. I can't believe my eyes. They've got paintings by Guttoso, De Chirico, Lojacono, and portraits of the Sicilian writers Pirandello, Sciascia, and Camillieri. Then there are paintings that I don't recognise. "You see, we are buying paintings by upcoming Italian artists, giving priority to Sicilians," Patrizia says.

Clara is bursting. She says to Patrizia: "This place is paradise! You know I'm an art historian and interior designer, don't you?"

"Yes, we know," Patrizia says. "You can come and stay here with us anytime you want. With Adele's help, I am opening a gallery in London."

"Another reason I'm going over to London is to look for premises," Adele says. "We were thinking of the West End. Somewhere around Regent Street."

"What about South Bank?" Clara says. "That's the trendy area for anything artistic now. And there's more space in that area compared to the crowded West End."

"You see," Adele says, "we need a Londoner to help us. We'd love you to oversee setting up the gallery and managing it when it's open. I can't do it. Though I love art, what I crunch best is law and numbers."

Clara is enthusiastic. "Directing a gallery in London is a dream for me."

"It's just come true," Patrizia says. "Who better to do that for us than a member of our family?"

Humps is uneasy. But he won't be able to stop this. Clara has a mind of her own and will go ahead with this project. I'm actually happy for her.

FORTY-FIVE

Friday 29th September – late afternoon

We drive Zia and Susi home. Peppina is there in the courtyard. Sitting on a chair with a long face, and arms tightly folded. Probably sulking because she hadn't been invited. Seeing her after all these years has brought back to me all the pain I went through as a young woman. I still hate her and, even though she's dead, I still hate my mother. It's because of Peppina that I've lived most of my life with only one kidney. I remember her stamping on my side, and me pleading for her to stop. I was so helpless.

"Don't accept anything to eat or drink," I whisper to Humps and Clara. As usual, Humps probably thinks I am being unfair, or even delusional.

"Let's go and sit in the garden," Susi says.

"Great idea!" I say.

Peppina huffs. She makes clear she can't be bothered to get up, but she does and goes with us all into the garden.

"I'll bring some cakes out," Zia says.

"We simply can't eat any more," I say. "Believe me, we've eaten so well. We don't have space for them."

Humps looks as if he could eat one.

"Look at your waistline," I say to him. "If you put on any more weight, you won't be able to get into your suits."

He disobeys, as he does more often than not. "I'll just have a little one." They are all a similar size. We are leaving tomorrow. I don't want nasty surprises stopping us getting back, but, rightly enough, he does what he wants.

Peppina asks me in Sicilian when we are going back. I say the next day. She answers that Sicily will be a better place once our plane has taken off. "You and your filthy English family gone." I don't answer that. Instead, I am seething. She has offended me repeatedly since I was a child, and played a crucial role in forcing me into an arranged marriage, along with my mother. Zia didn't have a hand in that. Peppina helped to weaken me so I became pliable enough to marry Luca and, as a consequence, I had to put up with the insults of his mother and sister. I was a nervous wreck, and my health was very poor, when I got back to England at only eighteen years old. She could have killed me.

But now Peppina is insulting my family. That is something else. That stings me even more. They are my world. How dare she? This is the drop of anger that makes the proverbial vase overflow. Humps, of course, hasn't noticed a thing. He and Clara are talking to Zia and Susi.

"I'd love to see the stables again. I have fond memories of grandpa taking his mules in there. Sometimes they didn't want to go in. Quite a performance."

Peppina says there's nothing to see down there. It's a storeroom, a wine cellar now. "Grandpa liked you less than I do," Peppina says. "Your father's shenanigans got on his nerves."

To be honest, I couldn't have cared less about my grandfather, nor about what grated his nerves. Susi suggests that we open a bottle of Sicilian white. Peppina lifts herself off the chair and says she'll fetch a bottle.

"Fine," I say. "Let's go down together."

The others decide they'll go to the bottom of the garden to look at the wide expanse of the rolling campagna. Susi has some binoculars.

Peppina goes to the top of the stone flight of stairs. I follow her, closely behind. When she is five steps down, and out of the line of sight from the others, I take a deep breath and give her the most almighty push in the small of her back. She falls. She screams. She tumbles down, like a sack of potatoes, rolling over and over, her head slamming on the stone steps as she goes. From top to bottom, her ordeal lasts less than ten seconds. It seems to take eternity. When she comes to a halt, blood is spurting from her mouth. I run down after her, to the bottom where she lies, crying out loud: "Oh, my God! Peppina! Peppina! ..."

She is moaning. In pain. Writhing. Her voice is hardly audible. "Maria," she keeps hissing.

"Oh, my God!" I hold her hand.

Then I shout: "Call an ambulance! Call a doctor!"

I look down at her and say: "This is for what you did to me when I was a child," as the others descend the stairs in shock.

Just before they arrive, Peppina utters her last "Maria."

They are all dumbfounded. Neighbours turn up, attracted by the mayhem. Peppina lies there in her own blood. I force tears out of my eyes. I ask Humps for a handkerchief. "She slipped," I wipe my eyes and nose. "She slipped from the top, we were about five steps down." I cry some more. "Oh, my God, oh my God!"

Humps holds me in his arms "Calm down, darling. Please calm down."

"No, I can't. This is too awful. A nightmare."

Eyes peer down at her. Incredulous.

A neighbour says how dangerous she's always thought that long flight of stone stairs were. "I warned Peppina, on more than one occasion. She should have had a landing built to break up the two flights. She didn't listen."

Susi seems as if she is in a trance: "This is terrible.

Terrible."

"What are we going to do now?" Clara asks.

"Not much we can do," Humps says.

It is clear to everyone here that Peppina is dead.

"Poor Aunt Peppina," I say, "poor woman. What a sad day!"

A couple of women nod in agreement.

We have to stay for the evening.

FORTY-SIX

Friday 29th September – evening

A doctor arrives. He concludes that she has indeed died from the consequences of a fall. Accident, he writes on the death certificate. "That's three deaths from accidents in the last two days," he says, "two men died in a trattorino accident in the countryside yesterday. I do hope this tendency is reversed soon. A sad time for our village."

A woman nods. The house is full, in no time at all, with women, mostly elderly, a few of them are accompanied by their husbands. They sit around, talking about something or other relating to life and death. How we're here today and not tomorrow. How we go from nothing to nothing with a short life in between. They list stories of anyone they've ever known who has died in accidents. They compare accidents, even ones in which nobody has died. Then another lady starts on illnesses... I have an audience and feel I have to say something. "I feel so guilty," I lie.

"Nonsense," one tall, plump woman, with flared nostrils, says. "You couldn't do anything about it."

"That's the point," I reply, crying, "I was there and I couldn't do anything to help. Peppina was in front of me one moment, and the next moment she was tumbling head over heels down the stairs. I couldn't reach her. Too fast for me. Oh, God, I wish we hadn't come here today. I wish I'd gone down to get the wine on my own. Tomorrow we're going back to London, and I have to take all this emotional turmoil with me. Oh, my God!"

Humps is getting worried. Maybe I should tone it down. I let the others carry on with their comments until late evening when one-by-one they finally go back to their homes.

Zia says she can't leave Sicily until after Peppina's funeral. She asks if we will stay.

"I'm sorry, Zia, we have to go back tomorrow. Humps's workload will be enormous after being away. I need to be there for him."

"We have funeral. You no see you mother grave. Crack in marble. Rain go inside."

"Sorry, Zia. I know you want me to get it repaired, and I know you want me to stay for the funeral. But I am willing to do neither. I'll tell you what I will do though. You can inherit the whole of the house. I don't want it. In fact, you'd do me a favour if you took it off my hands."

"You give me house?"

"Yes, then you can either keep it or sell it. If you decide to sell it, you can use some of the money to pay for Peppina's funeral and repair my mother's grave."

Zia nods.

I could have said more but Zia has agreed with my idea. What would be the purpose?

"Adriano and Giulio funeral?" she says, meaning: wouldn't I be attending those either?

"Zia, Adriano was your husband's nephew, he's nothing to me. And Giulio isn't related to either of us."

"But Provvi..."

I interrupt before she gets too mellifluous. "Provvi is relieved. She will go home and make a better life for herself and hopefully be able to take those sharp edges off her boys' personalities. With time they may come right. No, sorry, I'm leaving. I'm sure you can manage, you know everyone here. And Young Cushi will help you out. And you've got Susi."

"Susi, she different. She no like you."

"Maybe, it's just as well she's not like me," I say.

"Alright you go."

I kiss Zia on both cheeks. "I'll see you in London."

Her next comment chills me to the bones.

"Peppina go up down stair all life. She never slip. Never slip."

I am not going to bother answering that. Zia has nothing on me. Uncle Tony in the pantry is my insurance. She knows that.

We leave.

PART III

London and Dorset, 2017

FORTY-SEVEN

Weekend: Saturday 30th September and Sunday 1st October

Peering out of the porthole, I see a dark sky with clouds hanging down low. A miserable grey Saturday when we land at Heathrow. Hard rain bounces off the tarmac. Pouring down and not quite as romantic as crystal raindrops dripping from trees along the Thames towpath. What a relief to get back to the safety of our home. Though I am now feeling better than I did before we left. The ball of anger I've carried around with me all my life has gone. I've avenged the degradation Peppina and my mother put me through. I realise why Susi has never felt anger towards her father. It's because she killed him. Revenge relieves anger by dissipating it. I feel like a different person. One holiday is all it took. Never mind that Clara admired Peppina. And my family, who are about to disembark from the plane with me, don't know what I did in Sicily. But now they know about my family connections, and I won't be able to hide that from them any more. I also feel relief because I can now talk to Humps and Clara openly about my family, if not about what I did. Emma, however, will have to remain in the dark and, consequently so will Mark. Luckily, they didn't come to Young Cushi's house. And, hopefully, the Peppina episode in the piazza didn't resonate with them.

Sunday was one of those marital, stay-at-home days. I have always loved the calm and the serenity of our home. I don't know if I can reshape and recreate that contentment Humps and I had before going to Sicily. Now that he knows, will it be possible to find a route back to it?

Humps and I mostly talk about our recent holiday. What else? After all that bright sunny light, we are back to dim London drizzle. The kind that seems about to stop, but goes on incessantly instead. That's how I feel inside. I'm still thinking about what I did to Peppina. I felt a rush inside. Something that started at the bottom of my stomach and came up to my throat. My hand reacted to that. I simply don't want to think about Peppina's death, though it keeps surfacing in my mind. It was a spur of the moment thing. Everything she'd done to me culminated in that instant.

"We finally got around to visiting the place of your origins," Humps says, "how can I say... It was all very interesting."

"I'm glad you enjoyed it."

"I did very much. Apart from those bloody roads. Young Cushi's house! Never seen anything like it. Heaven on earth. And everything in it. The style of it."

"That would mostly be down to Patrizia's good taste, I believe. Plus, of course, it's easier when you've got the cash to splash around."

"Oh, yes. She's some woman," he sighs.

"Hey, what's this I hear? You're not to even let such thoughts enter into the anti-chamber of your brain. You as much as look at a Sicilian man's wife the wrong way, you know what happens, don't you?"

"I have some idea, but wouldn't like to imagine it in detail."

"No, of course, you wouldn't. Snip, snip," I say, making a scissor-like gesture with two fingers.

"Ouch, ouch, and bloody ouch."

"Would be a great pity."

We laugh together, kiss and cuddle on the sofa. My response is half-hearted. I don't deserve him. God knows what he thinks of me now.

The awkward questions don't take long to surface.

"What does Young Cushi do for a living?"

"He's a businessman of some sort."

"What sort?"

"The sort you don't ask questions about."

"He doesn't look like the kind of businessman who reads *The Economist* every week, and the *Financial Times* every day."

"For all you know, he could have them delivered," I half joke.

"They'll arrive one week late in that place. Though his English is good enough. He's even got a slight cockney accent."

"Yes, well, he lived in London until he was about fifteen. I still remember him well as a child. He was the quiet, pensive type. Not like some of the tearaways in our community."

"There can't be much trade there, in the middle of the back of beyond."

"In Sicilian, they'd say it's the place where Christ lost his shoes."

"Apt expression. Gives the idea of desolation well."

"Look," I say, "it's a different culture. You can't judge it by your parameters."

What he says next shocks me.

"Probably into fraud, extortion, drugs, or all three. He's a mafia boss, isn't he?"

I flap. "No, you mustn't use that word. Nobody utters it in Sicily. They say there's no such thing as mafia, no such thing."

Humps is, to say the least, surprised. "Why are you defending the mafia? Darling what are you saying?"

"I'm not defending anyone," I say. "So many countries are riddled with crime. Yet, this island, that hardly anyone outside Italy cares much about, is stigmatised, and automatically associated with what is called the mafia. Every Sicilian is suspected of being a mafioso. It's ridiculous."

"You see, you're still defending them. It's a 'family,' isn't it?" he says. "It's a 'family' that is more important than your own nuclear and extended family, isn't it?"

"I suppose so. Please, Humps. You wanted to go to Sicily, and now you're upset."

"I'm not upset. You're the one who's distressed. I am sorry to be the cause of that, but it's such an eye-opener. We have to talk about it. You can't just shove it under the carpet. I can't believe you're related to such people. Can you imagine if the tabloids got hold of the story: *Big Bonus Banker related to Big Mafia Boss.* That's national front-page headline stuff."

I react by getting angry. "It's not my fault. Why did you follow me there? I've kept you away from them for years and everything's been fine. But you just waded in."

"Yes, go ahead, as I said before, sweep it under the carpet. Trample on it so it doesn't crawl out. It'll all be hunky-dory. Just look the other way," he says.

"Don't tell me there are no dirty dealings going on in your bank. And other banks come to that. 'Oh, let's not look too closely at where the money's coming from.' No, it doesn't matter if the coffers are full of gold belonging to the world's nicest dictators starving their population to death. It doesn't matter because that's not mafia, is it? No, because The Mafia is only in Sicily. The original."

"Darling, please. Don't get so worked up. You do have a point. But it doesn't detract from the fact that a serious criminal organisation is present in Sicily. Call it what you will," he says.

"Yes, but it's the way of human beings – it's the way of the world. People clan together taking away the livelihood of others. Channelling state money to their powerful friends rather than using it to benefit those in need. Remind you of anyone in the UK? Give that a one-word definition."

He has a bewildered look on his face. The last thing I want to do is to upset my Humps. It's not his fault if he married a fake.

"Darling, can we stop this?" I say. "It's not doing us any

good. I'm not saying my family are angels, it's just that we are not the only ones. The caricature is that we have it in our genes. We're here now in our lovely home. Let's shut the door on the dirty dealings out there."

"You can't," he says. "What about Clara? You do realise that they are going to launder money through that art gallery they want to open here, don't you? That means my daughter will be helping the mafia clean their money."

"And if they deposit money in your bank from sales of works of art, would your bank refuse it?"

"We will if it's criminal money."

"But, if it's been laundered, it won't be criminal money any more, will it? So you'll take it?" I say. "Come on, darling, let's stop this. I don't want to argue with you." I try to hug him, but he's in a huff and doesn't respond.

"Why don't we have a game of Scrabble?" I ask. So we do. Humps's first move. Starting on a double letter space, he plays out all seven tiles: 'QUARREL' gives him 102 points. You couldn't make it up.

FORTY-EIGHT

Monday 2nd October

The holiday aftermath has well overflowed my washing basket. How many machine loads are there? Zia and Susi won't be back until next Monday. I am full of tension that cleaning seems to appease. I throw myself into housework. I hoover the carpets. And, also for the first time, I hoover our heavy curtains. I mop the kitchen and bathroom floors. And, for the first time, I also mop the walls of both bathrooms with bleach. I have a bleach addiction. 'Kill all known germs' has stuck with me. The cleaning frenzy extends to cupboards. Out comes everything. Each item inspected for the expiry date, shelves bleached, and everything back in again.

When I get round to washing the windows, Adriano comes to mind. He spent his adult life wiping windows. What was the point of it all, when he was dead and buried prematurely? His funeral is tomorrow. Zia and Susi will show a presence and be seen to care about Uncle Tony's nephew. Even if she wasn't involved in Adriano's killing, Susi has got her revenge. Unbeknown to Zia, she has avenged her daughter's rapist. Adriano's children and widow are no doubt already there to give their loved one a decent send-off. He will be buried in the same cemetery as his father, Teodoro. Probably next to him. Who, in turn, is buried next to an illegal immigrant posing as his brother Tony. I don't think they'll bring Adriano's body back to London. Dead bodies of the community are nearly always taken to Sicily to be buried. Like my mother was taken to Sicily. Zia already has her space ready. She will be buried with my mother and Peppina, miles away from Uncle Tony.

Then there'll be Giulio's funeral. I wonder how Provvi is coping. Relieved, no doubt. Why wouldn't she be? No more beatings. A peaceful life awaits her at long last. Just so damn unlucky she had to take that nasty decision. What else could she do?

What a holiday, eh? Three funerals and not a wedding in sight.

Unfortunately, I bump into Barbara in Waitrose. I am not in the mood to talk to anyone. "Were you on holiday? I pushed some of your post into the box so as people couldn't see you were away. Where did you go? Anywhere nice?"

"We went to Sicily. Had a great time. It's the first time Humphrey's been."

"Oh, I do hope you weren't hobnobbing with the mafia, dear." She has a good belly laugh. Now's not the time, I think. I give a fake laugh back, pretending her comment is funny. This woman ought to shut up. I probably will have to make her do just that, if she carries on.

"Well, I was worried about going because I thought you'd have all the London mobsters round while we were away," I say, and have an even bigger laugh than she had before. She looks shocked. "Oh, and thank you for pushing our post through. You never know who's keeping an eye on you, do you?"

"Are you enjoying your retirement?" she asks.

"Very much, thank you. You know, I've been so busy since I retired that I wonder how I ever found the time to work."

"Do you miss your students?"

"I've fond memories of them, but it was hard work and I wouldn't go back to that."

"You were teaching at some prestigious schools, I hear."

And on it goes. She is trying to extract information from me to relay to others, which only stops when I manage to get away.

Ironic, isn't it? I have taught at schools where as a child, they wouldn't have let me darken their tennis courts with my shadow. They'd have laughed at me then. But I'd gone on to teach the children of some of the most influential people in London. An achievement, or not?

Surprising what you can do when you're a chameleon.

FORTY-NINE

Monday 9th October

The day of Zia and Susi's return has arrived. Driving to Heathrow always stresses me out somewhat. I take the Mercedes. It's more comfortable than the Golf. On our way back home, they tell me a little about what happened after my family and I left. Young Cushi is going to deal with Peppina's estate. Apart from the house there is grandfather's piece of land out in the campagna. Amongst those barren slopes. I make it clear to Zia that I don't want my share of the land either.

"You good woman."

"No, Zia, I'm not a good woman. Land, house, or whatever, in Sicily, is simply of no interest to me."

"When in cemetery for Peppina, I see workmen put new marble on you mother tomb. Now her tomb new like Peppina tomb. I pay from house money. You no worry."

"Oh, it was such a sad holiday, Mary," Susi says.

"I know, it was all so unlucky." More planning than bad luck, actually. But I don't say so.

"Adele, she come next week. She stay at my house," Zia says.

"She couldn't come with us because she had to go to Switzerland first. She flew to Milan, then she's flying here," Susi lets on.

I will ask Zia about that when we are alone. She won't tell me the whys and wherefores while Susi is within hearing range.

"I'll come and see you tomorrow, Zia. If that's OK with you?"

"Yes, you come. I wait for you."

"And Susi shall we go for another Italian one evening. Humps is going out for a work dinner on Wednesday evening. What do you think? Are you free Wednesday night?"

"Yeah, I don't think I've got anything on."

"Wednesday it is, then. Seven o'clock at the usual place?"

"Yeah, lovely," she says.

"Oh, before I leave, I want to ask about Provvi? How did she take Giulio's death?"

"It was so sad, Mary," Susi says. "Provvi's now going to

have to bring those kids up on her own. I'm sure she wouldn't have gone to Sicily, if she had any idea he was going to die in an accident."

"She brave woman," Zia says, "she good mother."

"Yeah, and Adriano's family are already back in London," Susi says. "So sad for his family. Maybe Susi could tell Zia about Adriano now that he's dead. But that's for Susi to decide. I might talk to Susi about it.

FIFTY

Tuesday 10th October

It seems like such a long time ago, when, post-retirement and pre-Sicily, I visited Zia's so much. Here I am again going to see her. This has to stop, and it'll have to be gradual. For now, I want to know how she's taken Peppina's death. In the sense that, will she make trouble for me? Does she still think I pushed Peppina? And, if so, will she let it go? I will sustain the accident with my teeth. There is no other way. I need to stave off danger. Though I had enjoyed those walks by the Thames on the way to her house, dejection has taken the place of enjoyment now. Everything looks negative to me. The water is dark and dirty. The shouts of children on the football field irritate me.

When I arrive, Zia is behind the net curtains. I can see her outline. She must have been there waiting for me to arrive. She lets me in, kisses me on both cheeks and says how happy she is to see me again. No cakes today. Zia hasn't had time for baking. We have our usual tea. She is ready to tell me about Bella and Rosa. "Quick before some other women arrive," she says.

The events were related to Zia by Peppina who, in turn, had been told by Young Cushi himself. Nobody else would even dare mutter a word about this 'event,' if they hold their life dear.

The saying 'Let sleeping dogs lie,' in Sicily is extended to: 'Let sleeping dogs lie and let busy bodies lie, too.' You do not poke your nose into anybody else's affairs. If only people were to understand that, they'd keep themselves from entering into potentially lethal situations. You never know who you're talking to. You never know who's connected to whom. The most used sentence in the Sicilian dialect is: 'U ni saccio.' Which means: 'I don't know.' And if, unfortunately, you find yourself anywhere near a crime scene, or get tangled up in anything involving criminals, through no fault of your own, then you have the choice of either keeping your mouth shut, or accepting the dire consequences. That's the reason why the first thing you'd say would be that you didn't see or hear anything. You'd been distracted by something else in the diametrically opposite direction. Something similar came about in Bella and Rosa's case.

When the two arrived at Palermo airport they were intercepted by Young Cushi's men. "Young Cushi know everything. Young Cushi have men in airport. They take photo," Zia says. Then the women got on the long-distance bus to The Village. On the way it stopped at various small towns and villages. At one of these stops a man got on, bought a ticket from the driver and, as he was paying, told him that in five minutes' time he'd pull off at the next lay-by, say the bus had broken down and everyone had to get off. And so it was.

After a while, a minibus and two taxis arrived to pick them up, in the desolate campagna. The two sisters were bundled into one of the taxis. They were driven to a construction site in open fields, where some road building was in process. Only clouds of dust from the gravel as witnesses. Without any ceremony, the women were made to leave the car, were shot and thrown into the roadbed along with their possessions, including suitcases. The roller-compacter moved in to fill the crater with gravel, broken rocks and other fill material. And that was the end of Bella and Rosa. No gravestone, no lying in a peaceful cemetery – but simply decaying under speeding cars, tired lorry drivers, and excited tourists.

"Zia, what a terrible end," I say.

"I know but two sister want ruin me and Susi. I stop them. But picciotti shoot two sister they throw them in hole because they women. They throw men in alive."

On the other hand, I had pushed Peppina and caused her death. I wasn't much better than Zia.

Zia was bright and chirpy, her usual self. I wondered how many times she'd been involved in something like this. Is it possible that with time you get used to it? That you come to feel nothing for the victims, like I don't feel pity for Peppina. Nor any of the others, come to that. Only a sense of closure. Of having done what was right. I suppose if you fix in your mind on the fact that the victims have received their just desserts, then you can convince yourself that it was the right thing to do and have a clean conscience. The other thing I ask myself is how Zia and Susi, who are both practising Catholics, reconcile this with their religion. Zia goes to mass every single Sunday. Does she have no remorse? Or, maybe, as I've often been told, I think too much.

And I probably think too much about trying to deconstruct my feelings. What exactly do I feel? In the end I come to the conclusion that what worries me most is that I, who have strived to be an upright citizen and have taught others to behave well, have it in me to connive in murders and also to actually kill a person. I feel that if I can do it, anyone can. That's what gets me: the fact that human beings are flawed creatures. That it is easy to slip into evil for what we believe is a just cause. That we are only good, if we do not come in contact with evil in the first place. What would anyone else have done in my situation?

The doorbell rings. This time it's a young woman called Irene. "Irene," Zia says, "this my poor sister daughter. Sister die forty-two. Now other sister die in Sicilia. Eleven day ago. Peppina die." Zia beams a look at me.

Irene offers her condolences. Early thirties. Third generation Sicilian, I imagine. Pretty young woman. Dark brown, bobbed hair. Tall, slim. In a red dress, and white and red ankle length boots. Bangles on her wrist, wedding ring on finger. No watch.

"You no worry," Zia says to Irene, "Peppina she rest in peace. She say rosary every day when she alive."

Irene doesn't stay long. Zia gives her something in a bag.

"I see you again next week," Zia says.

Zia accompanies Irene to the front door. Looking around, I notice the pantry door is locked again. I thought I'd managed to persuade her to keep it open.

"Zia," I say pointing to the pantry, "have you gone back to locking that door?"

"Yes, I lock. I have thing in there."

The penny drops. Of course, it isn't about Uncle Tony's body. There is something, or things, she is trying to hide.

"Zia, I have an idea about what you've got in there."

"You no idea, silly girl."

Thinking of my mother's bag in the wardrobe, and Peppina's guns in that metal case under her bed, I say: "You're hiding cash, aren't you? You might even have a gun in there, too."

She blushes. Sits down. And is silent for a minute. "Cuppa tea?"

"No, thanks. Let's not get distracted. I'd like to know

what's in there," I say pointing to the pantry door again. "Please unlock it, Zia."

"You kill Peppina. You push Peppina."

"The door, Zia. We're talking about the door."

"I have little money in there."

"Bella and Rosa knew you had a lot of cash, didn't they? You would never have had to sell your house. And guns? You have guns, don't you?"

"Two. My gun and you mother gun."

"My mother's gun?!"

"Yes, you mother have gun."

"Why?"

"Defend herself."

"Defend herself from what exactly?"

"From no-good people."

"When my mother died, she left me a bag of cash..."

"I know. She leave you cash, and me gun. She say you no know how use gun."

"The only real guns I've ever seen were those under Peppina's bed in Sicily. Two of them."

"Adele bring."

"What? Do you mean Adele's bringing those guns here?"

"Yes, I ask her to bring, they family gun."

"I suppose 'family' has two meanings here."

I'm not sure she gets the pun.

"Family is family," she says.

"Grandmother gun and Peppina gun belong to me," she says.

"Yes, but do you realise that trying to smuggle guns into the country is very dangerous. If found, they could be traced back to you. And your house would be searched by the police. They might even find Uncle Tony's body."

"Ah, you silly girl. Uncle Tony like stay in his house. He love pantry."

"Zia, this is getting ridiculous. Because he liked the pantry when he was alive doesn't mean he wanted to be killed and buried there."

"Cemetery no-good. It rain on grave."

Has Zia gone completely mad? Were all three sisters mad?

"Zia, getting back to those guns, if the authorities trace you, God knows what consequences there'll be for all of us." That, of course, includes me. I am now getting terribly worried.

"They no trace to me. You no worry."

"They will. You're cousins with the Cushi family."

"And you cousin, too." Zia knows I am thinking of myself. Jesus. What on earth is happening?

"You no worry," comes Zia's favourite phrase. "We old tradition. We hundred generation tradition. Nobody can win us. We win. We strong."

"Zia, justice will catch up with us. Adele's just a girl."

"Adele, she clever. She fly Palermo to Milan. Palermo Italy, Milan Italy. No check. She go Switzerland with Swiss car. They no check. She take money. She arrive Thursday."

"What money?"

"Young Cushi money. He keep in Switzerland."

"What? Does she take bags of cash around with her? Where does the money come from?"

"Insurance. And other."

"Insurance? And other?" I repeat.

"They pay. He protect people."

"Zia, it's called extortion."

"Extortion? No. No, extortion. I no understand extortion."

"You do understand."

"You talk difficult," she says. "You posh. You read book."

"No, I distinguish between things, so we know exactly what we're talking about. People pay an insurance premium so that if something bad happens, they are compensated. You are saying that people pay so that nothing bad happens to them. The two are different."

"Second better. You sure nothing bad happen to you."

Jesus. What a mindset.

"And what else does Young Cushi get up to? It's not just extortion, is it? You said there was 'other.'"

"Transport and distribute," she says. "They take from Sicilia to here, to Germany, to France, to other European country. Lot of thing come on boat from Africa to Sicilia."

"What does he transport and distribute?"

"Lot of thing."

"Like? Drugs?" I ask.

"Maybe drug as well. I know he transport food. Best olive oil. Best Sicilian wine."

"So far, we've established that he deals in extortion and the international drug trade. Anything else?"

"No. He no touch prostitution. He think prostitution bad. He church man. If he no on front bench Sunday morning with wife, priest no start mass. No-good people do prostitution."

"Zia, drug trafficking is also done by no-good people. Drugs kill."

"People want drug, they look for drug. Nobody tell them take drug. You no take drug, my children no take drug. Cigarette drug, alcohol drug. You no smoke you no get drunk. People stupid. People kill themself."

"You help kill people," I say.

"We only kill no-good people," Zia says. "You kill Peppina."

"I did NOT kill Peppina," I say in a stern voice. "Please get that idea out of your head. Peppina slipped. There on those cursed stairs right in front of me."

She looks at me as if to say it isn't true. Zia is convinced I pushed her.

"Zia, I'd like to know where my mother got that money from. It was drugs, wasn't it?"

"Distribute."

"So the money my mother left me was 'distribute' money. Great, simply bloody, great."

"I show you mother gun." Zia goes to the pantry, and proudly pulls out a shoe-box. This you mother gun. I give you."

"No, Zia. I don't want it," I say shaking my head.

"Why you no want? Silly girl. This good gun."

"I don't want it because we're not that sort of people."

"You same blood as you mother. We gun sort of people."

"You keep it. I don't want it," I say.

"Good gun self-defence. What you do when robber come in you house?"

"Report him to the police, what else?"

"I shoot him. Ah, police," she sighs, "they no have time for you, they no have time for me. Keep away police. Police dangerous people."

"Cuppa tea?"

"Yes, please. I really need one."

I follow her into the kitchen. "Irene. Does she distribute?"

"Yes. Silly girl, all women come here distribute. But Provvi, no yet. Now Provvi no husband she can distribute. I need speak to Provvi. She can sell to some mother at school. She need money now she have no husband."

"What if she doesn't want to? Not everyone is without morals."

"Provvi have to. I organise kill husband. She must pay lot money to Young Cushi. He have to pay men. No thing free in life. No thing free in death. She distribute, you no worry. She no choice. Good money."

I put my head in my hands. Look at my shoes. Take a deep breath.

"Sorry, does that mean that Olga, Giusy, Bella, Rosa, Angelina and the others I've seen here all distribute?"

"Yes. I tell you already. You no listen to you Zia. Giusy she have hairdresser. She best distribute in salon."

Oh, yes. Those free samples weren't free at all, were they? How could I have been so naïve? No wonder Giusy didn't offer me any, she thinks I am in drugs up to my neck. My reputation stinks by now.

"What about Susi?"

"No. Susi no-good distribute. She have big mouth and many men. She tell to men."

"Zia, so you know about Susi and her men?"

"Zia know. Zia know everything. People tell me. Susi no good take on my patch when I dead. Giusy do that. Giusy clever. You know, I boss of my patch. Other nationality people try take patch from me, but I send picciotti and they soon calm down."

But Susi had been good at keeping the rapes quiet. Zia underestimates her.

"And, is that what my mother was doing? Dealing in drugs?" I'm asking myself, rather than her. So all my university was paid for by filth. And all those clothes, all that spending. Simple filth.

"I was a teacher, a protector of the young. I've spent money that has damaged young people. The easily influenced, who'd do anything to look cool. No, no and no. It can't be."

"If you no money, you no go university. You no teach. You no marry big banker." She changes the subject, "Young Cushi like you. He think you clever woman. He say pity you no part of family when you young."

"You talked to Young Cushi about me?"

"Yes, he talk to you, too. He think you know about distribute."

"That's ridiculous. I don't want anything to do with trafficking drugs."

"You husband rich. You no need distribute. Everyone distribute if they no money and have chance. When I young, I come to England. I clean every public toilet. I clean English people shit. And you mother clean shit. You think all easy. Nobody give us no thing."

"Zia, look I know it hasn't been easy for you, or for my mother. But there are a lot of modest people out there, who never turn to crime."

"When you born you mother and father live in one room in house of Englishwoman. You mother alone with you all time. She eat only in kitchen. Englishwoman no let you mother in living room. You mother no go out. She no money. She in room or kitchen all day with you. You mother love you."

"No, she did not," I say sternly. "Just don't say that again. She hated me. Whipped and hit me black and blue. Made my life a misery. You don't know how Susi and me have suffered. You and my mother chose to come here. You chose to do that. Not us. We were born here. We were innocent children and our parents took out their frustration on us. Zia, you're doing my head in. I've got to go."

"Not Zia fault. Zia hit by Tony, you forget. You mother no say to me she hit you."

"Well, she wouldn't would she? And Peppina did, too. They forced me into an arranged marriage. I lost a kidney because I wanted to come back home. Zia we're a terrible family, can't you see that? You have to stop what you're doing. Our family moved to England for a better life. Being criminals is not being better. Being better is not only about money."

"You no be better without money," Zia says. "I no know about you kidney. You no tell me."

"Look, I really have to go," but I sit there instead.

"You come back Thursday. Adele here. You talk to Adele. If you no come, Young Cushi be cross with you."

Yes, of course. All this respect business. Be careful not to slight them, otherwise they'll make you pay for it. I will come and see Adele, but that will be the last time I go to Zia's. I have to get out of this viper's nest. Without giving any of them reason to hold anything against me.

"He no know you kill Peppina. Young Cushi fond of Peppina. Better he no know. He love Peppina all his life. Since he in short short. He love Peppina and he love me. If I tell Young Cushi you kill Peppina, he kill you, for sure," she makes a cutting gesture across her throat.

"But I didn't kill her," I say again, "and you can't prove otherwise. It's your word against mine."

"Yes, what you think? He believe you word, or he believe my word?"

"Zia, keep in mind what you have in the pantry. Let's stop this, please!"

The situation is black for me. If she decides to tell Young Cushi, he will turn against me, but I am more worried he will harm my family. Organise an accident. We can't go to Italy any more. We must sell the chalet in the Dolomites. Also, I have to cover my tracks, just in case. I don't think Zia will say anything to Young Cushi. I need to get her to promise she won't utter a word about this to anyone. What do I do in case she doesn't co-operate? I have to start laying the ground.

More than once, I've seen old people being suffocated in films with a pillow. I need to find out more about that.

FIFTY-ONE

Wednesday 11th October

Susi and I meet inside our usual Italian restaurant. I am already sitting at a table with an aperitif in front of me. Punctuality was never Susi's strong point. Ten minutes after the appointed time, she comes bouncing over. White bandage dress. I think that's what it's called – so tight must be uncomfortable. Though it's stretch. "You want to watch how you sit in that dress," I say. Low cut with two lunar shaped bulges trying to get out, and thick-off-the-shoulder straps. Vertiginous black stilettos.

"Darling, good to see you again," she says.

"Oh, it's so good to see you again, too. You're looking good. Wasn't necessary to get dolled up like that. You're only having dinner with me, you're not on the pull now."

"You never know, Mary. Always good to be smart. You never know who you might meet, and when."

The greasy-haired waiter comes over. "What will it be for madam?" he says to Susi, tunnel vision straight down her cleavage. She notices, smiles coquettishly and says, pointing to my drink with a long purple-varnished nail, "I'll have one of those."

I'm embarrassed that she's flirting with a man half her age. "He could be your son, you know?"

"Yes, but he isn't, is he?"

I turn the conversation to Sicily. "Terrible time you had in Sicily. All those funerals. What a holiday, eh? The ending of my holiday was traumatic witnessing Peppina's death. That was so sad."

"I know," she says. "Poor Peppina, dying in her own house like that."

"Problem is accidents come suddenly. One moment you're here, and the next you're gone," I say, echoing those women paying condolences while Peppina's body was still warm.

"Are you ever going to tell your mum about the rapes?"

"What's the point? Let's let sleeping dogs lie, eh? Anyway, it would only upset her. She doesn't need that now she's old and weak. By the way have you seen my mum yet?"

"Yes, I went to see her yesterday. She's OK, isn't she? But, you're right. She is a bit weak. I noticed she was having trouble breathing. She had to sit down once or twice because she was giddy. Don't mention it to her though, she got very uppity when I talked about her health."

"Yeah, she's weak. I didn't notice the breathing problem, though."

"She must have caught a bug on the plane back," I say. "Takes a few days to surface. Even a mild illness can be lethal in old folk, you know?"

"Yeah, I know. And on top of that she's still grieving about Peppina."

"Time is a great healer," I say. "It will mellow with time. I told your mum that she can have Peppina's estate. I don't want anything."

"I don't want that house and land, either," she says. "Who's going to buy them?"

"Well, your mum's very attached to the house. It's her childhood home. She's the only sister left, so it rightfully belongs to her now. Italian hereditary law passes property down to me, even though my mother's dead she still has a right to her share. Not like in England, is it?"

"I don't know," she says.

"I'm not sure either, come to that. I'll have to ask Humps. He knows everything."

"Maybe my brothers'll do something with the house."

"Silvio and Stefano haven't been there for years, have they?" I say.

"Silvio has. Franca has family in The Village. She grew up

there don't forget. She has old friends, like Patrizia – they went to school together."

Of course. Silvio was in the transport and distribute trade as well. How stupid of me not to make the Patrizia-Franca connection. What could be easier than handing out little plastic bags of powder from an ice-cream van? Silvio went from your ordinary, kill-me-if-I-hear-that-jingle-again, ice-cream man, to a man at the head of a popular ice-cream brand. Who financed that? Whippy flakes? I don't think so.

"Susi, in confidence, have you ever taken drugs?"

"Course not. I'd tell you if I did. I've never even seen drugs, never mind take them. You know what my drugs are, don't you?"

"Men."

Susi knew nothing of Zia's doings like I didn't know about my mother's.

"How's your brother Stefano getting on up north?" I ask.

"Oh, they're fine."

"They're in the restaurant business, aren't they?"

"Yeah, they're doing really well. They've got three restaurants now. His wife, Romina, is the boss there. I've never seen a man so scared of his wife. That's how I'd be if I ever got married again. I'd keep the reins on him," she says.

We giggle.

"Not surprised she's keeping him under her thumb. What, after nearly abandoning her at the altar."

"No worries, Mary. She got her own back."

"Both your brothers have done well, haven't they?"

"Yeah, well they always were determined. Me? I'm just having fun. We're all different, eh?"

"Very much so. There's a lot to be said for your way of life."

What I meant was keeping out of the 'family business.'

"Oh, yeah, I've had a smashing time. Still am," she says.

The waiter turns up to take our order. You'd think that the menu is stuffed down Susi's décolleté. He is studying it quite hard now. "That's off the menu tonight," he says when I ask for their Uccelli scappati.

"Won't you look at the arse on that," Susi says, watching the waiter's pert bum walking back to the kitchen. We giggle again.

"Hey, the application for the grant to set up a women's helpline has been approved. Seba phoned me last night. We're meeting up next week to discuss the project."

"Wow." I say. "That's some achievement, especially as the government are pulling the purse strings tight in this period."

"He put the claim in years ago," she says, "and it's only come through now."

"Come at a convenient time, if you ask me?" I say. "Susi I would have loved to have worked with you on that project. To help women in need would have been so rewarding. But I'm not sure now. I need some time to think."

"Oh, come on, Mary," she says, "it'll keep you busy. I tell you what, why don't you manage the telephonists. That shouldn't be too much work. Appoint the right ones and so on. I don't know how many we'll need at this stage. We'll work it out as we go along."

"I need to think about it, Susi. I've got some sorting out to do. I'll let you know OK?"

She leans over the table a little, and says: "Hey, Mary, let me tell you about my recent lovers."

"Go on, then," I say.

Andy first – a teacher, poet, abstract artist, trombone player – not her sort, too arty farty. His great involvement in the arts, according to Susi, was down to the fact that he didn't have a dick. "Mary, I shit you not, it was a spread-out blancmangey mess, with a little pinnacle on top."

Agog. I try to imagine it.

"I pitied him, Mary. Fancy being so unlucky. I mean, what's the point of being a man if you haven't got a proper dick. Poor man nearly cried when I stared at it."

It's no good arguing with her by saying that life wasn't all about sex. I've tried that, many a time, and got nowhere. This man has lots of other interests. But, you just have to let her talk about her new lovers, until she's got it out of her system.

"Then what happened?" I ask.

"He went to the bathroom and took a tablet, must've been a Viagra. I wouldn't know, no-one's had to use one with me before." She laughs. "And, you know what?"

"What?"

"When he came back, it was like a normal one. He has a wife and two kids, but imagine being married to that!"

"Poor bloke," I say, shaking my head as if to say 'life can be so unfair, can't it?'"

"Did I tell you about Jim, the black banker?"

"Yes, you did."

"You should have seen it, Mary. It was ginormous. Must have been about half-a-yard long." She tries to figure out what length half-a-yard is by holding up her index fingers and moving them along an imaginary line.

We giggle like a couple of schoolgirls. "That's impossible, Susi."

A man at a nearby table, early-sixties, looks over. "See, you're attracting attention," I say laughingly. When his head turns back in the opposite direction, she whispers loudly, "I always did like a man in a nice suit!"

"Stop it," I say. She was way over the top. Or, some might say, it is me who's too prudish. The truth is that although I think I'm above such talk, I listen with interest.

"Haven't told you about the Detective Chief Inspector yet. Mary, you should have seen it. Short and wide it was. About the diameter of the rim of this coffee cup..."

We are interrupted by the waiter bringing us two flutes of Prosecco.

"Oh," I say, "very nice but we didn't order them."

"Offered by the gentleman over there," the waiter says, pointing to the man in the suit.

"I couldn't possibly," I say.

"Come on, Mary, don't be such a misery guts, I'm having mine even if you're not drinking yours."

"OK. Well, if that's the case, I'll keep you company. Let's seize the glass," I say, as I reach over for mine. I figure out that he'll most probably get his value for money from Susi.

In no time at all, the suit is sitting at our table. And guess what? He is all over me. I glance at my watch. "Oh, it's nearly ten o'clock," I say, "my husband's picking me up soon. He might actually be waiting in the car. I'll pop out and have a look." Once outside, I phone Humps. "Darling, can you come and fetch me, please?"

"So sorry," I say to the suit, my husband's out there. I have to go. Nice meeting you. Susi, I'll give you a buzz whenever."

Out I go, leaving them there laughing, flirting and drinking more Prosecco. They have a bottle of it on the table now. No doubt I'll hear about his reproductive parts in due course.

FIFTY-TWO

Thursday 12th October

Adele is pleased to see me. I give her a hearty welcome. Her mother, Patrizia, has sent me a beautiful jewellery box, engraved with magna-Greek gods. "It's silver," Adele says. I can't refuse it. That would be seen as a total lack of respect towards her, and her family. The gesture would be taken to mean I don't want to have anything to do with them; that I refuse them and what they stand for. These are dangerous people. I have to conjure up every shred of diplomacy I have in me. "I can't believe how beautiful it is," I say. "You must thank your mother very much."

"You can call her yourself, if you want. She'd love to hear from you. Here's her number," Adele says, passing me a business card saying she's an art dealer.

"I make ricotta cannoli cakes again this morning," Zia says. Celebrate Adele arrive in England. Later I give you two to take to you husband. Cuppa tea?"

This has gone beyond a pastime. Beyond a cosy cup of tea and home-made cakes. That 'cuppa tea?' is beginning to grate.

"My mother has great respect for you, you know?" Adele says.

Wrong kind of respect, I think.

"Yes, I'm fond of your mother, too. We were best friends during that time I spent in Sicily. We shared all our girly secrets."

"I'd hate to think what they were," Adele says.

"Well, I'm not letting on," I laugh.

Zia comes back with her tray. "We tell Maria, you other present for her," Zia says to Adele, while she turns to me and gives me a sly grin – one that reminds me of Peppina's. I've never seen, or maybe noticed, that smirk on Zia's face before.

"Yes, it's exciting," Adele replies. "Look, I have here Peppina and your grandmother's guns."

"This Peppina gun," Zia says, picking one up. "This my mother gun. I tell Maria take her mother gun. She no want."

"It's a very old model," Adele says.

"She keep souvenir of her poor mother," Zia says, "she must take gun. She must respect mother."

Adele looks at the gun and says: "This old model wouldn't

be much use. The only thing it's any good for is as an ornament. Like in a glass-fronted cabinet. Dad's got a great gun collection, up in the attic. You must have your mother's for keepsake," Adele shoves it into my hands.

"Yeah, you take gun and two cannoli for you husband when you go," Zia says to me.

Defeated, I take the gun. I'll throw it in the Thames on my way back home. Drop it into the Thames when nobody is looking.

"Giusy take my patch business," Zia says, "Adele come to speak to Giusy. She good girl. She work with me. She got experience. She clever. My Susi no so clever. Silvio and Stefano work with me. They do good business. But they no time to take my patch. They wife busy busy."

"Now, I hope that day is as far away as possible before you go, Zia" Adele says, Adele gives Zia a kiss.

If Zia tells Young Cushi, I am the cause of Peppina's death, he'll believe her, rather than me. I can't antagonise him. Uncle Tony's body in this house was no longer insurance for me at all. I couldn't use that now. First, because Young Cushi knew about it. His father had buried Uncle Tony there. If I disclosed that, I'd end up with Bella and Rosa under the motorway.

Have the three venomous sisters won? They have struck through Zia. They have slithered towards me, tracked down their prey and pounced on me. Am I locked in their tight grip again? Drawn into their world? I have been a good student, a good teacher, a good wife and mother. All in vain. The evil in them has ultimately raised its ugly head in me. I'd let down the good people in my life: Auntie Marge, Humps, my daughters, Mark and little Benjamin.

I manage to get away and take the gun, irritated that I will have to go to Zia's again. But the next time must really be the last time.

"Humps, now that I'm retired, I'd love to go and live in our lovely thatched cottage in Dorset. What's the good of having it, if we don't make the most of it? All that peace. I so long for some peace and quiet."

"Well that's unexpected. I'm still working, you know that. And you've always been happy in London."

"I know but I need to get away now. I need to get away to think straight. I'd miss London an awful lot if I couldn't get here when I wanted to. But it's perfectly feasible to get to London and back in a day."

"What brought all this on, then? You've always loved London."

"I know but I need to get away now. I need to get away from the whole Sicilian community. I was wiser when I was younger and steered clear of them all. Now I've let my defences down, and look what people we've been in contact with. I want to go back to being out on a limb. I don't want to see them again. I'll go and say goodbye to Zia. Then that's it."

"You're being rather harsh, aren't you? Zia's not that bad, surely. And Susi's the sister you never had. It's the people in Sicily, you want to be away from. And you're far enough here."

"It's not that easy, darling. They're all linked. Having contact with one of them is having contact with all of them. I'll miss Susi. But she badgers me about going to see her mum. I need a complete break."

He lowered his head and looked at me over his glasses. Like he does when he's disagreeing with me.

"Look, darling," I say, "I don't want to keep on digging up reasons why, but please just take it from me that we'll be better off in Dorset. When there's a play or exhibition here we want to see, or if we want to visit the kids, we'll come up for the day or stay for a night or two."

"It'll probably be more than one or two nights we'll be staying. But, Mary, if that's what you want, we can spend more time down there. It's an easy move. Just take a few clothes with you and go and stay there."

"And what about your work?"

"I'll see how I can shift my work around so I can be there as much as possible. I can probably get away with being in the office once or twice a week. I can do a lot of work from home, like writing, conference preparations and even take phone calls. But I'll have to travel back here for meetings."

"Oh, that's great," I look around the flat. "This place is far too big for us, anyway. I'm not getting any younger and soon won't be able to clean it all properly. I'm tired. I want some peace, reading, walking, cooking and so on. And you can go back to a bit of gardening. Like you did when we first got married and had a garden."

"Now, that does appeal to me," he says, "but I'm not happy about not having a bolthole in London. We could get a smaller place here. You might want to come back, darling. You never know."

"I don't think so. Also, my retirement has made me think back through my life. It's been a turning point, if you like. I'd like to do some writing. My head is full of ideas. That will take a lot of time and I need to be in a place with no distract-ions. The calming effect of fresh sea air."

"To Dorset, it'll be then. Lots of fresh air and exercise, walking in the woods and by the sea. What could be better?"

"And, also we need to sell our chalet in Italy. I don't want to go to Italy any more," I say.

"Now, that's overdoing it," Humps puts his foot down. "Let's gradually switch over part-time to Dorset first. Then we'll think about the chalet. You're a little depressed at the moment. You haven't been happy lately. We can't take important decisions like this now."

FIFTY-THREE

Friday 13th October

This is the final time I am going to Zia's. I do hope that she has no other visitors there. Zia opens the door, kisses me. I go in and Giusy is there, all tits and holy cross. She is about to leave. That's a relief. I'm not in the mood for false chit-chat.

"Zia, I have something I need to talk to you about. It's about this Peppina business. I've been worried that you've got into your head that I was somehow responsible for her death, which is totally unfounded. It's been keeping me awake at night."

"Ah, Peppina business! You no like Peppina, Peppina no like you. You go down stair, she die."

"Yes, but the point is, I need to know what your view is about how she died. Do you think I killed her? I came here for that purpose. I want an answer. A promise, even."

God knows, I will kill Zia before Young Cushi gets me.

"I do no thing. I no know about you kidney. You no tell me. You daughter my poor sister. What I do?" Zia answers her own question, "I no tell Young Cushi. He second cousin. You are what left of my sister. I think you push, but if you say she slip, she slip." Zia often came up with these contorted contradictions. In essence, she was saying that she thinks I pushed Peppina, but she wouldn't tell anyone that.

"Thank you," I say to Zia, and kiss her. "So you promise?"

"I promise. Look I swear on Bible. I no tell anyone," she moves to fetch it.

"No, Zia, that won't be necessary. You've promised. I take your word for it."

"You know word of Sicilian is like pillar in cement with steel inside," she says.

Zia is well up on Sicilian construction work. That brings all sorts of connotations to my mind.

"Yes, secrecy is in our blood," I say. "And, I promise I will never tell on you or Susi," I glance over at the pantry. Which is under lock and key again.

"We let dog asleep lie," she says.

"Yes, let's let sleeping dogs lie. And sleeping bodies lie, too: Bella, Rosa, Giulio, Adriano, Peppina and, of course, Uncle Tony, too."

"Yes, they all rest in peace. I bless them. God look after soul of them," Zia says. Zia is completely without remorse. At least, I have a little guilt.

"I'm not too sure about their resting in peace," I say. "They are probably turning over in their graves crying out for revenge."

"Ah, revenge? Revenge for living people. If you have saint in paradise, revenge easy. If you have no saint in paradise, you lose."

Others might not understand this, but a Sicilian does. Her 'saint in paradise' is Young Cushi. It used to be Old Cushi. With a little help from her saints, Zia had got rid of her husband and decimated his family. Another reason why Zia is letting me off the hook is that she knows that if I had it in me to kill Peppina, I could do it again – I could very well kill her. She is now quite frail.

"Cuppa tea?"

"No, Zia. I have to go. I've lots of organising to do. Humphrey and I are moving to the south coast."

She is shocked.

"You London girl. What you do there?" she says, nearly crying.

I ignore her reaction.

"Oh, there's lots to do there. I'll be reading, walking, writing."

"I tell you, quiet life not for you. What you write?"

"I don't know. I'll find something. My head's always

buzzing with ideas. A book probably."

"You no see you Zia. Me family."

"I need to get away from the hustle and bustle of life here," I say. She knows what I mean. And she knows I won't be back to see her.

I kiss her on both cheeks, go down the path to her gate, and fasten it firmly behind me. Wave goodbye to her. She's standing there in the porch of her house in her pink slippers. Small, grey, and frail. Nothing like you'd imagine a murderer.

"Zia wait for you," she calls after me, "you come back and see you Zia."

Without answering, I walk away with conviction. Without looking back.

During the weekend, Humps and I talk about going to Dorset. He understands that I need to get away. Actually, he doesn't look too happy either. "Are you OK?" I ask.

"Yes, yes, just tired. You know, end of the week and all that."

"We'll have a good rest this weekend. It will do you the world of good," I say.

"I certainly agree to that," he says.

By Sunday afternoon, Humps perks up a little, so I think I can ask him, if he minds if I go to Dorset tomorrow. He is surprised at first, but readily agrees. "I'll come down after you whenever work permits," he says.

"Great," I say, "I don't want to be away from you for too long. I'll go and pack a few things. I'll take the Golf. Is there any petrol in it?"

"I'm not sure," he says, "we haven't used it for a long time."

"Well, I hope the battery's still working, then."

FIFTY-FOUR

Monday 16th October

The Golf starts up and I set off for our cottage. Driving along the M3, I think that I will stay in Dorset for as long as it takes me to sort myself out. Think through everything that happened in Sicily. Hopefully, Humps can join me soon, then we'll have a lovely time together.

Everything just as we left it last time we were here. The grandfather clock in the entrance shows the right time: 1.25. I open the living room curtains to let the daylight in. The lawn is overgrown, weeds everywhere. I must remind our odd-job man, Nigel, to come and cut it. He doesn't seem to have been for a while. I open the windows to get some fresh air into the place. It's just started to drizzle. There's wood stacked up on both sides of the fireplace. It's quite chilly. I could light a fire when I've been to the local shop to stock up on food. I must get a bunch of fresh flowers to brighten up the living room. There are little bulges in the wallpaper due to humidity. We must have it stripped off, waterproof the walls, and put up new wallpaper. A white background with little coloured flowers dotted about on it would be nice. Which bag did I put my umbrella in? Ah, here it is. I think I'll have a brandy before going out. I get a heavy crystal tumbler from the drinks' cabinet and pour a smidgen into it. I hold the bottle up to the light – there's not much left, I'll buy another one.

When I get to the gate, Yvonne from next door comes out and says: "Maria, I saw your car in the drive and thought you must be here."

"Yes, I only arrived about an hour ago," I say.

"Well, I was saying to Henry, we haven't seen Maria and Humphrey for a while. Welcome back."

"Thanks, Yvonne. Humphrey isn't actually with me, I came down on my own. He'll be here as soon as his work allows him to be."

"Oh, well, you enjoy yourself, dear. Do pop round and say hello to Henry. He gets so lonely now he can't get around much."

Henry used to work for the ministry of defence. All very hush-hush work. Now he's bedridden.

"Of course, I will," I say. "I'll pop round after dinner this evening. Is 7.30 alright with you?"

It is still raining. There's nobody else on the beach. The only company I have are the gulls squawking and the waves breaking. I fight with my umbrella as it turns inside-out several times. Humps hasn't answered my text message yet – he's usually very quick. Maybe he's busy working. After we came back from Sicily, Humps shunned me when I tried to hug him. That had never happened before. He was enthusiastic about my coming to Dorset. We've had such a good marriage. The trip to Sicily might have changed all that. Humps and my daughters now know the truth about my family. In a sense, it's a relief. Emma reacted like me when I was a girl, she wants nothing to do with Sicily. Shut it out. Whereas Clara has embraced it. Humps? I don't know which way it'll go. He's seen me in another context, and he may not like that added facet. Another reason for coming to Dorset is that I want to see how long it takes him to follow me here. The ball is in his court. If he's here after a couple of days, all will be good, but if he doesn't come then I'll have to look reality in the face. Resign myself to the idea that he doesn't want me any more. The rain is much heavier now. I make my way back, stop at the deserted bus shelter to check if there's a text from Humps. Nothing yet.

"How's Humphrey," Henry asks.

"Oh, he's fine," I say. "He's very busy nowadays."

"So, when's he coming down from the big smoke?"

"Maybe in a couple of days. It depends on his workload."

"When he's here, he'll have to come and have a little tipple one evening. Even two or three. Evenings that is. And tipples as well..." he jokes. Yvonne and I laugh with him.

"I'm sure he'll love that," I say thinking how much nicer our neighbours here are than in London.

"Nigel hasn't mown our lawn, or tidied up our garden," I say. I must phone him.

"Oh, of course, you don't know," Yvonne says, "the poor chap died."

"What!" I say.

"Yes, the poor man had a big heart-attack," Yvonne says. "I tried to phone you a few times about a couple of weeks back. I thought you must have been on holiday. We've found a young man to do our garden. I tried phoning to ask if you wanted yours doing as well. His wife takes on cleaning jobs, if you're interested. Mind you, we hid our number, so you wouldn't have known I phoned; habit, you know. Then our son and his family came to stay, and I forgot all about it."

"Thank you for trying," I say, "I'm so sorry about Nigel. Can't have been more than fifty, surely. He was a jovial sort. It must have been awful for his family – all of a sudden like that. I'd love the new man's phone number. The cottage can do with a good clean as well."

"Where did you go on holiday?" Henry asks.

"To Italy," I say.

"We love Italy, don't we?" Henry says to Yvonne looking for consent.

"We spent some happy times there on holiday, didn't we, love?" Yvonne says.

Henry nods and says: "Those beautiful rolling hills of Tuscany, the wine and food. We love it. We could go back, couldn't we, love?"

"Oh, I'd like that," Yvonne says.

We chat for a while longer, then I leave.

It's 9.30 and Humps hasn't answered. I try to phone home. He's not there. Then I try his mobile. He's not answering. I switch on the TV, see if there's anything worth watching. I'm so confused, I can't take in a thing, instead I get ready for bed. Have a shower, brush my teeth, and apply night cream. I'm getting so old, I think, as I look in the mirror. I go to bed with my Kindle, place my mobile on Humps's pillow in case he calls. I scroll through the items on my Kindle and settle for Shakespeare's Sonnets. No way I can concentrate on a novel. I then lie awake listening to the wind and a tree branch scratching against the window. Sleep overtakes me. It is about midnight when a text message wakes me. It's Humps: *Sorry darling for not replying before. Mayhem at bank. Been in meeting all evening. We have huge problem. Will call you in the morning. Good night. xxx*

FIFTY-FIVE

Tuesday 17th October

After my porridge, I try to ring Humps. The house phone rings on and on. At last, he answers. "Hi, darling."

"Oh, my darling. What happened yesterday? I've been so worried." I say.

"Absolute chaos at the bank. We don't know which way to turn."

"Why? What's happened?"

"I'd rather not talk about it on the phone, I'll tell you all about it when I'm there." His comment briefly reminds me of Zia not wanting to talk about important issues on the phone.

"Fine," I say, relieved that he seems to feel the same about me. "I'll have a nice dinner waiting for you. And Henry next door's looking forward to having a chat and a drink with you."

"Have to love you and leave you, darling. Must get to the bank. I might be able to come tomorrow evening, if things settle down at work."

"That's brilliant," I feel revitalised. I phone the new gardener. His wife answers. She says that he's busy all day today, that he might find time tomorrow to mow the lawn, but nothing more than that. The rest of the garden will have to wait. But she can come over to clean our cottage late afternoon. She'll take her kids to her mother after she's picked them up from school, then come here.

FIFTY-SIX

Wednesday 18th October – evening

The Mercedes has just come into the driveway. I rush out to greet Humps. He's happy to see me, but his face is drawn. He can't have had much sleep. Maybe he hasn't eaten much either. Because I didn't know what time he was arriving, I made vegetable lasagne, which will keep in the oven.

He looks unsettled. I know my Humps. "Darling, what on earth's the matter?"

He sits down on the sofa in his dark blue suit. He's come straight from work. That's a first because usually when he gets home, he comes and says hello to me, then changes into his jeans. He sighs.

"Darling you must tell me."

"There's an enormous problem at work."

"Well," I say, shaking my head, "what is it? Tell me."

"It's not easy..."

"Maybe but just try and tell me."

His voice shakes: Money's gone missing – a great big

hole."

"Oh, my God! How much?"

"Just over fifteen million pounds."

"You what! Fifteen million? And how did it happen?"

"We have some dormant accounts and..."

"What's a dormant account?"

"When there's been no movement on an account for a long time. Maybe because the holder is elderly and doesn't need the money, or for whatever other reason."

"And?"

What he says next chills me.

"And, together with some of my colleagues, we invested money on the stock market and lost it. Problem was that we had to keep taking more and more money and investing it to cover the losses, hence making more losses. As I said, we've now lost fifteen million."

"Just a moment. Let me get this straight. What you're saying is that you took money, which wasn't yours, from savers' bank accounts, and took risks with it."

His head is in his hands, and his gaze is fixed on the fireplace. "If we keep throwing money at it, the loss will probably get bigger. Essentially, that's it"

"What do you mean, 'that's it'?" I get up and pace up and down the living room. "Humps you've stolen money. Money you don't even need for God's sake."

"It went wrong."

"I know it's gone wrong. But, you stole money!" I'm livid, I wring my hands. He sits there like a battered dog.

I put my hands in my hair and say: "Never, ever, in my life could I have imagined that you of all people would steal! I'm astounded."

"I'm sorry, but it went wrong."

"So, who are the other people involved?"

"Essentially, Frank and Jimmy. We operated together. But

all the members of the board know about it."

"Great, bloody great! Because you're all senior you cover each other's arses. Have you done this before?"

"Yes, well, not so often, but it always worked out."

"That is to say..." I wave my hand towards myself, meaning come on tell me the rest.

"Exactly as I said. We've done it before..."

"...and you always got away with it." I finish his sentence.

He looks down at his Church's.

"So, you three contrived, and made illegal money although you have big salaries, bonuses, and perks." He's now looking at me, an imploring look, as if I shouldn't be so harsh.

"...and what did you do with this money?"

"Well, we're running three houses, and two cars, for starters, we've been on expensive holidays, the girls' school fees... and we didn't always make that much."

"Are you telling me that you've been doing this since our daughters were girls? Jesus, I don't believe it. Tell me it isn't true."

He fixed his gaze on the flowers on the pine chest. "I'm sorry."

"Yes, and so am I. Bloody downright bloody sorry. And all the time when I was feeling guilty about not telling you of the dirty dealings in my family, you were thieving. It had to go wrong sooner or later, didn't it? If the authorities find out, you're finished. It'll be all over the papers. You might even go to prison."

"I suppose so."

"And, you couldn't stop, could you? And, another thing. You can't say you did it to keep me. I grew up in poverty, so poor that when I was little I had ice on the inside of my bedroom window in the mornings in winter. My father only let me have the infra-red on while I changed into my pyjamas... I can do hardship... No, no, no, our lifestyle more or less matched our earnings. You didn't spend it all on me and the girls. What else did you do with the money you made?"

"Well... public relations... We, um, the main reason why we did it was so we could organise PR parties – all the senior people at the bank took part."

"Parties! Parties!" I am seething. "You organised parties! Your bank took money from accounts and organised parties? So these were the so-called working dinners, were they?"

"I'm sorry. I should have told you they were parties."

"Where were these parties held? I don't remember being invited to any parties."

"In the big plush London hotels. Wives weren't invited. It was policy, no wives or girlfriends. We invited businessmen, politicians, oligarchs, CEOs, high-ranking civil servants... all influential men."

"Just a moment! I don't for one second believe that you organised parties for men only. Were there no women there at all?"

He swallowed hard and didn't answer.

"So..." I say.

"We procured women from escort agencies..."

"What?" I start crying.

He gets up from the sofa and comes over to where I'm standing. Putting his arms round me, and holding me close, he says: "Mary, I'm so sorry."

So he's been to bed with these escorts? That's why he feels he needs to come over and hug me – to deaden the blow.

"No, Humps, no. Please tell me it isn't true," I say sobbing into his chest, "please tell me you haven't been with other women. Please. I couldn't stand it."

"Mary, I'm so sorry."

I untangle myself from him, pushing him away from me by hitting his chest with my fists. I go over to the flowers, grab the vase and, with all my might, throw it straight through the window. Shards land both inside and outside the cottage.

"Please don't..." he says.

"Please don't what? Don't you dare touch me," I growl at him. "Just don't fucking touch me." I grab the gold carriage clock off the mantelpiece and throw that through the second pane of glass together with the Wedgwood ornaments, and the Capodimonte figurines. The fireplace tool set is next, I hurl it through the third pane. Then, I seize the frame holding the photo of us on a cruise ship, happy and smiling; I yank the back off, rip the picture out, tear it into little pieces, and throw them up in the air. I slam the frame on the floor and stamp on it. He is gob smacked. "Yes, that's right," I howl out: "It's my Sicilian temperament. I'm letting it all gush out. None of your stiff-fucking-upper-fucking-lip. I'm going back to London!"

"You're in no state to drive, please..." he pleads.

"Don't you dare touch me," I hiss. "Don't you fucking dare touch me."

I storm to the corridor, take the keys off the table, get my coat and handbag, look back and shout: "And don't you dare fucking follow me back to our flat." I slam the front door behind me, kick it, then get into the Mercedes and drive away.

FIFTY-SEVEN

Thursday 19th October 2017

I sobbed into my pillow during the night. My eyes are red-raw. I must pull myself together. Calm down. Straighten out my thoughts. I pat cold water on my face, then make my porridge. I pick at it for a while, then go and throw it down the toilet. What am I going to do? I need to speak to someone about Humps betraying me. Is there anyone other than Zia? Emma or Clara? No, he's their father, they shouldn't know about this. That would shatter the image of their precious daddy. Susi? She'll wonder what the fuss is about.

It has to be Zia. I go to her, see if she'll open the door even if it's morning. I ring the bell and then shout "Zia," through the letter box knowing that she can't hear me through two doors.

"Ah, Maria!" she says opening the door. "I no think you come back to see you Zia again. What matter with you? You look like ghost."

"Zia, I'm gutted."

"What you problem? You white. You no worry. Zia sort for you."

"It's Humps," I say walking down the corridor, past the row of popes, to the living room. "He's been with escorts."

"What you say escort?" she doesn't understand.

"Prostitutes, bagascie, whores, troie, tarts, puttane, sluts, zoccule..." I shout.

"Minghia!"

"Yes, minghia, Zia. I could strangle him."

Zia points a finger at me and wags it four times, to the beat of each word, as she spells out: "You – no – kill – him."

"Zia! The thought never crossed my mind. Really! I would never kill Humps. Not even now that he turns out to be as big a minghiuni as any other man."

"You never say never." And imagine my surprise when Zia starts singing: "Only you, and you alone can fill my heart with love... A-ha, A-ha."

Zia, stop it. Are you taking my pain seriously, or what?"

"You sing no more love song." Zia doesn't know, but she's just near enough quoted James Joyce. "I tell you he put it in, and you say me: 'No, no, my Hump he good man...' Only you, and you alone... "

"Zia be serious I've had my life shattered."

"Oh, you shatter, " she says. "I tell you what is shatter. My husband Tony is shatter. He no tall, he no handsome, he no rich. And he hit me. That is shatter!"

She's even getting angry at me now. She's impossible, but at least I can speak to her and know she won't tell anybody.

"So, he futtiri puttane," she says, "you go home give him nice kiss, you futtiri another man. What the problem?"

"What, Zia? Are you saying I should go with another man?"

"I sure, it make you feel better. If you find man you like, you futtiri him. Occhio per occhio, dente per dente, *meaning:* eye for an eye, tooth for a tooth, she says quoting the Bible.

"But you've always been against adultery."

"This time it no adultery, this time it revenge. Capisti?"

"I can't," I cry.

"Why you no can?"

"I love him."

"Ah, you silly girl. Next week when you get over, you find nice man."

"Zia! Uncle Tony cheated on you. Did you go with someone else?"

She lowers her eyes: "Maybe."

Oh, God. Am I the most boring person in my family? Apart from Emma that is.

"Now you go buy three fish and chip on corner shop, and we have lunch. Adele say she come back for lunch. I no have time for cook."

"Yes, of course, Zia. Is Adele still here?"

"Yeah, she go shopping. She tell me, she here for lunch."

Zia puts the fish and chips on vividly-coloured, flowery plates.

"I pop Adele plate in oven." But as soon as Zia is about to do so, Adele rings the doorbell. She comes in loaded with shopping – all designer items in large paper carrier bags. Well, she'll have no problems getting through customs in Palermo when they see her name.

"I had to get a taxi back, I couldn't face going on the underground with all this shopping," she says. Anything will look good on her tallish, slim figure.

"You come eat. Fish and chip ready for you."

Adele comes and kisses us both. As we're eating, I wonder when I can tell Zia about the missing money at the bank. But, I can trust Adele, and I might well get some help.

"When we went to Sicily, your father said that if I ever needed help I was to ask."

"Sure," Adele says, "we're family. Fire away."

"It's just that... there's money missing in Humphrey's bank. There's a gaping hole of more than fifteen million pounds."

"Stra-minghia!" Zia says.

Adele is eating chips with her fingers, one by one. At the sound of fifteen million a chip stops in mid-air. "Wow! Are you kidding me?!"

"Humps and his colleagues have been taking money from accounts to organise PR events. They bought and sold shares. They've done it before, but this time they lost money instead of making it. They might have lost money before but managed to recover it. This time it's got out of hand."

"Vaffanculo, when you husband rob, he rob big," Zia says. "He no rob olive jar from supermarket."

"You're telling me!" Adele says.

"I know, I was shocked when he told me. All the top-tier people know about it at the bank," I say.

"I'm not shocked that they took it, bankers play about with money. But I'm shocked that they lost it, whoa!" Adele says. "We should be able to help you out. Leave it with me. I have an idea. I'll talk to dad about it when he gets here. Does this bank have an Italian branch?"

"I don't know. I'll find out," I say.

"Don't worry, I'll find out myself. Mom and dad are getting here on Monday. They're coming to see the premises Clara found for the art gallery. Sounds like it's a great location. Did Clara tell you?"

"Eh, no. I've been away for a few days and haven't spoken to her," I say.

"Yeah, she found this awesome place near the Thames, on South Bank. Mum's coming over to see it and sign the contract, if she likes it. Dad's coming as well because he has things to do here."

"Adele she sort for you. She clever girl," Zia says.

"Would you and your parents like to come to ours for dinner one evening?" I ask.

"We'd love that," Adele says. "Which evening are you thinking of?"

"How long are your parents staying?"

"We're going back together on Saturday.

"What about Thursday?"

"OK. I'll ask mom when she phones this evening and let you know."

That gives Humps a week to get back home and get his act together, and come back to London after he's got the windows fixed.

"Zia, you come, too. Young Cushi will be delighted if you're there."

"I come later. I bring dessert."

"Fine, Zia, as you wish. I'll give Susi a call and see if she wants to join us."

FIFTY-EIGHT

Sunday 22nd October

Humps has been texting and phoning since Thursday. I've ignored him. And I've just received a text saying he's on his way home and will arrive soon. I don't answer. He'll get his answer when he's home. What a mess he's got us into. Humps together with Jimmy and Frank couldn't rustle up that kind of money, and now they will have to accept Young Cushi's help, that is if he and his daughter can find a way to do it.

But what hurt most was his escapades with call girls. I could get over the bank business. Betrayal is different. I didn't realise how much it hurt. I have always been faithful though I have had a few indecent proposals during our long married life. I even resisted the constant overtures of that sensual music teacher. Those escorts were probably beautiful, long-legged, long-haired blondes from eastern Europe, or cute petite women from Asia, or voluptuous Brazilians. And what sweet nothings did he purr into their ears? The same as he's murmured to me? Or was he simply animalistic, got on with the job and said nothing to them? How debauched can you get? Oh, Humps, I hate you.

Zia says having an affair myself would make me feel better. I'm in my early sixties for God's sake. Men my age look for younger women. Anyway, that's not on the cards right now. I hear the key in the lock. Humps walks in. He's in his jeans and dark blue suit jacket, looking like a million dollars. In his arms a huge bunch of red roses. "These are for you," he says, holding them out to me. It would be churlish to refuse them, though I feel as though I could cut their heads off and stuff them in his mouth. I take the roses, say a cold "Thank you," and take them into the kitchen. Then I ignore him, and he is sensible enough to realise now's not the time to talk to me. He goes to the bedroom and stays there for a while. When he comes out he says: "Don't those roses look beautiful?"

I want to hug and kiss him, and I want to punish him at the same time. So, I just utter a "Yes."

I didn't get any lunch for myself, so I'm not cooking for him either. He notices there are no smells in the house and says: "Shall we go to a pub and get a Sunday roast?"

"No," I say, "we have things to talk about that can't be discussed in pubs."

He gives a sigh of relief because at least I'm speaking to him.

"Fine," he says, "I'm ready when you are."

"I don't want to talk about your antics at parties. The less said about those the better. Even if we talked about them at length, the fact remains and there's nothing you can say that'll make me feel better."

I try holding my tears back but they triumph and start running down my cheeks. He puts his arms around me, but doesn't say anything. It would feel so good, if he weren't such a bastard. I wipe my tears, go and sit in my favourite armchair, and say: "Young Cushi and his family are coming to dinner Thursday evening. Zia and Clara are coming as well. Susi can't because she's got a date."

"I see. So they're here in London, are they?" he says.

"Yes, I've spoken to Adele who's still at Zia's. She says she might be able to find a way of solving the fifteen million problem. You're going to have to speak to your colleagues before Thursday and tell them that you've probably found a solution. And if that doesn't work, and a journalist finds out, the papers will have a field day and your face will be on the front pages for all to see. Your elderly parents will choke on their breakfast when they see your picture plastered all over the *Daily Telegraph*. I mean, although your colleagues hold senior positions, you're number one and the buck ultimately stops with you."

"I know. I'm so sorry for dragging you through this."

"Whatever happens, I'm standing by you. I love you, and my life without you would be meaningless."

"As mine would be without you," he says.

"Is that offer for Sunday lunch still valid?"

"Yes," he says and jumps to his feet.

"Amuni," I say.

"And what does that mean?

"Let's go, in Sicilian."

"Amuni," he says.

While we're waiting for our roasts, Humps says: "By the way, I got the window fixed. It needed changing. I chose the Tudor style lattice panes – you know, they're reinforced in case of any more tempests."

"Well, I am not apologising."

"I'm certainly not expecting an apology. Quite the contrary. I thought that was a stonking performance. What was it you said: "Stiff-fucking-upper-fucking-lip?"

The waitress overhears him as she arrives behind him with the roasts. I didn't tell him she was coming. She smiles.

What did you tell the window suppliers?"

"Vandals. And that's what I told Yvonne, too. Of course I had to pick up all the objects and the shards on the lawn first, otherwise they'd have realised the glass had been broken from inside to out, and not the other way round."

"Will you be making an insurance claim?"

He smiles that smile that makes me melt. "We'll let this one go, I think. I'm not sure they have a claims form for Sicilian tempests."

We laugh.

"Buon appetito," I say.

"Buon appetito."

FIFTY-NINE

Thursday 26th October

Thursday soon comes around, and I've hired help to get the house ready. By midday, it's sparkling. I've ordered food from the best Italian restaurant in the neighbourhood, and have asked them to bring the right wines along, too. They are bringing the food and sending a waiter and a cook. We've agreed that they will leave after the first course has been served. So it will be all small talk up till then.

Clara arrives with a cardboard tube under her arm. "I've got the gallery plans in here," she says, waving the tube about. "Where's daddy?"

"He's in the shower. Our guests will be here soon."

"I've chucked my job in," she says. "The bloody pittance they were paying me wasn't worth my while working out my notice. I phoned them point blank, and told them I wasn't going back. He said: 'Clara, you're in the middle of a project.' And I said: 'Someone else'll have to finish it off then, won't they?' Oh, I can't tell you how good that felt."

"Well, they're hardly going to take legal action, are they?"

"No, they definitely won't do that. And, if they tried, I'm sure our family can find a way to put them out of business."

"But you won't get a reference," I say.

"They can stick it. What do I need a reference for? My reference for Patrizia's gallery is that I'm your daughter."

"I see."

"Mum, I'm over the moon. I've already got some designs in here to show Patrizia. I've put a lot of work into this. Do you know what my new salary is?"

"No, idea, darling. I suppose it'll be pretty high judging by your enthusiasm."

"Mum, high? It's astronomical! And added to that I'll be getting commission..."

"That's great, Clara, that really is great. I'm so happy for you," I kiss her.

"Have they signed the contract?"

"Yes, they signed two on Tuesday. Straight after Patrizia, Adele and me had seen the premises. They signed the gallery contract, and my work contract."

"Wonderful! Sorry, darling, I need to change. They'll be here any minute. Dad'll soon be out and you can talk to him."

"Are you getting all dolled up?" she asks.

"Yes," I say, looking at her in her jeans.

"Well, don't overdo it."

"No, I won't. I'm wearing that light-blue shiny dress. By the way that'll be an excellent choice for the opening of the gallery, too."

"I'll be wearing my black and silver weirdo stuff. It's allowed when you're an artist."

"Ah, here's dad," I say. "I'll be back in a mo.' Do tell him about your new job."

As soon as I finish dressing, the intercom rings. They're here. They come out of the lift loaded with presents.

"Ciao, bella!" Patrizia says, kissing me first, then Clara.

"Young Cushi comes in holding two bottles of wine, while Adele is embracing a beautiful bouquet of flowers.

"Oh, you shouldn't have," I say. I am so happy to see them. "Do come in and sit down. We'll have our aperitif in a moment. Humps and Young Cushi shake hands. This is going to be an incredible evening. I can feel it.

After our second course, Zia arrives in a taxi armed with cannoli. Susi phoned me to say Zia had left, so I worked out how long the journey would take and waited for her at the gate. "Ah, Maria, you take cannoli. I get out of taxi." When we walk in, Zia is welcomed with cheers. "You my wonderful family," she says. I place the cannoli on a large Spode oval serving dish. The waiter and cook have left. I don't have time to get the dessert plates, and they're all taking a cannolo each. Now, in other times, Humps would have thought that untoward, but he's joining in as if he weren't a toff. I hardly recognise him lately. It took a Sicilian tempest to loosen him up. Humps gets the port out. "Fill your neighbour's glass to your right and then pass the decanter around to your left. And we keep going round until the decanter's empty. You start, Cushi, there's a good chap," Humps says. Some things never change.

"Fill up," Zia says, when Young Cushi is serving hers.

"Quick drink up, Zia, before the decanter comes round again," Humps says.

"I drink, you no worry," she replies.

"Let's get to work," Adele says. Zia wants to watch television because she always watches television in the evenings. She sits on the sofa, and I give her the remote control. She's happy. Patrizia and Clara sit on the carpet, then Clara spreads sheets out for Patrizia to see. Humps invites Young Cushi and Adele into his office. I go too. I want to see what all this is about.

"Can you design a structured product based on something that fluctuates wildly like the crude oil price?" Adele says to Humps.

"Yes, the derivatives desk does this all the time," Humps says.

"What my father wants to do," Adele says, "is to deposit twenty million euros in an investment account with your bank. Then we close the account when it's down to three million euros. So that means seventeen million euros can be used to cover the loss. Your people will have to design the product so that my father's loss is your bank's profit. The only unknowns are how long the transfer takes, which depends on the fluctuation of the oil price, and any recovery in the pound against the euro," Adele says.

"We can design structured products so that the bank wins whichever way the price goes," Humps says.

"I'll need to see a draft of the contract to make sure there are no hidden surprises," Adele says.

"Adele, I'm relying on your legal knowledge to get this right," Young Cushi says.

"Oh, we will get it right. No worries," Adele replies.

"A man of mine has examined the books and business of your bank's branch in the south of Italy," Young Cushi says. "We are prepared to offer your head office eight million euros to buy the branch from you."

"That branch is worth more like forty million euros," Humps says.

"That's the offer. Your bank's not in a strong position to argue," Young Cushi says.

Adele intervenes: "Eight million plus seventeen million makes twenty-five million we're paying. It's a decent sum given we're getting you top people out of the media limelight and the law's clutches."

"I'll need to get it through the board. There are ten of us. The board knows hell will break loose if the press get hold of this story. The media hate us bankers as it is. I will argue at the board meeting that there's too much risk in owning a small branch in the south of Italy, so we'd be better rid of it. We save our bank in London from a scandal and reduce our risk profile."

"Tell them I don't barter" says Young Cushi. Don't come back with a counter offer. And tell them we'll need to open an account for the new gallery. There'll be a lot of money going through that. If our offer is refused, we can take our custom elsewhere."

So if I've understood correctly, Young Cushi is making

fifteen million euros, while adding a bank to his portfolio. Humps shakes hands with Young Cushi and Adele to seal the deal. "Let's go back to the living room, join the others and open a magnum," I say. "We must celebrate." I give the bottle to Humps. He turns it upside down and shakes it vigorously. Then he pops the cork which flies and is followed by a champagne spray. He opens his mouth wide and tries to catch the champagne in his mouth before it hits the floor. With the result he drenches his face and hair. The man is decisively going insane. Long may it last.

We hold our flutes into the middle of the circle we've formed, raise our glasses high, "To our family, and viva la Sicilia," Young Cushi says.

"To our family, and viva la Sicilia," we all repeat.

Zia looks admiringly at Adele and Clara standing together, and says: "Salute e figlie femmini. We drink to you two young girl. If Ziuzza can see you, she be so proud of you." Zia raises her glass to them. "To two young clever lady. You future of our family."

Sparkling Books

We publish:

Crime, mystery, thriller, suspense, horror and romance

YA fiction

Non-fiction

All titles are also available as e-books from your e-book retailer.

For current list of titles and direct links to stores visit:
www.sparklingbooks.com

@SparklingBooks